The Gentle HEARTS

S.A. Khan

INDIA · SINGAPORE · MALAYSIA

ISBN 979-8-88704-359-3

Contents

Disclaimer

This book is a work of fiction and is written solely for the purpose of entertainment. The plot isn't related to any real-life or historical incident. Names, characters, businesses, places, events, locales, and incidents are either products of the author's imagination or used in a fictitious manner. Any resemblance to actual persons, living or dead, or real events is strictly coincidental.

Certain institutions, agencies, and public offices have been mentioned, but the characters are completely imaginary. The views expressed are those of the characters and should not be perceived as that of the author. Any conversation among the characters within the book is not intended to offend the sentiments of any individual, caste, community, race, or religion or denigrate any institution or person, living or dead.

The information provided in this book on various topics should not be judged as accurate and reliable as it was gathered from articles written by professionals; also, the content was not evaluated for accuracy and genuineness.

Preface

I dedicate this book to all my family members, neighbors, and friends who failed to fight with Covid and left me to mourn till I breathe. This ordeal wasn't alone; I felt overwhelmed with anguish and grief for the millions who perished worldwide. This phase of my life was dreary and heart-wrenching and deeply devastated me.

In addition, the collateral damage of this phase was that I failed to write the sequel of my first book, *The Invisible Protectors*, which I had planned to do. The constant encouragement from friends, family, and well-wishers, the excellent reviews on Amazon and Goodreads, and even the tag it earned of becoming the top 10 Amazon's best sellers for a while, nothing helped me to hold the pen.

When things began to improve, I was able to rediscover my passion for writing. However, I opted to write about the kindhearted people I have met and read in my over seventy-plus years of existence instead of writing a sequel. Beautiful people who worked relentlessly to better the lives of unknown persons, sacrificing all they had – their time, their money, and family life – without expecting a reward.

Before I conclude, I must thank my creator for bestowing me with a squad of stimulators; my six grandchildren reside thousands of miles away but are a constant energy source and joy for my wife and me. We feel happy and blessed when we reminisce about them, watch their videos, or see them on flat-screen.

Chapter One

Manjula Rao

My name is Manjula Rao; I was born in the year 1964 in Mahbubnagar District, 110 kilometers away from the state capital Hyderabad. My father was a wealthy landlord and a businessman, who owned hundreds of acres of agricultural land, two power looms manufacturing cotton dhotis and sarees, a real-estate company, and a civil contracting company dealing with large government projects. My twin younger brothers are only a year younger than me; Mom had a couple of miscarriages after the second birth and failed to produce more progenies. I was my father's darling, and according to my mother, he had made me a rotten spoiled brat who would come back from her husband's home within no time. After completing my secondary education, I told Dad I wanted to do my graduation from a college in Hyderabad; the idea behind this request was to enjoy the city and hostel life; heck, with that brilliant idea.

Dad conceded my plea; however, instead of putting me in a hostel, he bought a villa in Hyderabad, relocated the entire family to the city, and admitted me into a women's college for the commerce degree course. Our new home was a newly constructed, luxurious two-storied building with a vast lawn, plush backyard, servant quarters, two car garages, etc.

Dad deftly avoided telling Mom that I had shown interest in studying in Hyderabad. Mom would've skinned me alive if he had told her, but she guessed it and cursed me the whole time, claiming it had to be me who had given father this mad idea. We were all unhappy at first but gradually began enjoying the city life; Dad was commuting between Mahbubnagar and Hyderabad but doing his best to be with us as often as possible. Finally, Mom stopped whining, and we overcame the initial longing to return to our roots. When I was in my final year of graduation, I met with Nageshwar. It was a cold evening in January. I was sitting on the lawn to enjoy the chilly breeze with a cup of tea, taking a study break as I was cramming textbooks in college and at home because the fear of impending final exams increased day by day. While engulfed in my thoughts, I saw the watchman walking toward the main door. I asked him what he wanted, and he said, "A young man wants to meet with your dad."

"Bring him here," I said, surprised as I had never seen any young person visiting Dad.

The person, who looked to be in his early to mid-20s, was brought by the watchman. He was tall, around five feet 10 or 11 inches, lean, of whitish complexion, wearing well-pressed formals – a white shirt tucked into navy blue pants, a blue half-sleeve open-neck sweater, and polished black leather shoes.

"Why do you want to meet with Dad?" I inquired.

He said, "My bank manager asked me for it, and I've no clue why your dad wants to meet with me."

I asked him his name and the bank manager's name, and he said, "I'm Nageshwar Rao, and the SBI bank manager's name is T.K. Seshadri."

"Have a seat, and let me check with Dad, whether he's free to see you," I said and went inside. Dad was in his home office; he had converted one room into his office, where he kept himself busy on the three phone lines and a pile of files.

I informed Dad about the visitor.

Dad said, "Let him wait for a while and offer him some drink."

"Who's he, and why does he want to meet with you?" I inquired – my inquisitive nature compelled me to ask the irrelevant question.

"Oh, he's a young entrepreneur seeking funding for his generic medicines manufacturing business," Dad said.

"Can I talk to him to know what he's looking for and why we should invest in his business, a little grilling to see whether he knows what he's doing?" I asked.

"You're a lifesaver! I'm waiting for an urgent call, and it could take at least 20 minutes before I would be free; you grill him as much as you want, and I'll join you when I'm done," Dad said.

"Fine, I'll speak to him till you join," I said.

Nag was sitting erect as if someone had plastered a rod to his back; he had sharp features, protuberant eyes, a clean-shaven face, a side-parted thick flock of black hairs – with any yardstick, a handsome lad.

I said to Nag, "Dad will join us in the next half an hour as he has to attend to some important phone calls. He asked me to inform you that he's willing to consider offering you funding for your business expansion, provided he's satisfied that you're in control of your operation and it's being run satisfactorily. Before Dad comes, could you fill me in about your education, how you entered into the pharmaceutical business, what you're manufacturing, how many employees you have, your current monthly sales, your expansion plan, and any other information that would help us in understanding the operation and ascertaining that expansion would boost the sales and profitability?"

Dad wanted me to be a businesswoman; he had made me spend most of my summer holidays in the Accounts Department of power looms for the past several years, which resulted in me acquiring valuable insight into how the business processes work.

"Sure; if it's okay, would you inform me about your dad's line of work and whether you want me to tell you in brief or detail how I've got into the pharma business and how it's doing now?" Nag said.

"Okay, let me begin with my introduction. My name is Manjula Rao, and I'm the firstborn in the family. To answer your question, we're from Mahbubnagar, where we've several businesses; the major ones are two power looms that produce cotton sarees and dhotis, a real estate company, a construction company, agribusiness, and a few other businesses. Regarding your business, please share in detail whatever you want us to know to make your case convincing for injecting the needed funding," I said.

"Glad to know about your business activities. I'll share all the essential details from my college days to this date. I'm from a small town which is 80 kilometers from here. My dad is the wealthiest man in the village and owns lots of agricultural lands and quite a few tractors and trolley trucks that he rents out to other farmers for plowing and taking their produce to the market. We're three brothers and one sister; the eldest is my sister, and I'm the youngest. We all studied in a convent school at the district headquarters, 15 kilometers from our village.

"My sister graduated in English literature, married a doctor, and migrated to the UK, and my brothers joined Dad's business after completing secondary school. I graduated in Commerce from a prestigious college in our city and decided to settle here and do business.

"When I was in my final year of graduation, I met with one of my friend's guests from Bombay. During our conversation over dinner, the Bombay lad knocked down a few whiskey pegs, abandoned his inhibitions, and bragged about his family business. He claimed that they manufacture generic medicines, and it is highly lucrative. They offer their drugs for less than half the price of branded drugs and still earn a profit of more than hundred percent. They produce Paracetamol tablets and syrup, Amoxycillin, Azithromycin, and a few slow-moving products, like cough syrup and vitamins. Most of their customers are in small villages, the RMP, BUMS, BAMS, and even quacks.

"While listening to the Bombay guy, I decided that this is the business I should do when I'm through with my studies. So, after graduating, I told Dad that I wanted to investigate the possibility of starting a drug manufacturing company. And for my feasibility study,

I want to go to Delhi, Ahmedabad, and Bombay for a couple of months or a little more. Dad attempted to persuade me to join the family business but, upon my insistence, gave permission.

"I spent around two months in these cities and learned almost everything about machinery suppliers, raw materials, and the manufacturing process. I understood that I needed between 15–20 lakhs seeding money and a couple of experienced workers to start the business, which has massive growth potential.

"When I was in Bombay, I visited a small pharma company manufacturing both generic and branded products; the visit was to know whether I could be their distributor for my state. My reasoning was that if I worked as a distributor for a while before taking the plunge, it would greatly assist me in understanding the nitty-gritty of the pharma industry. Unfortunately, they already had a distributor who, according to the owner, was doing an excellent job. He gave me a factory tour; while walking through the factory, he suggested selling their products under my brand name; I promised to consider his proposal.

"After the factory tour, I left, and while waiting for a train to take me to the city center, where I was staying in a budget hotel, a middle-aged man approached me. He introduced himself as Ashok Karmakar and informed me he works as a production supervisor at the pharmaceutical plant I visited and mentioned he overheard the owner suggesting that I buy his drugs under my label. He said that if I accept the proposition, it would be an utter waste of time and money, as I would be lucky to break even, let alone make a profit. But if I want to establish a profitable pharma business, I could start with a small manufacturing unit with an investment of 10 lakhs, and he could help me set up the machinery and the products I should begin with and ensure that we produce the best quality medicines. He has a diploma in chemical engineering and 22 years of work experience in the pharma industry.

"I took his contact number and home address and promised to get back to him if I managed to arrange the needed money.

"After returning from my trip, I told Dad my feasibility study revealed that the pharma industry is growing tremendously, and it's an excellent time to enter this business. However, to establish a small manufacturing unit to produce a few fast-moving drugs, 20 lakhs of investment is needed, which I requested him to give me from my share of the property.

"Finally, after lots of deliberation, the family consented to give me the money on the condition that I return it with interest from my share of the property whenever the distribution would occur, which I agreed to. Dad had a lawyer buddy write the contract, which everyone signed, and I received the check.

"I came to Hyderabad, bought a six-acre road facing barren land in the outskirts at a bargain price and contracted a builder to build a sizable steel shed. While the shed was under construction, I invited Ashok Karmakar to come to Hyderabad to discuss the possibility of utilizing his services. The following weekend he came, and I offered him his asking remuneration without negotiations and agreed to hire one of his colleagues who would assist him.

"Exactly after seven months from the date I got the money, my factory was up and running. It is now a little over two years since I started the operation, and we're working with seven employees – two sales executives, Ashok, his assistant, a cleaning lady, a watchman, and me. We're not only covering our expenses, but the company has earned more than 70,000 in net profit in the last two years, which I've put in a fixed deposit account.

"With my firsthand knowledge of the pharma business, I'm confident I'll double the turnover if I increase the production capacity and add a few more fast-moving products to our portfolio. Bulk-pack generic medications are in high demand everywhere, from small towns to major metropolia, and we often can't cater to the market needs because of our limited production capacity. Considering this, I wanted to increase the manufacturing capacity and add a few other fast-moving medicines, for which I requested a loan of 20 lakhs from the bank, but they refused," Nag said with a smile.

"Okay, it's good to learn that you're in a good business. Do you have anything more to share?" I asked.

I was captivated; the way he spoke – slow, articulate, and in a firm tone – was pleasing to the ear and indicative of his uprightness.

"Nothing more, Ma'am; I've informed you everything you must know about how I entered the pharma business and where I stand now," he said.

"Let me check what's holding Dad," I said and went inside.

Dad was busy on the phone, and after a few minutes, he disconnected the line and said, "I'm still busy and cannot leave this room because I've to make a few important calls. Just brief me on what input he's given about his business."

I told him everything he said, including the growth potential.

"Honey, I want to give you this project. This Sunday, go to his factory with our chief accountant and let him examine his books, and you check on his products, machinery, land and inform me your comments regarding whether it would be a good opportunity to invest. I noticed that he's a slick talker, so don't get fooled by his polished demeanor, and even if you notice a minor discrepancy in what he's said today and what you see at his factory, then forget about him. However, if you find him an honest and committed boy, we will consider lending the required amount," Dad said.

"Dad, why do you want me to involve in a business venture in which I don't have any experience or knowledge?" I asked.

"Honey, you don't get experience unless you work, so do what I ask you to do," Dad said with a smile.

"Dad, you're too much! I've not finished my graduation, and you want to involve me in your business," I said.

"Go, darling, analyze his business thoroughly; investigate the market potential of both the unbranded and the branded medicines and give me your feedback," Dad said.

"Fine, but don't blame me for any gaffes," I said and left the room.

Since I was so taken with Nag's polished, earnest, and good demeanor, I was delighted that Dad had assigned me to look into his business.

Nag was sitting in the same erect posture; maybe he was uncomfortable in the swanky environment. I told him Dad was busy with important calls, but he or I would visit his factory coming Sunday to look at his operation and decide whether we could further our discussion. He left after giving me his business card.

Sunday was only three days away, and I decided that I should better prepare myself by learning as much as I could about the pharmaceutical business. The next day, first, I went to the market and purchased a trade directory in order to know how many pharmaceutical factories were operating in Hyderabad. Unfortunately, there were only two in the entire city; one was a branch of a multinational pharmaceutical that produced cough syrup and a few vitamin tablets. The other company was in the industrial area, manufacturing generic drugs. The next day, after finishing college, I asked the driver to take me to the generic pharma factory in the industrial area. It was a woeful place in a factory's name, perhaps around 300 to 400 square yards of steel shed; there were four tablet-producing machines in one corner, and the other had heaps of raw material boxes.

Machines weren't kept in a dustproof room as was essential, and they were dirty. The limestone floor tiles were grimy and broken in many places, the paint was peeling from the tin walls, and there were no workers. A bald, heavily built man was sitting in a small glass cabin, and before he could come out and speak to me, I walked out.

The next day, I spoke to various medical stores and doctors and gained valuable insight into the sales of branded medicine. I gathered it is a highly cutthroat business, primarily when selling newly established pharma companies' medicines. The markup medical store demand is very high compared to what they receive by selling the established brands. In the initial stage, drug stores could help promote the new brands, as many low-income patients, instead of going to a doctor, go to a medical store and ask for medicines to treat their illnesses. As a result, they push the brands that give them substantial margins. Quite a few doctors could also help you develop the business by prescribing your brand, provided you offer them the needed incentive. The essence of my investigation was that branded medicine business could be developed, provided you invest heavily in marketing activities.

On Saturday evening, I briefed Dad on my findings on the pharma business and about my visit to the generic medicine manufacturer.

Dad said, "Good work, darling. Tomorrow morning, go to Nageshwar's factory with Murli Saab, our chief accountant, and let him check the account books, and you give input on what you see and think of him and his business."

"Fine, and thank you very much for testing my abilities in messing up things royally," I said with a chuckle.

"Honey, go and have fun; I'll not take your or the accountant's recommendation without checking on everything. I want from you an unbiased opinion about the boy and his venture and nothing more," Dad said.

"Okay, Dad, wish me good luck," I said.

"Good luck, and have fun," Dad said with a big grin.

Before leaving the house, I informed Nag we should be at his place in an hour. Due to Sunday's thin traffic, we arrived at the factory in less than 45 minutes. He must've spent a substantial amount of money constructing the ten-foot-high concrete boundary wall with a one-meter-high barbed-wire fence at the top to make it difficult for anyone to climb. The entrance had an approximately 15-foot-high iron gate with the metal signboard of his company, "Super Pharma," on its top. After a couple of honks, a young man of around 30 years opened the gate. On the right, I saw the factory shed, and on the left side, beside the entrance, were two housing units of equal size, and the remaining area was a vast span of land covered with dried grass.

The driver parked the car in front of the steel shed where Nageshwar was standing; he welcomed us and took us inside. Half of the shed's left side was partitioned with glass and aluminum walls; installed inside were various sizes and shapes of stainless-steel drug-making machines. In the open space of the far end of the right side were piles of neatly placed raw material corrugated boxes and plastic buckets of liquid chemicals, and close to the right side of the entrance was a large glass cabin with several tables, chairs, and cabinets. He guided us to the glass cabin and said, "This is our office, where the part-time accountant, sales executives, and I sit. Sales staff are not coming today, but Ashok, our production supervisor, and the accountant should be here any minute."

A young woman came with a tray of cold drinks and biscuits and asked whether we wanted masala tea. I accepted her offer with thanks, and my chief accountant settled for a cold drink.

I opened the conversation and said, "Nageshwar, allow me to introduce you to Mr. Murli Rangaswamy, the chief accountant of our group of companies. I've brought Murali Saab to review your account books, and while he attends to it, you give me a factory tour, with input on what you manufacture, etc. Lastly, my apologies to you and your staff for bothering you on a Sunday."

Nageshwar said, "For me coming on Sunday is no botheration, as this is my house also, and for my staff, it could be a little inconvenient, but sometimes you have to put up with such inconveniences."

"You stay on the factory premises?" I said astonishingly.

"At the entrance, you would've seen two housing units; one is my residence, and the other is for the watchman and his wife," Nag said.

I was impressed with his dedication, as living in this jungle couldn't be anything other than pain.

Two persons entered the room before I could say anything; one was a middle-aged man, around 45 years of age, and the other could have been in his late twenties or early thirties.

Nag introduced them to us – the senior person, Ashok Karmakar, the factory supervisor, and the young man, Prabhu Ramachandra, a part-time accountant. He then said to his accountant, "Prabhu, please show all our account books to Murali Saab, and inform everything Sir wants to know."

"Manjula Ma'am, please come with us; Ashok will tell us about our current manufacturing and what new products we intend to produce," Nag said.

We came out of the room and went inside the dustproof glass-partitioned area, covered with an artificial ceiling made of aluminum panels; we had to wrap our heads and feet with disposable caps and foot covers at the entrance.

Once inside, Ashok briefed me about the machines and their products.

I gathered from Ashok's briefing that they primarily produced Paracetamol and Amoxicillin antibiotics. Moreover, the business has enormous potential to grow both in generic and branded medicines.

When we came out of the manufacturing area, I saw Murli Saab and Prabhu busy sifting through the source documents and ledgers. I wanted to know a few things from Nag, and conducting our discussion in the office in front of the accountants won't be appropriate. So, I asked Nag, "Can we sit somewhere other than your office, as I need to discuss your financial requirement?"

He thought for a moment and then said, "If it's okay with you, we could sit in my tiny studio apartment, which is more comfortable than any other place on the premises."

"Fine with me," I said, and we walked toward his house. I saw a white Ambassador car parked under a tin shelter next to his house unit's wall.

It was a rectangular single-room of around 20 feet by 30 feet, with shining marble floor, snow-white walls, on the left-hand side a sitting area with a one three-seater and two one-seater sofas, and before that a small round dining table with four chairs. On the right side were a queen-size bed, a bedside table with an alarm clock and telephone, and one small wooden temple two feet wide and four feet high. Two walls were decorated with two landscapes and seascape paintings. On the left side in the corner was a wide frosted glass sliding door, which must be leading to a dresser-bathroom, as I didn't see any cloth cabinet in the room.

He kept the entrance door open, asked me to sit on the single-seat sofa, and inquired whether I cared for another cup of tea or a cold drink, which I declined.

I decided to compliment the room fixtures and furnishing, which impressed me, and said, "The room is spacious and aesthetically furnished, and I believe you're a God-fearing man."

He smiled and said, "I don't know whether I'm a God-fearing or religious man, but every day in the morning, I spend a few minutes thanking my Lord for whatever he's given and for waking up my family and me in good health.

"I cannot take the credit for the room furnishing, as my mom did it. I used to stay in a hostel in the city, and one evening I stayed here late to finish pressing paperwork. By the time I was through with the work, I was exhausted, so I slept here. This room wasn't in use, so there was no telephone or furniture except one ceiling fan and a cotton rope cot. It was routine for my mom to call me every night around ten-thirty, and as usual, she called me that night at my hostel; when she didn't find me there, she called on the factory number, and I didn't answer as I was sleeping in this room. She panicked and came here in the middle of the night with the entire clan. After seeing me intact, she decided to stay here for a few days to make my room inhabitable and get a telephone extension. Mom stayed in a hotel almost for one month, making this room comfortable and safe for me to spend my nights. For my safety, she bought two ferocious German Shepherds to guard us during the night; they're caged at the back of the factory shed in the daytime. She also purchased an Ambassador car, so she doesn't have to worry if I'm shuttling late at night."

"Is your mom educated?" I inquired.

"Mom graduated in English Literature; Dad didn't go to college but speaks fluent English because of his convent school education from kindergarten to tenth grade," Nag said.

"Could you please tell me how much you've spent to set up this facility?" I asked.

"Little over 14 lakhs and close to three lakhs in the raw material and purchase of two delivery vans, office furniture, and a few other pieces of equipment. I've kept two lakhs in a three-month rollover fixed deposit account, and the remaining cash, I've kept in the factory account to cover salaries and miscellaneous expenses," Nag said.

"How much do you need if we ask you to expand both in generic and branded drugs?" I asked.

"It is difficult to give you a figure, as it depends upon how many products you want to produce. For example, my business needs around 20 lakhs to increase current products' manufacturing capacity and add at least ten new drugs. But, on the other hand, if you construct a medium-size factory to manufacture around twenty or more branded products, I trust you would need at least 50 lakhs," Nag said.

"If we agreed to lend you 50 lakhs or even more, how long would it take to get the machines and start the production?" I asked.

"If we decide to manufacture superior quality products, we've to construct a steel-reinforced concrete slab building and cover the inside with aluminum composite panels to make it completely dustproof and fully airconditioned. Building construction could easily take at least a year, and to start the manufacturing, it would take anything between 18 and 24 months. If we encounter delays for unforeseen reasons, then keep another six months to overcome such nags," Nag said.

"Is it possible for you to prepare a business plan, giving a brief input on what you've done thus far, how you intend to expand, and the amount you need?" I asked.

"Sure, I could do that, but you need to give me at least two to three weeks to prepare and get it typed," Nag said.

"Take as much time as you need, but prepare an impressive document, as omissions or inaccuracies could lead to rejection. If you need assistance preparing the plan, I suggest you take guidance from Murli Saab. He could tell you how to prepare, and if you need, I'll ask him to give you copies of some of the most adeptly prepared business plans that he may have in the company records," I said.

"I've not seen any business plan as of this date, and I would be much obliged if you tell Murli Saab to give me copies of one or two plans," Nag said.

"No issues; I'll instruct Murli Saab to give you the plans and provide any assistance you need," I said.

"Much obliged and appreciate your help," Nag said.

"I will call you in three weeks, and if the plan is ready, you could bring it, or I could send one of our staff to collect it from you," I said.

"I'm sure three weeks should be enough to prepare the plan," Nag said.

"Fine, let's go and see whether Murli Saab has completed his review of your records," I said.

"I want to organize lunch if you care to eat here, or we could go to a decent restaurant," Nag said.

"Thanks for asking, but we must go now," I said.

By one, we were back, and along with Murli Saab, I sat with Dad to give our input about the factory premises and the business. Murli Saab confirmed everything Nag informed, starting from establishing the company with a capital of 20 lakhs. He gave Dad copies of bank statements, machine purchasing invoices, and the audited balance sheets and left with a "Have a good day, Sir."

Dad said, "Shoot, I want to hear your comments on what you saw and think."

"Dad, he's done an excellent job setting up the factory; you know, he stays on the factory premises. I was amazed by his dedication and commitment, and everything he said to me was true," I said.

"It looks like he's impressed you tremendously; do you want me to meet with his family for your alliance?" Dad said with a booming laugh.

"Dad, don't joke; we're in serious discussion, and next time I'll not do any of your work. The last input is that I've asked him to prepare a business plan; if needed, he could take help from Murli Saab," I said.

"When we're lending him money against collateral, why do we need a business plan?" Dad questioned.

"Dad, I want the business plan; I wouldn't judge him with the language or any other content. Instead, I would be looking into the products he wants to add and whether he has a solid justification for investing so much into business or not," I said.

"How come you've become so knowledgeable about business! I'm impressed, and I agree with you that we should know whether he's justified to pump in so much money for the projected business growth," Dad said.

"I must remind you, in case you don't remember, about your child's education and experience. I'm in my final year of the Bachelor of Commerce degree course. The knowledge you're impressed with was acquired by slogging and sacrificing my several years of summer holidays in my dad's accounts department," I said.

"I'm pleased that my child has grown physically and intellectually. You tell him that Dad is willing to lend him the money on mutually acceptable terms but that he'll only do so after reviewing his business plan," Dad said.

"Sure, but why do you want to get into the money lending business?" I inquired.

"The boy is desperate for the money, and I don't think there's any harm in helping him," Dad said.

"Fine, I'll convey your message," I left the room, saying I was hungry.

I felt happy with Dad's decision to lend him money. Dad had too much money, and 10 or 20 lakhs for him was nothing, and if my assessment of Nag's character was correct, then for sure, he'll return every penny with the agreed interest rate. While I was taking my lunch, Mom joined and said, "What's going on? The driver told me he took you and Murli to a factory this morning."

"Dad sent Murli Saab and me to a drug manufacturer, who wants some funding to expand his business," I said.

"Why has he involved you in a business activity where you lack experience or knowledge?" Mom asked.

"Mom, you should ask Dad about it, and for your information, I didn't want to do it either, that much I told Dad, but he refused to accept all my reasoning and instructed me to take up the task," I said.

"You and your dad are getting on my nerves; you complete your graduation, and I'll find a boy and push you out of the house," Mom snarled.

"I love you, Mom; I also don't want to be a part of Dad's business; tell him to give me the two power looms, so I could survive with the income of the looms and feed myself and the boy you want me to marry," I said.

"Shut up, and don't make me angry. Otherwise, I'll not wait even for your degree," Mom growled.

"Okay, Mom, do whatever you think is right," I said.

She left the dining table, huffing and puffing. Mom subscribed to the old school of thought that girls shouldn't enter the male domain; they should learn house chores, get married, and raise children. Dad was entirely opposed to Mom's ideology. According to him, girls should be given equal opportunity to work in every field, and raising a family and running a house shouldn't become a barrier to whatever they want to do with their life. Mom never agreed with Dad's thinking and told him that he would regret his bad decisions one day, mainly related to me, who has completely gone out of her hands. Blah, blah, blah.

Dad was walking barefoot on the lawn in the evening; he believed walking on the grass helped him reduce stress. I joined him, and after walking for a few minutes, Dad said, "Shoot, I'm listening."

"Mom is upset with me because I'm getting involved in the business; she said you and I are getting on her nerves. She wants to push me out of the house by marrying me off as soon as I complete my graduation. Instead of learning the business, she believes I should learn how to handle the household chores," I said. "We were always on her nerves, so don't worry about that, but I believe she's right; we should find a suitable boy for you, as I'm looking forward to playing with my grandchildren," Dad said.

"Dad, you're too much, but take my word; I'm not going anywhere and will always be with you," I said.

"We will see about that; let's go inside; it is getting cold here," Dad said, and slowly we walked toward the house's main entrance.

I was continually thinking about Nag; his dinky accommodation and the immaculate factory premises reflected the thoroughness with which he worked. His devotion to his business was another thing to admire. I also noticed his manicured nails, combed hair, well-pressed clothes, and shined shoes, loudly announcing that he valued and practiced cleanliness and personal hygiene, which was commendable.

I tried to sleep but couldn't; his factory, flat, and smile without showing teeth kept popping in front of my closed eyes. I had to suppress my urge to speak with him with brute force; I wanted to hear him talk. He never fumbled in search of words or to gather his thoughts, which was enticing and captivating. I was sure Nag would go places with or without Dad's money. Moreover, at such a young age establishing a manufacturing business is no child's play; you need to be well-organized and highly disciplined and have a strong urge to succeed, supported by the capacity to work hard and, last but not least, the talent to interact with a wide range of people. Dad always used to tell me, "Manju, working alone is the easiest thing in the world, but taking work from many people and guiding and extracting the best out of them is the most challenging thing to do. For this, you need to have multiple personalities molded into one, got to be a disciplined, organized hard worker, a hard-hitting administrator, and, most of all, a humane, humble, loving, and caring person." I don't remember when I stopped thinking about Nag and drifted off to sleep.

The next evening, I couldn't resist my urge to speak with Nag, and around 10:45, I called him, and he answered on the second ring.

I said, "Sorry if I'm disturbing you, as it is late at night."

"Please always feel free to call me; generally, I sleep between 11:30 and 12:00, but you could call whenever you've got a free moment," Nag said.

"Thanks; I called to convey Dad's answer to your request. He's agreed to lend you money on mutually acceptable terms provided you furnish a business plan," I said.

"I already started my work on it; yesterday, I received from Murli Saab a copy of a business plan prepared for your father to invest in a garment manufacturing company, which is very detailed and impressive. Murli Saab is a real gem; this morning, he called me and gave several tips on writing the plan, what to emphasize, and how to prepare the cash flow, sales, profit projection charts, and a few other vital points that must be addressed," Nag said.

"Great, I cannot be of much help, but if you think I could assist you in any way, please ask," I said.

"Certainly, I'll ask your assistance in reviewing the plan once it is ready," Nag said.

"Okay; please feel free to take Murli Saab's assistance whenever required," I said.

"Thanks, he's a knowledgeable and kind person, and I'll definitely seek his assistance when needed," Nag said.

"Okay then, I must say goodnight as tomorrow I've got college," I said.

"Goodnight, Ma'am, and thank you very much for your call," Nag said.

I slept, thinking about why I was getting so attracted to him. Is it because of his civility, physical appearance, or being bitten by the crush bug? From my early teens, I heard Dad mention to Mom that he wanted an educated boy belonging to a financially sound family for Manju. But unfortunately, I don't think Nag fits into Dad's set criteria. To begin with, he's just a graduate; there's nothing much to talk about in the money department except mounds of ambitions, and whether he would succeed in converting his dreams into reality is a big question. I don't know when I slept but woke up to my mother's shouting, "Manju, lazy girl, get up; you have college." I quickly freshened up, took a sandwich bite from the table, and rushed to get in the waiting car.

At the beginning of the fourth week, I called Nag late at night, and he immediately answered; I said: "Hello Nag, how are you, and how's everything?"

"I'm doing well and very pleased to hear from you, Ma'am," Nag said.

"Nag, please call me Manju, as your Ma'am makes me feel like an old person," I said.

He laughed and said, "It is difficult, but I must do that, as I don't want you to be an old lady."

"Tell me, have you finished your business plan, or are you still working on it?" I asked.

"By tomorrow evening, I'll complete it, and before giving it for typing, I want you to review it. Is it possible for you to have lunch with me the day after tomorrow? I know a very exclusive family restaurant, where they have a vast buffet lunch of both veg and non-veg dishes," Nag said.

"I'll call you tomorrow night and inform you whether it is possible or not," I said.

"Please do your best to accept my invitation; I'm certain your feedback will immensely assist me in tightening the loose ends. Manju, allow me to say that I've felt extraordinarily confident and energized since I met you. I feel you're all around me and encouraging me to work hard and be a successful entrepreneur. I'm sorry if I offended you with my comments, but this is not a made-up story but an honest admission of my current mental state," Nag said.

"It's nice to hear I'm motivating you, but I guess it's your fantasy only. You're a hardworking guy, which I noticed the moment I walked into your factory. I'm confident that if you achieve your goals, all of the credit will go to you alone because no amount of motivation will work unless you've got an in-built burning desire to achieve your objectives," I said.

"Thank you for the encouraging comments, but I'm truthful in telling you that you've pumped in my body tons of energy, pushing me to put up long hours without feeling tired or lethargic," Nag said.

"Okay, Nag, I must say goodbye and goodnight; time to sleep," I said.

After hearing his goodnight, I disconnected the line.

I thought this boy was creating problems for me, as I was continuously thinking about him and missing focusing on my studies.

The next day around five in the evening, I went to Dad's office: he was busy reviewing some papers, and without looking at me, he said, "Shoot."

"Dad, yesterday I called Nag to inquire about the progress on his business plan. He said he would complete the task by this evening, and before giving it for typing, he wanted me to review it. He invited me to have lunch with him in an upscale family restaurant where we could sit comfortably, have our lunch, and review and discuss his document. I don't know if I should go with him, and even if you permit me to go, if Mom comes to know, you bet she'll roast me alive," I said.

Dad laughed loud and asked, "Do you want to go?"

"He's requested me to look at the draft, even though I told him I'm not qualified to comment, but he's insisting. You tell me, Dad, what I should do?" I asked.

"You go and judge him as a person, how he is, how he treats you, his motive behind asking you to look at the plan, and whether he wants you to recommend him for the loan or ask for any other favor.

"To hide your luncheon date from Mom, do one thing, send the car back once you reach the college tomorrow. I'll ask one of my friends to lend a car and driver who'll follow you to the restaurant, and after lunch, come home in that car and cook up some story to tell Mom about the delay and the reason for sending the car back. Don't mention the luncheon to your mom now or ever; else, she'll turn us into dead meat," Dad said, and we laughed aloud.

I called Nag in the night and asked him to pick me up from the college at 1:30 in the afternoon.

When I came out of college the following day, I found Nag standing in front of the entrance gate. He took me in his shining Ambassador car to a restaurant in a luxury hotel. We found a corner table with no noise, so we could talk without yelling.

We had our lunch, mostly talking about my studies and the final exams due in three months, his business, and what kind of growth he expected in the next few years without injecting any new money. While having our tea, he pulled out two files from his handbag and gave them to me. One with the label "Generic Products" and the other with "Branded Products." It took almost 15 minutes to go through both files. The Generic Products file had the executive summary, company profile, products, market potential, projections, current financial standing, and expansion requirement based on the addition of fast-moving drugs. In the end, I found the quotation for the supply and installation of needed machinery.

In the Branded Products file, he had written about the products they should manufacture, the cost of constructing a dustproof concrete structure on at least one acre of land, the machinery needed, and the running costs. Lastly, attached is a factory blueprint designed by an architect and quotes for the factory construction and the machinery.

Nag's handwriting was good, and the entire text was in caps, making it crystal clear for anyone to read.

Once I finished reading, he gave me a letter addressed to Dad that mentioned he would like to borrow 15 lakh rupees to expand the generic medicines business. He would pledge his land and factory to guarantee the return of lending.

In the next paragraph, he mentioned that 70 to 80 lakhs were required to set up a factory to manufacture 30 or more branded products. The construction of the factory would cost around 30 lakhs, machinery about 35 lakhs, and for the raw material and a few months labor wages, at least 10 or 15 lakhs.

Since he had no money to venture into branded business, he could offer his services as a managing partner for a 20 percent share in the company. The investor should handle the finance and procurement of raw materials, and the rest he would manage. He had done a thorough job; impressive, as I don't think you need to know anything else to decide.

I told him I would take the files and his letter, and there was no need to get it typed, and on my way home, I'll make a copy of all the papers and give it to him for his records. He wanted to drop me home, but I said my car was here, and with a goodbye and promise to call him in a few days, I left.

Nothing happened for almost two weeks, and during this period, only once did I speak with Nag to inform him that I had given the papers to Dad and that he had said after reviewing, he would decide.

On a Sunday morning, Dad called me to his office and said, "This afternoon, we're going to Nag's village, and your mother will also accompany us."

"Why mother, and why are we going to his village and not the factory?" I asked with surprise.

"Your mother will brief you, and no more questions. Go," Dad said smilingly.

I found Mom in the kitchen, busy with a few servants putting various items in several trays placed on the kitchen island table.

"Mom, why are we going to Nageshwar's village, and what are you doing?" I asked.

"Please don't disturb me, go to your room, and I'll be with you as soon as I finish arranging the trays," Mom said.

I decided not to push her for an answer in front of the servants; however, I smelled the rat, which filled my heart with mixed emotions.

Usually, a boy visits a girl with his parents, but that is not the case here. Mom would have insisted on seeing Nag's home; after all, I was her only daughter.

We were at Nag's house around four in the afternoon. The house had a cast-iron gate and high boundary walls and must have been spread on three to four acres. The house was on the right side, a typical large village house of the rich, and on the left side, under a tin shed, I saw several tractors and trolley trucks. Nag and his father and brothers welcomed us at the house entrance and guided us to a large living room, where the ladies greeted us by showering rose petals and spraying rose water. The living room was furnished with shining wooden furniture and beautiful paintings; I recognized two giant replicas of Raja Ravi Varma's *Hamsa Damayanthi Talking with Royal Swan* and *Goddess Saraswati*. In addition, two cradled panels encrusted in thick glass contained photos of ancestors. The room was proclaiming the amazing taste and affluence of its owners.

We all sat on the comfortable, stylish sofas, and Nag's Dad introduced his family, and my dad did the same. Nag's Mom gave me the feeling of a sweet and docile person; she was slim, with olive skin, her face reflected as if wearing a permanent smile, transforming her into a mellowed and lovable person. Nag's two sisters-in-law were beautiful, plump, and donned plentiful gold and diamond jewelry. In contrast, Nag's mother had only a single-string pearl necklace, diamond trinkets, two diamond bangles on her right hand, and a wristwatch on her left hand. Nag's father and brothers wore well-pressed formals and talked with genuine welcoming smiles. I was seated beside Mom and felt very uncomfortable because three ladies' eyeballs were penetrating my body. I had no clue what they were trying to ascertain by focusing on me; nonetheless, they made me uneasy, which I believe Nag's mother sensed and asked Nag to show me the house.

Nag rose from his seat and gestured for me to follow him; I looked at Mom, who signaled me to go, and I let out a sigh of relief and happily followed him inside the house. The back door opened into a large courtyard, the central area had a lovely carpet of green grass, and various flowering plants and creepers surrounded the edges.

Nag said, "We've six flats in the house, five of which have three bedrooms, and one serves as the kitchen, dining, washing, and storage. Three units are for the three sons, one for my sister and one for Mom and Dad. At the back of the house, we've quarters for domestic help.

"I needed to talk to you about the purpose of your visit, so we will go to my unit, where we can speak in privacy."

With a gesture to follow him, he walked toward the courtyard's left side, opened a door, and gave me a way to enter. It was an aesthetically furnished living room; I saw two large vases stuffed with long-stemmed, colored roses, filling the room with a relaxing fragrance. We sat on the comfortable sofas facing each other.

"I'm sure you must've been briefed or sensed that our elders are considering the possibility of our alliance," Nag said.

"Unfortunately, no one has uttered a word, but I understood the purpose," I said.

"Great, my mom informed me late last night that you're coming, and I should be here before noon.

With no offense, allow me to open my heart to you. The day I saw you, I prayed to God to give me a wife like you; you have everything a man could ask for: beauty, brains, and an excellent upbringing. I don't believe in miracles, but that's what's happening. Luckily, instead of getting a wife like you, I was presented with the possibility of marrying you. You must've ascertained by now that there's nothing in me that you could appreciate except for our matching cast. If you say no, then no hard feelings from my side, and I would consider myself lucky even if we could remain on talking terms," Nag said.

I remained silent for a few minutes and then said, "You're a good man; however, I've not looked at you from any other angle except as a businessperson. Therefore, it would be best to give me time to think, and in the meantime, you also seek your elders' feedback on my family and me."

"My mother already gave me a thumbs up, which means no one could dare challenge her decision. She never interferes in Dad's business, and when it comes to domestic decisions, no one, not even Dad, dares to question her. So, you could surely consider a big yes from my family, and I assure you that I'll always keep you happy and satisfied if you accept the alliance. But please don't take any pressure from my side or your parents, and, if you want me to say no, I could do that too," Nag said.

"Nag, give me some time to think. At this moment, I'm blank and unable to absorb whatever is happening," I said.

"Fine, Manju, but allow me to reiterate, don't take pressure from anyone to decide against your liking. You don't have to upset your family; I'm willing to be the bad person," Nag said.

"Thanks for being so kind, and as I said, at this moment, I'm blank, and you need to give me time to make a well-thought-out decision. If you don't have anything more to say, then can we go," I said.

"I've nothing more to say except that if you want a loving, caring husband who would stand with you in your thick and thin, you don't have to look far," Nag said with a chuckle.

I also laughed and said, "Nice try, Nag. I promise to check all the near and dear with a microscope."

"No, dear, I don't want you to check the near and dear; instead, look for a young pharma company owner who would pamper you like a princess and will always attend to your wish as a command. On a serious note, I don't think I deserve you; our upbringing and socioeconomic standing are worlds apart. You're wealthy and accustomed to a life of luxury, which I cannot provide; therefore, I implore you not to decide in my favor. Please take my comments as an honest admission of my limitations," Nag said.

"I heard you loud and clear and will decide considering everything that would be in the best interest of both of us," I said.

In the late evening, I went to see Dad in his home office and found him reviewing papers filed in a bulky file. Before I could say anything, Dad said, "Honey, your call; if you say yes, I would invest heavily to establish a large factory to manufacture branded drugs. The factory will be in your name; your hubby will be a working partner with a 20 percent stake. You take your time and decide, with no pressure from either your mom or me, but allow me to say we liked the family very much. They're hardworking, upright, and fairly educated. They have no demands whatsoever, and anything we'd give to our daughter is fine.

"Regarding Nag, I've made an extensive check on him starting from his hostel days and found him free from bad habits; he seems upright and studious, a man of few words, and very helpful and generous. According to one of his classmates, he helped many students with anything they wanted and used to pay quite a few poor students' college fees but never mentioned to anyone about his generosity. Your mom is pleased with Nag and his family, but I've told her we'd respect Manju's decision, so the ball is in your court. You decide and tell us."

Now I'm 55 years old, wife of the super-rich Nageshwar Rao, and mother of one son and two daughters. The elder daughter, my bundle of pleasure, was born after one year of my marriage and is married to an industrialist; she's also working as a senior executive in the Manju Group of Companies, which owns one of the largest Pharmaceutical Companies and several other businesses, such as food processing plants, cold stores, fish farming ponds, stitched garment factories, shopping arcades, and a 100-bed super specialty hospital for the opulent. Second is my son, who's studying MBBS. He is tall and of whitish complexion like his father, a slim and very handsome-looking boy, my heart. Finally, my last child is my doll, four years younger than my son, studying in the USA.

Chapter Two

Rama Rao

I was born into a wealthy family; my father, Nageshwar Rao, and my mother, Manjula Rao, built the Manju Group of Companies, a diversified conglomerate. Today, we're among the top 100 well-heeled families in our country. However, I never took pride in my family's richness. I was allergic to most family friends and relatives who persistently talked directly or indirectly about their wealth or the wealth-making ventures one should explore or undertake.

I derived pleasure by ensuring I remained the class topper and, in my spare time, playing with our servants' children, helping them with their homework, and seeing them smile thankfully at my gifts of chocolates or cakes. Mom used to taunt my father, saying his son has brought his genes, and that he's comfortable in the company of the servants' children and never invites or visits his schoolmates. Dad used to smile and tell Mom, "I'm proud he got my genes."

I have two sisters, the elder is four years older than me, and the younger is four years younger than me.

My father and mother are fitness freaks, and from a young age, they taught the three of us the importance of a nutritious diet and regular physical activities.

I am not a sportsperson, but Mom made me addicted to jogging, swimming, tennis, and shuttle badminton. My daily routine from class 8 has been to sleep at 10:30, wake up at 5:45, go for a thirty-minute jog at 6:00, and in the evening, 10 minutes of body warmup exercises, 15 minutes of jogging, and 45 minutes of shuttle badminton or tennis. My swimming is mostly restricted to weekends or holidays.

Mom used to play with me, run with me, swim with me, assist me with my homework, and sing beautiful lullabies to put me to sleep when I was a youngster. She was always my best friend, teacher, and loving and caring mother. Still, her love and care were on one side, and on the other side, I was getting groomed by her with an iron fist to make me capable of holding the responsibilities of a large business organization. She monitored all my activities from morning to evening, which wasn't restricted to what I ate or my homework. In addition, she was always in touch with my school teachers and the headmaster, ensuring that I maintained my grades and behaved well with my friends and teachers.

At the age of 14, when I was almost 5'8" tall. Mom hired several teachers to assist me in my school subjects and teach me banking, business process management, stock market dealings, martial arts, etiquette, how to become an influencer and lead a stress-free life, ballroom dances, yoga, and, lastly, public speaking. Most of the instructors were non-native and employed for being the best in parting the skills they mastered and earned a reputation for excellence.

I was learning all the teachings to my teachers' satisfaction; however, I couldn't develop an interest in running the empire for which she was grooming me.

My pleasure wasn't in making money but in serving the needy and bringing joy to the less fortunate souls. I decided to become a medical doctor at a tender age and build a charity hospital to provide free medical assistance to the needy. I was unsure whether I was right or wrong, but I couldn't or didn't want to adjust my perspective and alter the path I believed would lead to contentment. I think Mother Teresa has returned to the world and decided to relive in my body.

When I joined medical college, I asked Mom for a bike, which she flatly refused, and after lots of debate, she conceded to my subsequent request for a small used car of my choice.

Mom took me to a used car dealer and forced me to buy a three-year-old Honda Accord; even though I protested, it was too flashy and not a small car, but she refused to listen.

I hardly mingled with anyone in the college except a few male class fellows and no girlfriend, as most of them aimed to make loads of money or go abroad with or without a husband.

I met with Madhu Priya when I was in the fourth year of MBBS; she was a fresher. One morning, I parked my car and was about to step out when I jolted with a bang. My car was hit on the right-side rear bumper by a glitzy BMW X7. A ravishing young beauty in light blue faded jeans, a pink tunic top, and wearing shimmering shades came out of the car and said, "Is this your car?"

I said, "Yes, Ma'am, and I think you forgot that this is a parking area, and you need to drive slow."

"Oh, shut up, go to a repair shop and ask how much it would cost and take that money from me. My name is Madhu Priya, and I'm a fresher," Madhu said.

"Wait a minute," I said, got into my car, backed out of the parking spot, accelerated ahead, and slammed into the BMW's left side rear door, damaging it severely.

"You idiot, you'll pay dearly for your foolishness. Stay here for a few minutes and see what happens," she yelled.

I said, "Sure, Ma'am, I could wait as long as you want, and please inform me what it would cost you to repair your car and take that money from me. My name is Rama Rao, and I'm a fourth-year student."

"You wait here, and I'll make sure every bone in your body is smashed into tiny fragments," she shrieked, took out her mobile, and called someone.

I should call Mom or Dad, as this girl must be a rich brat and could call a gang of goons to come and beat me up. But I decided against it as Mom would come with 50 or 100 people to ensure I'm safe, and then she'll send me to college with bodyguards in a bulletproof car. Suddenly, I remembered that the director-general of police had come to our house for dinner a few months earlier, and as he was leaving, he gave me his mobile phone number and said feel free to call him for any assistance. Best to ask for help from the DGP, so I walked a few meters away from the car and called him; when he answered the call, I said, "Uncle, this is Rama Rao; I met with a car accident in my college parking area and wrecked a rich girl's BMW X7 car. She's calling some thugs to fix me. Could you assist me in sorting out this matter?"

He said, "Don't worry, I'll ask the assistant commissioner to look into this matter personally; stay calm and wait for the policemen to come. And, give me her car registration number."

"Sure," I said and gave him the plate number of her car. I disconnected the line after thanking him in advance for his assistance.

I heard the girl shouting on her mobile, "Dad, the stupid idiot damaged my car door on purpose just because he got a minor dent in his car while I was parking. Please send a few of your friendly police officers to break the bones of this duffer." Then, after a pause, I heard her saying in a low voice, "Okay, send the traffic police, but I want to press charges for damage to my car with the intent to inflict physical injury."

A traffic police inspector and a couple of constables arrived within a few minutes at the site, took Madhu's version of the accident, and then came to me to take my input. I said, "While parking, I lost control of my car and failed to apply break on time, which caused the hit to her car."

Before the inspector could ask further questions, a police car pulled up alongside our vehicles, and a police officer came out and took the traffic inspector aside. They whispered for a couple of minutes, and the traffic guy came to us and said, "The Commissioner's Office will handle your case; please go with the police officer, who has come to fetch you and Ma'am."

Madhu and I parked our cars as they should be and sat in the back seat of the police car. While seated, Madhu said to me, "You'll know who I'm when they lock you up and beat the hell out of you; my father, Venkateshwara Rao, is a prominent industrialist and a well-connected person."

I didn't respond to her utterance.

In 20 minutes, we reached the police headquarters. The inspector took us straight to the assistant commissioner's office, who welcomed us and asked us to take a seat on the sofa in front of his desk, and instructed the inspector to send tea for us.

"Before I settle your dispute, we will have tea, and Ms. Priya, we've spoken with your father and briefed him about the accident, and since he knows Mr. Rama Rao and his family well, he said he'll come here to sort out the issue. He's promised to be here in the next 15 to 20 minutes," the ACP said.

A well-dressed teaboy brought us tea and a variety of biscuits. I noticed that Madhu was perplexed and probably curious about how his father knew the family of this duffer.

While we were sipping our tea, a plump man pushing forties or in his early fifties, wearing a gray suit without a necktie, entered the room and, with a hello, came and sat beside me. "I'm very sorry, my son, as I'm sure it must be an oversight of my daughter. Please tell me what happened," he said.

I remembered seeing this man and his wife at one of our house parties long ago, so I decided to address him as Uncle. "Uncle, please ask your daughter what transpired, and then I'll give you my version," I said.

"Sure, Madhu, please tell us exactly what happened; before you relate the incident, allow me to mention that Rama's father is a God-sent angel to me, and whatever I'm now, it is due to his patronage," said Madhu's father.

She was giving surprised looks to her father and me. I think she never envisaged something like this to arise, and this garbage of a person could turn out to be the son of a VIP. After a few seconds, she said, "I want to withdraw my complaint. I accidentally damaged his car, and he also damaged my car. Since I was a little abrasive, I apologize if my behavior offended him."

"Rama, please forgive her, and I assure you, in the future, she'll not give room for a complaint to you or anyone in the college," Madhu's father said.

"She apologized, and I accept it; you don't have to apologize. Let's move on without any hard feelings, and I must go now as I've got a couple of important lectures," I said and rose from my seat.

We shook hands, and the ACP said, "I'll ask the driver to take you back to your college."

The police car dropped us at the college entrance gate, and while walking toward our lecture rooms, she said, "So you're the son of a VIP; your father must be a teacher of my father, as such respect you show only to your gurus."

"Please ask your father if you want to know about my dad. I'm just a student of this college and nothing more. So forget about me and the episode, and I wish you all the best in your future endeavors," I said and walked toward my lecture hall.

The next evening, when I reached home, I saw a brand-new BMW 7X parked on the porch with a gift wrap ribbon and a large bouquet of red roses on the front passenger seat. I asked one of the domestic helpers what was going on, and he expressed his ignorance.

I found Mom in the TV lounge and inquired about the BMW, "Venkatesh Saab's driver brought it, and I talked to your dad about it, and he said he would tell everything at the dinner table," Mom said.

"Whatever reason he may have given, I'm not going to accept it, period," I said.

"I wholeheartedly support you, as I believe we should never accept such expensive gifts from anyone or give such gifts. It is nothing but corruption," Mom said.

"Okay, Mom, let's not accept any justification from Dad and return it," I said.

"Fine with me," Mom said.

Dad asked me to tell him about the car accident at the dinner table.

I said, "Dad, that girl was driving fast and couldn't control her car while parking and hit my rear bumper. When I told her she should drive slowly when in the parking area, she got upset and, in an abusive manner, asked me to shut up and tell her how much it would cost to repair and take that money. Her arrogancy infuriated me, and I retaliated by smashing her car door, telling her to repair the damaged door and take the repair charges from me."

Dad didn't respond to my comments for a few minutes and then slowly said, "I don't appreciate your avenging attitude; particularly when dealing with a lady, you must be highly cautious. Of course, I accept that she shouldn't have acted the way she did, but still, you cannot justify your action. It would've been nice if you had forgiven her abusive behavior, assuming she must be in a terrible mood because of an unpleasant early morning occurrence that caused her to lose focus. Nobody likes to hit someone's car on purpose, particularly when driving an expensive car."

"Dad, I also felt the same afterward, but I got carried away in the heat of the moment," I said.

"Venkateshwara Rao, her father, has been a longtime friend of mine. He's sure his daughter must've wronged you, so as a gesture of apology on her behalf, he gifted you a decent car. I flatly refused to accept the gift, but he was adamant and said he'd given it to his son, and I couldn't deny him that pleasure. We don't have an option but to keep it because of his uncompromising stance, but don't worry; we'll return his gift with interest at an appropriate occasion," Dad said.

"Dad, we already have a fleet of expensive cars, and if I'm not mistaken, we've two top-of-the-range BMWs, so what would we do with this new toy," I said.

"You're right, but we don't have a choice," Dad said.

"Fine, Dad, but don't expect me to drive it," I said.

"Your call," Dad said.

After a couple of days, I got my car with the repaired bumper and took it to college: otherwise, I was shuttling in a taxi. After parking the car, while I was walking toward the main building, Madhu appeared from where I couldn't see and said, "Why you're not driving the expensive toy you got as a reward for damaging my car? And you know, as a punishment, I'm not allowed to drive my car, and a driver has been assigned to take me wherever I have to go."

"Miss, I feel sorry for you, and your dad's valued gift is inconsequential to me. I don't need it; I wouldn't drive it, and thanks to you, most likely, the whole college knows who I'm, which is very upsetting," I said.

"Let's forget whatever has happened and be friends. You're my senior, and I could learn a lot from you," Madhu said.

"Please keep away from me, as I don't have time for idle chat, particularly with a discourteous person," I said.

"Why you're so upset? I already accepted my stupidity and apologized. I urge you to close the chapter and move forward as good friends," Madhu said.

"I don't see any common ground to be friends. Your father's money has gone to your head, preventing you from understanding that you must be polite while dealing with less fortunate people. Try to bring a smile to a poor person's face with any act of kindness and witness the pleasure trickling through your body that no amount of material possession could ever give you. I also understand your motives to have friendly ties with me, in which I don't have any interest," I said.

"Oh, Mister, get off from your high horse and don't ever imagine that I want to be friends with you for any ulterior motive that probably you're cooking up in your ineffective upper chamber. I thought you were a sensible person and being senior to me; I could learn a few things if we became friends. However, I was hugely mistaken; you're a nasty person, and having any relationship with you would be foolish," Madhu snarled.

"Ms. Priya, don't you think you're taking too much liberty in expressing your views as I don't allow and appreciate someone being disrespectful or throwing insults at me," I said.

"You've started with a barrage of insults and humiliation, and when I retaliate, why you're objecting?" Madhu said.

"Ms. Priya, I wish you good luck in all that you're aspiring to achieve; please spare me, and don't bother to meet with me again, for whatsoever reason," I said and walked toward the college building.

She didn't initiate any conversation with me after that encounter; however, I noticed she stood intentionally in the corridors from where I passed to my lecture halls. Further, after a few weeks, I noticed she switched to eastern dresses from her usual jeans and tops. To say she was beautiful was like lessening her beauty; she was a gorgeous drop-dead classy dame, a little plumpish – typical rich well-fed girl, height about five feet six or seven inches, pale white skin color, sharp features, and brilliant bright white eyes.

I wanted to accept her offer to be friends with her; she's beautiful and intelligent, or else she wouldn't have got a free MBBS seat in this prestigious college. Regrettably, my perspective on life was the polar opposite of hers. Her outward appearance showed that she placed a high value on luxury and excess in her life, and her obnoxious behavior revealed that she was used to wielding her wealth and power.

My primary goal was to make the world a better place for the disadvantaged, and I preferred an unassuming way of life to a pretentious one. Even friendship would be impossible to maintain because of our divergent approaches, which would only lead to friction and strains. So, despite her beauty and intelligence, I decided not to squander my time in her company.

Until I completed my MBBS, I saw Madhu almost every day in the corridor, canteen, or library. However, I neither tried to recognize her nor attempted to get into a dialog with her.

I did MBBS and MD Medicine and went to a reputed Mumbai college to do DM (Cardiology). After securing the Doctorate, I went to Sydney, Australia, for a one-year internship with a world-renowned Interventional Cardiology professor.

Upon completion of my internship, I returned to Hyderabad, and one evening, I had to sit with Mom and Dad to discuss my plans.

I said, "For a few months, I want to work in Manju Super Specialty Hospital under one of our senior cardio doctors. I'll also work with various charity hospitals who need my services until I get into a position to establish a large multi-specialty charity hospital."

Dad said, "Whatever you want to do, I'm with you, but you must give the company two to three days every week."

"Dad, even two days is too much; initially, I'll give one day from nine to two, and in the late afternoons, I would attend the board meetings or any meeting that requires my presence," I said.

"Please find a way to work one day in the morning and two days in the afternoon from three to six or seven. You must be aware that Manju Group is a multibillion-dollar company with branches in more than 100 countries. Soon, you'd to run this mammoth organization. Primarily, you'd be responsible for maintaining profitability, continually increasing market share for your products, venturing into new territories, adopting new technologies, and adding new products," Dad said.

"Dad and Mom, please understand; I've been pursuing my aspirations to serve the less fortunate and build a charity hospital for them since I was young. We've only one life in this form; if we spend it to accumulate wealth, we wouldn't have time to accomplish our objectives and leave behind a legacy that future generations will remember and follow. Money-making is perfectly fine, and to do that, we've hundreds of highly paid executives who are hardcore professionals that understand how to increase profitability, expand product lines, and keep the business efficient and lean. You know well that I cannot say no to you for anything, but I beg you to allow me to use my skills and make the lives of the needy happier," I said.

Dad looked at Mom, probably asking her to respond to me; after a while, Mom said, "Give us a few days to get back to you."

After a couple of days, while having dinner, Dad said, "Rama, tomorrow morning, you come with me to the office, as I wanted you to meet with a few senior executives."

"Fine, Dad," I said.

As agreed, the next day, I went with Dad to the corporate office, and instead of taking me to his chamber, he took me to the meeting room, where Mohini, my elder sister, and three men wearing well-pressed suits were sitting. Dad introduced the men as Manju Group's chief operating officer, chief financial officer, and chief executive officer. Mohini was the head of pharma companies and real estate. He then said, "From now on, every Monday morning from 11:am to 1:pm, all of us would meet here to give my son an update on how we're performing, what issues we're facing, the status of new ventures in the offing, any new projects that we intend to undertake, which are the untapped markets and what's holding us to do business in those markets, and any other matters that senior management must be aware of, or whether any action is needed to tackle them. In addition, he'll work here for two days in the afternoon, and if any of you need to update him or seek his input, feel free to contact him," Dad said.

After 20 minutes of feedback on various business fronts from my sister and the executives, Dad excused the three executives, and the meeting room turned into a family chat room. My sister expressed extreme pleasure in my business participation – though it wasn't enough, it was a good beginning. While we were on family matters, Dad received an intercom call, and after hearing it, he asked the caller to send him to the meeting room.

A middle-aged, semi-bald, gray-haired man dressed in a sky-blue suit and a matching silk tie entered the room. Dad welcomed and gestured to sit beside him and introduced him as Ajit Kumar, one of India's most renowned architects, particularly well-known for designing hospitals and dustproof buildings for pharmaceutical companies.

He then addressed me and said, "Rama, you're aware our hospital has 12 acres of land, but it was constructed on approximately one acre. The remaining space was set aside for future expansion. I want to utilize the vacant land to construct a charity hospital for you on the extreme left of the entrance. Please inform Ajit how you envisage your hospital building or buildings and based on your input, he'll prepare drawings for your approval."

All of us spent nearly two hours with Ajit to come to an understanding of what I wanted. Two five-storied hospital buildings with separate entrances and a three-storied basement for parking. Each hospital building should have 300 beds for inpatients, with provision to increase the bed capacity. One hospital would provide pro-bono services to the underprivileged; the other would serve middle-income people who can afford to pay a reasonable amount for their medical treatment and care. Then, at the back of the hospital, two five-storied large accommodation buildings for outstation medical staff. Doctors' accommodation will have 60 apartments, 56 flats on four floors, and the top floor will have only six large apartments for the senior-most doctors. The paramedic and support staff building should have 120 two-bedroom flats.

I excused myself after Ajit left as I had an afternoon meeting with the Manju Hospital's cardio doctors.

Mom had been pushing me to get married since my return, but I refused, saying let me settle down, and then we would discuss it. Now I got another excuse, saying let the hospital get ready, and then I'll think. Somehow, I couldn't find myself mentally prepared for marriage.

My daily schedule became so hectic the day we started construction of the hospital buildings that I had little time for leisure activities, even on Sundays. Everyone participating in the hospital project worked 12–14 hours a day, and the construction contractors worked two to three shifts. As a result, it took less than two years to complete the infrastructure.

A couple of months before the tentative date of opening the hospitals, we advertised in pan-India English daily newspapers to fill doctor vacancies. I established a panel of four doctors, including myself, to hire qualified doctors genuinely interested in serving the downtrodden and destitute. In addition, Manju Hospital's HR department was assigned to recruit technicians, paramedics, administrative, and support staff.

A Hyderabad-based doctor, Madhumati Priya, MD (Medicine) DM (Nephrology), caught my eye while I was going through a large bundle of doctors' resumes. She was 28 years old, single, and worked for several charitable hospitals in various parts of the city. I figured she was as crazy as I was for choosing to work for charity instead of a corporate hospital where she might make a lot of money and gain fame. Despite lacking the needed experience, she was a well-qualified nephrologist to head the department, so I decided to call her for an interview.

Daily in the afternoon, we took interviews for 2–3 hours; on the fourth day, Dr. Madhumati Priya came. I instantaneously recognized her; she was the same Madhu I had encountered almost nine years ago. She must've lost between 10–15 kilos; yet, she looked stunningly beautiful in her simple off-white cotton salwar-kameez and wore no jewelry except diamond ear trinkets and a wristwatch sporting inside the wrist.

Her looks and appearance announced that she was a changed person: from the chirpy, aggressive, glamorous, and well-fed, she now appeared malnourished, with her sunken cheeks and slim body. I signaled the senior doctors to proceed with the interview.

"Ms. Priya, I noticed from your resume that you only work for various charity hospitals. Do you get paid for your services, or you're offering them for free?" one of the panel doctors asked.

"I offer my services for free," Madhu said.

"If you're providing free services, then how are you making a livelihood?" another doctor in the panel asked.

"I own real estate, which gives me enough rental income to meet all my needs comfortably," Madhu said.

"Could you tell us your expectations toward salary and perks? And remember, it's a charity hospital, but still, we don't want anyone to work for nothing or peanuts," commented one panelist.

"I don't need any salary; however, I would appreciate it if I could get accommodation. My house is at least 12 kilometers from here, and considering the peak traffic, daily shuttling would be inconvenient and time-consuming," Madhu said.

The interview lasted over 20 minutes. The three doctors asked her several questions regarding her professional experience, hobbies, whether she would be interested in becoming the head of the Nephrology Department, and so on. She stated she had little over one year of experience working independently. She had no issues heading the department; lastly, she had no time for hobbies, except for reading medical journals to stay updated and jogging in the morning for an hour, six days a week.

I didn't ask her any questions during the entire interview, and nor did she look at me – very strange! However, she impressed me with her unpretentious appearance, poise, and charity work.

When she switched to casual Indian attire, I thought she did that to seek my attention – but now, seeing her still wearing salwar-kameez after so many years was remarkable, especially given her credentials as a highly accomplished medico. She truly amazed me.

I requested a 10–15-minute break from my panelists to ask her a few questions about my college days when I was her senior.

After they left, I said, "So, Ms. Priya, how's your dad and everyone, and why do you want to come and stay here in a small two- or three-bedroom apartment?" I asked.

"Sir, I'll answer questions related to my job application," she said admonishingly.

"Sorry if I offended you; please tell me why you want to join this hospital when you already work with several charity hospitals," I asked.

"I've to visit quite a few hospitals every day, and this ritual is causing me to spend at least 2–3 hours hopping from one hospital to the next, which is inconvenient and a waste of valuable work hours. In addition, the lack of qualified support workers who could satisfactorily manage inpatients is another dismal aspect of these small facilities," she stated.

"Why didn't you join one of the large charity hospitals to avoid wasting your valuable time?" I inquired.

"There are no large charity hospitals in our city," she snapped.

"Madhu, allow me to ask one personal question, and it is up to you to answer or refuse. Did I hurt you so severely that you decided to transform from a glamorous, bubbly girl to a serious and unassuming person?" I asked.

"I don't want to answer you; however, because you've played a role in helping me become the person I'm today, I'll respond. Yes, your comments caused me to reevaluate my lifestyle, which was no different from any other person in my circle of friends. I decided to follow your suggested path to see if it would assist me in becoming a better person. It wasn't easy at first to make the transition to something I had never done or experienced before. Still, slowly, I started enjoying my new avatar of an ordinary-looking run-of-the-mill person who enjoys the company of the less fortunate and makes them happy by extending a helping hand to provide for their needs. Thank you very much for whatever you said, as that enabled me to become content and happy. Please don't ask any more personal questions; I'll not answer," Madhu said haughtily.

"Fine; however, I must commend you on becoming someone who wants to bring joy to the suffering people. The panel would decide and revert to you regarding your job application," I said.

She said "fine" and left the room. I've no idea why, but I felt a little disheartened by her abrupt exit.

The panel unanimously selected her as the head of the Nephrology Department, and I instructed HR to send her the appointment letter, which they did and received acceptance in a few days.

I was overjoyed when HR informed me that Madhu had accepted the job offer.

However, I had no clue as to why I was delighted with her coming on board. I was tempted to phone her and say welcome but decided against it because she might not take it well. She must be a strongminded person; in anger, I made a few annoying comments, and she reformed herself and never bothered to speak to me again. Had she approached me again in her changed appearance, I would've yielded her desire to establish a friendship bond.

Since seeing her at the interview, she had been on my mind and had kept popping up for no apparent reason. Finally, after spending a lot of time thinking about her, I concluded that the only way to let go of my remorse for mistreating her was to form a friendly relationship. To begin with, I decided to do excellent interiors for her hospital accommodation, which would hopefully soften her up for the friendship.

The top floor of the doctor's accommodation had six apartments of 6,000 square feet for the senior doctors. Out of the six flats, one was much more spacious as it had a huge balcony that could easily accommodate 50 persons; I allocated that for Madhu. I engaged a highly praised home decorator firm known for its exorbitant charges and high-quality work. It took them a little over ten weeks to achieve the task. When I inspected the flat, I was pleased with their work: light pink granite floor, open kitchen living room, lovely motorized curtains, comfortable electric recliner sofas, a large TV, surround home theater, and gorgeous carpets. The kitchen had everything one could dream of, exquisite tableware and kitchenware and state-of-the-art equipment. The bedrooms were aesthetically decorated, and the teak furniture gave a grandeur look; walls were decorated with eye-soothing lovely sea and landscape oil paintings. The study room and the gym were furnished with expensive furniture and equipment. The living room had an 8' × 8' replica of Sobha Singh's *Sohni Mahiwal*; opposite that wall was a replica of Jamini Roy's *Mother And Child*. The balcony had a motorized acrylic retractable roof and sidewalls, and it was decked with exotic outdoor plants and outdoor cane furniture. I had no idea what prompted me to spend such a large sum of money or whether I expected anything from her for my generosity.

Three days before the hospital's opening, in the evening, I was sitting in my office with a few supervisors who were hired to maintain the entire Manju Hospital, accommodation buildings, and the surroundings. I received a call from the receptionist that Dr. Priya wanted to see me, and I asked her to send her in and excuse the supervisors. Within a few minutes, Madhu, with a knock, entered the room, Dressed in sky-blue cotton salwar-kameez, with no makeup whatsoever but still looking gorgeous.

I gestured her to a chair, and before she could say anything, I asked, "Have you moved into your accommodation, Doctor?"

"Yes, and would you please tell me why my flat was furnished lavishly compared to the other flats, which have bare-bone furniture and furnishings?" she said sternly; anger and dismay were visible from her facial expression.

"Doctor Priya, you're used to living in a plush place, and an uncomfortable dwelling would slowly reflect in an unacceptable underperformance, which we do not want," I said.

"No, Sir, I disagree with your assertion; I would be happy if you allocate me a two-bedroom flat with basic furnishings, and I guarantee you that it won't affect my performance," she said firmly.

"No, Doctor, I refuse to accept your request. If you want to work in this hospital, you must stay in the assigned accommodation," I vehemently said.

"This is too much. When my father gave you a BMW, you refused to use it, and now you're forcing me to accept something I don't want. I would highly appreciate it if you reconsider your decision, as I've decided not to stay in that flat," she said indignantly.

"I'm not giving you a choice; if you want to work here, you must stay in that flat only," I said mutedly.

"Sir, I don't understand why you're forcing me to accept something I don't want," she said faintly.

"Madhu, I've spent a lot of time ensuring that your nights and weekends are comfortable and relaxing. And, please, don't forget, your body is not used to the beating you want to give, so don't make an issue of your accommodation," I said.

"Tell me how I'd explain to my peers why I got such a nice place compared to what they were provided," she scoffed.

"You could tell them that was the condition for accepting the job," I said.

"I insist you reconsider your decision, and I'll also think of my options," she said and left the room without saying a word of courtesy.

On the hospital's opening day, she was present and attended the luncheon organized for the doctors, which was a significant relief to me; I wanted her to work for the hospital for incomprehensible reasons.

I asked the admin to inform me of her daily schedule, and after a few days, they reported that she comes at nine, goes to her inpatient ward, and then attends the outpatients till three. Afterward, she takes an approximately forty-five-minute lunch break and returns to the hospital around four, checking patients till six. Then, before calling it a day, she checks her inpatients and leaves the hospital.

Day by day, her patients' inflow increased, and within two months, I noticed that she was working 12–14 hours, six days a week. To reduce her workload, I decided to hire one or two junior doctors to work under her; otherwise, it could destroy her physical and mental health if she continued to slog this way.

One evening, around five, I called her to check whether she was free to see me, and she said she would come to my room after a few minutes.

The few minutes turned out to be three-fourths of an hour, and when she arrived, she didn't say a word about keeping me waiting for so long. Instead, without any preamble of a courtesy word, she said, "Tell me why you wanted to meet me."

I said, "I heard you're putting up very long hours because of the substantial increase in patient inflow."

She took a few moments to respond and then said, "Yes, it is true; sixty-plus patients come every day. And, unfortunately, I'm finding it difficult to give enough time to every patient."

"We had budgeted for three assistant doctors and a Department Head, so you've got the option of hiring one, two, or three more doctors to assist you," I said.

"At this time, I only require one assistant; however, if and when I require additional support, I'll revert to you," Madhu said.

"I'll tell HR to put out an ad for an assistant doctor, and you conduct the interview and choose a suitable candidate. Are you dealing with any other challenges that require my assistance?" I asked.

"No, everything is okay; I'll inform you if I encounter any issues needing your assistance. Can I go now, as I still have some work to finish?" Madhu said.

"Is it possible to come to your apartment this Saturday, say around seven? To check all is well and you're comfortable," I asked.

"I spend the weekends at my parents' house. Rest assured that all is well in the hospital and at the apartment, and if I need your help, I'll approach you. Thanks for offering your assistance, and I must leave now," she said and rose from the chair.

I said, "If you're not available over the weekend, tell me when you would be free to see me; I just want to check the apartment and have a cup of coffee with you."

"I'm busy in the evenings; apart from that, I've no time for friends or idle chat. You have a good evening, Sir," she said, emphasizing "sir," and left the room.

Even though I wasn't expecting such rudeness, it didn't offend me. There was no reason to get upset when she merely returned the coin I had given her almost a decade ago. Reports of her being a highly accomplished professional were pouring in from her support staff, colleagues, and patients, which increased my yearning to know more about her. I had no idea what I wanted to know and why, but I was longing to spend time in her company, which looked challenging. A girl who could sacrifice everything on a minor condemnation of enjoying her parents' money could stand firm forever on her decision to avoid my companionship.

When she was in college, the entire population of male boys must've chased her for being a prized catch; she had everything to go after her – beauty, intelligence, and, to top it all, a money bag. She must've turned down even the best of the best marriage proposals, demonstrating a punishing control over her passions combined with an unwavering determination to help the impoverished. When I compared myself to her, I didn't think I was anywhere near her. I was born with a gentle heart, and from a tender age, I enjoyed lending a helping hand to the less fortunate. However, it was unimaginable for me to give up all the luxuries and become a Lord Buddha at the age of 18 or 19, especially when you come from an affluent family and accustomed to a lavish lifestyle. Every passing day, this girl was becoming an obsession for me; I was trying to find ways to meet her, talk to her, learn about her likes and dislikes, and take her out to wine and dine. Refusal of my advances by this girl made me more assertive in my quest to develop friendly ties with her.

While going home, I decided not to contact her for a few weeks and see whether she regrets her despicable behavior. Then I thought she must've felt about me the same way years ago when I treated her disgracefully and never apologized or bothered to say hello when we crossed our paths.

Within two weeks of my meeting with Madhu, she hired Dr. Nazia Khan, who had just secured her MD in Medicine, to assist her, but she didn't thank me; I wasn't expecting her to call, but it was depressing. I couldn't erase her from my system; she was propping up whenever I got a leisure moment. This scenario was annoying, and I had no recourse to mutate this befalling. Moreover, I had no clarity about what I wanted from her; I wasn't in love with her, nor did I want to marry her, but I was dying to spend time in her company.

Mom was exerting immense pressure for marriage; she was willing to find a suitable girl; otherwise, I must tell her about anyone I liked.

Neither Mom nor Mohini could help me find the girl of my choice, and if left to them, they would come up with at least a couple of dozen beautiful, educated, rich brats who would make my life pitifully miserable. It was better if I looked around for my choice, but it was almost impossible to find someone of my liking.

It seemed like I was trying to zero in on Madhu, and all my excuses and set criteria were just bullshit. She had occupied my heart and brain so intensely that I continuously thought about her. If this was what it meant to fall in love, I was profoundly in love and attracted to her beauty, intelligence, and commitment to serving the poor, all of which were the virtues I wanted in my wife. Suddenly, I felt like my brain had shed a mountain of weight and released dopamine, oxytocin, serotonin, and endorphins instantaneously, all the happy hormones! I had found my life partner, but persuading her to marry me seemed challenging. If I ask Mom to talk to her parents about the alliance, and if Madhu refuses, Mom will be mad at her, causing unnecessary issues which could become hard to iron out. On the other hand, if I approach her with the proposal, I may fail in my first attempt, but my continuous chase may yield a positive result.

I decided to start my journey of a thousand miles; strangely, I was nervous about the arduous task of winning her over.

I called the building supervisor and asked him to inform me of Dr. Madhu Priya's daily routine. A couple of days later, he informed me, "She comes out at 6:00 every morning and spends an hour exercising and jogging. Then at quarter to 9:00, she leaves for the hospital and returns around 3:00 for half an hour to 45 minutes for lunch and again goes to the hospital and returns anytime between 6:00 and 8:00. Every day around 2:00 pm, a driver brings a lunchbox from her parent's house and gives it to the building guard."

The following evening at 7:30, I armed myself with a bouquet of red roses and a large Swiss chocolate box and went to her apartment. After a couple of minutes of continuously pressing the bell, she partly opened the door and, in a hostile tone, said, "Good evening, Sir, what can I do for you?"

I couldn't think of anything to say; however, I summoned the courage and said, "As I informed before, I'd like to check the flat to make sure you're comfortable and don't require anything."

"I believe I mentioned that I'm comfortable and don't need anything. And please tell me, is it a part of your duty to go to every resident, check their flat and ask whether they need anything to make their stay comfortable?" she said sarcastically.

I kept my cool and said, "Can I come in and talk about my duties, responsibilities, and everything you want to know?"

"I shouldn't allow you, you're uninvited, but if you insist, please come; however, I cannot spare more than five minutes, as I'm in the middle of some important reading that I must finish before I go to bed," she said in the same unwelcoming and hostile tone.

I walked in and said, "This is for you." I offered her the red rose flower bouquet and chocolate box.

She didn't take them and said, "Sorry, I cannot accept them, as I don't want to spoil our beautiful relationship of employer and employee; please take them with you."

I kept both items on the living room table and made myself comfortable on a recliner sofa. Madhu sat on a sofa opposite where I sat and said, "Sir, I don't think you go to every flat to find out whether they're comfortable or need any assistance to improve upon the facilities. So, please tell me why you're so kind to me?"

"You're the only one I'm concerned about because of our family ties, as I don't want your dad to complain that I didn't look after you well," I said.

"Oh really? I'm much obliged by your genuine concern for my wellbeing. Now for the last time, allow me to reiterate that I'm comfortable and don't need any assistance to make my stay further enjoyable. So please look at whatever you want to see; if satisfied, I must be excused," she said caustically.

"I haven't come here to look at anything; instead, I'm here to check whether you need any help to make your stay more comfortable. For example, do you want me to provide you with a cook, or any other assistance, so you don't miss anything that you were very much used to having?" I asked.

"I appreciate your overwhelming concern and benevolence, and as I said earlier, I don't need any help, and when I want something, I'll contact you," she said tersely.

"Madhu, can you not forget what happened between us years ago? Then, I was immature and living in an idealistic world, and anyone who wasn't subscribing to my approach toward life wasn't worthy of my friendship, which was pure stupidity. I've felt bad for misbehaving with you since I met you, and I'm disappointed that you changed your life to prove me wrong because of my adolescent folly. I want you to show your inner beauty by forgiving and becoming my lifelong friend," I stated solemnly.

She kept quiet for a few moments and then said, "Sir, whatever I'm doing today is not to prove you or anyone else or under coercion; my work has become my fountain of pleasure. As long as I'm alive and active, I'll continue to do whatever I'm doing now. So please, take credit for your guidance instead of feeling sorry for me and apologizing. Becoming your buddy is out of the question; I don't have the time or interest to form any relationship with you or anyone."

Insulting response, but I maintained my calm and said, "My absurdity has been haunting me since I interviewed you, and I regularly have sleepless nights. I urge you to reconsider your decision; now we both have common grounds to talk and enjoy each other's company, which will also assist in easing out my burden of not treating a lady with respect?"

"Sir, I don't have time to spend with you or anyone; during the working days, I get very little time to relax, and I spend weekends at my parents' house, catching up with my sleep and family affairs. I'm sure you would find plenty of girls who would blissfully enjoy your company. If you've nothing more to discuss, then allow me to resume my reading," she said.

"Okay, Madhu, I say goodbye for now, but do reconsider your decision, and please note that I don't want any other girl's company," I said.

"Good night, Sir, and in the future, please call me before you plan a visit to see how comfortable I'm. My cell number is in my resume," she said cynically.

I didn't respond and walked toward the door, and she shouted, "Sir, please take your flowers and the gift box."

"Throw them in the garbage bin," I said and walked out.

I wasn't expecting anything else to happen, but it did leave a sour taste in my mouth. Madhu seemed hell-bent on making me pay for how I wronged her a decade ago. However, before starting my aggressive chase, I must determine whether she was engaged or in a relationship. And, if the road was clear from such impediments, sarcasm or naysaying shouldn't deter me from marrying her.

I told Mom to come to my room before retiring, as I needed to talk to her about a possible alliance. She was thrilled, kissed my forehead, and promised to come after her dinner and stroll.

Mom entered my room around 9:30 with two cups of herbal tea, which she used to sip every night while watching TV. "Tell me, darling, every detail about my soon-to-be daughter-in-law," she said.

"Mom, you remember I fought with Venkateshwara Rao Saab's daughter, and he gifted me a BMW, as it was his daughter, Madhu Priya, who rubbed with me," I said.

"Yes, I remember it very well," Mom said.

"Have you seen Madhu immediately after that or in the recent past?" I asked.

"I met her only once at her house, and this was before your fight. Her father invited us and a few business associates for dinner to celebrate the opening of a new factory. I remember her as beautiful, bubbly, and full of energy. Are you interested in her?" Mom asked.

"Mom, she's now a nephrologist, working for Manju Charity Hospital, and heads the Nephrology Department. She's an altogether changed person. Before joining our hospital, she worked for various small charity hospitals. I'm incredibly impressed with her competence, dedication, and simplicity. If she's unattached, then I'll talk to her, as it's not going to be easy, and the possibility of a flat refusal is very high," I said.

"What? Why on earth do you think she would turn down your proposal? If I told her mother about the alliance, she would die out of extreme pleasure. If you like her so much, tell me why we cannot approach them with the proposal, which they would accept without asking for time to deliberate among themselves," Mom said.

"Mom, after our fight, she tried to be friendly with me, and at that time, she was nothing but a rich brat, throwing insults probably at everyone owing to her father's money and stature. I refused to interact with her and told her not to bother me as our life approaches were oceans apart. The next year, until I completed my MBBS, she did her best to be visible to me by standing in the corridors from where I would pass, the canteen, or near my car. She even switched from jeans and tops to a simple cotton salwar-kameez, but I completely ignored her. She's now a brilliant doctor who has dedicated herself to serving the poor and needy and most likely decided not to marry, as she's now 28 years old and still single. A few weeks ago, I tried to be friendly and asked her a personal question. She flatly refused to answer and cautioned me to behave. Considering this, I believe she would refuse my alliance; I don't want you to approach the family unless she commits to me. Before talking to her, I wanted you to find out from her mom whether she's engaged or involved. To get the information, tell her mom a family friend is looking for a girl, or cook up whatever you think is right, but don't say your loving son is taking an interest in her," I said.

"Okay, so if she's unattached, you want to woo her and chase her till she says yes. But, in the light of what you said, I believe you may have to spend a lot of time to soften her up, and unfortunately, I could give you only a few weeks," Mom said smilingly.

"Mom, one day at a time, first give me the good news and then let me worry about your deadline," I said.

"Okay then, good night, and I hope to give you the good, bad, or ugly news tomorrow when you return from the hospital," she said and left the room after kissing my forehead.

The next evening, when I reached home and looked at Mom inquisitively, she said, "After dinner, I'll come to your room."

Mom came to the room with the usual two cups of herbal tea and said, "I've good and bad news. Which one do you want to hear first?"

"Mom, you're a sadist, but I know both the good and the bad news. She's single but refusing to marry," I said.

Mom laughed aloud and said, "You're my son; yes, that's the answer I got. Her mom was in tears and asked my help to make her agree to the marriage, and it seems she rejected some of the best suitable proposals that no sane girl would refuse. The entire family is upset with her, but she's not budging from her decision to remain single and serve the poor. Good luck to you, and don't forget you only have a few weeks; whether you woo her or anyone, I don't care, but do it fast, or else I'll get a girl of my choice."

"Mom, you're not only a sadist but cruel. Instead of helping me find a solution to this problematic scenario, you're talking about the deadline. Please help me, Mom; you know I'm not good at chasing girls; guide me on how to begin this journey of improbabilities and succeed in my mission," I said.

"Honey, your problem, you fix it whichever way you think it could be fixed. You have everything to make any girl on earth agree to marry you, so don't get nervous by one unfriendly response. Smart girls generally don't cave in easily; keep hammering until you crack. Best of luck, my love; I may come to your rescue only if you fail in all your attempts and still want to marry her," Mom said.

"Thank you, Mom, for giving me the strength to pound on her encased hard shell," I sincerely said.

As usual, Mom kissed my forehead and left the room.

I called the florist shop owner of our Hospital; asked him to put a large bouquet of exotic flowers in Madhu's consultation room every day, before 9:00 in the morning, and every evening at 7:00, send a bunch of 10 long-stemmed red roses to her apartment.

The next day at 3:00 in the afternoon, I got a call from Madhu, asking why I had asked the florist to put a flower bouquet in my room every day.

"I wanted to thank you for your hospitality," I said.

"Sir, I don't appreciate your flowers, and your gestures won't help you either, as I've no interest in developing friendly ties with you or any other person," she said curtly.

"Madhu, don't be stubborn; I've decided to be your friend for life. I'll come in the evening to have a cup of coffee and to continue our dialog, to overcome this stalemate," I said.

"I'll not open the door, so it is better for you if you don't come," she said in the same hostile tone.

"I'll knock on your door till you open it, and it doesn't matter if the whole building comes to the floor to check on what's happening," I said with a chuckle.

"You won't find me in the apartment; I'll go to my parents' house after finishing the day," she said firmly.

"No, you're not going anywhere, or it won't be difficult to find your parents' house. I bet they would be thrilled with my visit and welcome me with open arms," I said with a loud laugh.

"What wrong have I done, and why do you want to disturb my peaceful life; please, I beg you to leave me alone," she said.

"Madhu, you're fooling yourself, don't let an idiot's rant destroy your beautiful personality. Instead, enjoy life like any other normal person," I said.

"Fine, I'll do that, but not in your company," she snarled.

"So, you're saying you believe in harboring grudges and taking revenge?" I asked.

"Look, if you bug me, I'll resign. I'm content and happy with what I'm doing and would highly appreciate it if you keep your nose out of my life," she roared.

"Madhu, whatever I'm telling you is for your good; please behave and be reasonable. Of course, we all make mistakes, but that doesn't mean that you punish yourself or others because of a silly omission of an irrelevant person in your life," I said, maintaining my calm.

"You don't have to preach to me what I should or shouldn't do. It's my life, and I've every right to lead a life I idealize," she growled.

"Madhu, I'll see you in the evening to continue our discussion," I said.

She disconnected the line without a word.

At 7:30, I was at Madhu's apartment, and after five minutes and several times pressing the calling bell, she opened the door, just enough to show her face, and before she could say anything, I pushed the door hard so that it opened wide and walked in without her permission. She thundered, "There's something called manners; entering someone's house without permission is ill-mannered and unlawful."

"Thank you for enlightening; please feel free to complain to law enforcement authorities. Is my coffee ready?" I asked.

She didn't answer my question, so I went toward the kitchen to help myself, but before I reached the espresso machine, she came rushing and said, "Don't dirty my kitchen; go and sit in the TV lounge for a few minutes, and I'll prepare your coffee."

"Thanks, that's like a good girl; I take my coffee with one spoon of sugar and no milk," I said and went to the TV lounge and lodged myself on a single-seater sofa.

Within a few minutes, she came with a coffee mug and gave me and said, "Sir, I'm in the middle of some important work, so please finish your coffee and excuse me."

"Go and get ready; I'm taking you for dinner," I said.

"What makes you think I would come with you for dinner? It is not part of my contract, binding me to wine and dine with you," she barked.

"I've resolved to undo what I did ten years ago and turn you back into the person I quarreled with. I'm not saying you shouldn't serve the underprivileged; please continue to do that but be normal, get married, and enjoy family life, like our parents. Cherish the pleasure of raising kids, take them around the world, expose them to different cultures, and ask them to carry forward the mission you've taken up. Now enough of the philosophical dose, go and get ready, or else I'll take you out in your nightdress," I said.

"This is too much; I don't want to go out with you, and you're threatening to use force, but take it from me: if you take me under coercion, you'll see my resignation tomorrow morning. And make a note, marriage is not on my bucket list and never will be," she shouted, her eyes shot out with rage.

"Fine, just go and get ready," I said.

Without saying a word, she went to her bedroom and returned within 10 minutes, wearing a cotton beige salwar-kameez and light makeup but looking stunningly beautiful.

I took her hand and walked toward the entrance door; she pulled her hand and said, "I'm coming; there's no need for you to hold my hand."

I had been using the BMW car gifted to me by her father for the past few days. I asked her whether she recognized the BMW when we sat in the car.

She said, "Yes, it is the same car my father gifted you, as I still remember the color and model, so why are you using it now when you refused to use it when given to you?"

"You're right; when it was given to me, you were a different person, but now you've become a person from whom I would love to take anything, regardless of its value," I said with a chuckle.

"Please yourself, but if you're thinking of having a friendly relationship with me, you're hugely mistaken. Today I'm coming with you, as I wanted to avoid an unpleasant scene. However, tomorrow I'll decide whether to move out or resign," Madhu snarled.

"Even if you resign, I'll not accept it, and if you move out of the apartment, I'll come to your house, and I assure you that your mom and dad will be excited to see me. Of course, once I put you on the right path, I'll not bother you, but till then, you must follow my guidelines on how to lead a normal life," I said, smiling.

"But, Sir, why don't you put your house in order? You're now possibly in your early thirties and still unmarried. So first you marry and then come to preach to me or others about the benefits of being married and normal or whatever you want to call it," Madhu said curtly.

"I'm working hard on that, and you bet you would soon learn I'm happily married," I said with a chuckle.

"Great, then go and have fun with your soon-to-be wife, and stop torturing me to spend time in your company," she barked.

"That's what I'm doing, honey," I said with a loud laugh.

"In your dreams. First of all, I'll not marry anyone, and even if I decide to marry, you bet it will not be you," she said contemptuously.

I ignored her comments and said, "Madhu, I'm not against enjoying a good life or earning money. However, I'm against the ostentatious display of affluence; mainly, I'm dead opposed to showing off your wealth in front of less fortunate people. From 9th grade, I used the school bus, as I saw envy in the eyes of many fellow students while I was alighting from my shining expensive cars. When I joined college, my mother insisted I go to college in a chauffeur-driven vehicle. I refused and requested a motorbike, which she flatly denied, and in the end, she agreed to buy me a small used car and no chauffeur.

"I got angry with you because you were throwing insults at me instead of apologizing, and you were doing that because of your family's riches. Today, you've become my ideal, as this is the life I subscribe to and enjoy.

"Madhu, like my parents, I too want to earn massive amounts of money not only to maintain the lifestyle that I've grown accustomed to but to spend a significant part of my earnings doing charity work. My support to the underprivileged gives me the satisfaction of living a purposeful life," I said.

"Sir, I'm comfortable with what I'm doing and the life I've chosen to lead, which is no different from your preaching," she said.

"Madhu, I know I'm nobody to tell you how to lead your life and what's good or bad for you. I'm mentioning what's noticeable to others, which is not looking good. Please come out of the hard shell hiding your beautiful personality; not only that, but it's inflicting utmost pain on your parents and all your loved ones. I'm also a boring person. From an adult age, I either buried myself in books or spent time serving the needy, and I never thought that I should also find an outlet to unwind by going out with family or friends to a picnic, eating out, watching a cricket match, or doing something that would relax the mind and body.

"I propose we amend our lifestyle to make our families and colleagues happy and remove the stigma of being a nutcase. To overcome our current personality deficit, I suggest we meet regularly to watch movies, spend evenings and weekends with our loved ones, and go for a long drive to far-flung scenic places, etc.," I said.

"Sir, I'm very happy with my life and don't need to bring any of your suggested changes," she said harshly.

I didn't respond to her comments; convincing her when she's unwilling to hear a word from me is just a futile attempt. But her responses reflected that she's a free-willed person, and softening up her rigid stand could take a long time. Nevertheless, I firmed up my decision to marry her regardless of how long she would take to say yes.

I took her to a fancy Italian restaurant; she ordered minestrone soup and skillet chicken; I asked the server to make it for two and give us panna cotta for dessert.

"Madhu, tell me about your social life, hobbies, food preferences, and any other routine that you must do daily, weekly, or biweekly," I asked.

"Sir, with due apologies, I must tell you that I don't like to answer any questions related to my personal life, and if you want to know anything related to my work, then do ask," she said tersely.

"Please, Madhu, be a pleasant person. Holding grudges doesn't suit your lovely personality," I pleaded.

“Sir, you’re my employer, and you should only evaluate me in that context. You’re intruding in my personal space, which I don’t appreciate. Allow me to reiterate, I’m thankful to you for giving me a soul-satisfying purpose in my life, which is keeping me happy, motivated, and content, so please stop giving any of your wise suggestions,” she said.

“Madhu, I know I’ve hurt you badly, and you have every right to be upset with me; however, I cannot undo what has happened. My mom owns 80 percent of the Manju empire, but she only attends board meetings and never challenges Dad’s decisions. I remember her saying I want to spend time only on two things: first, grooming my children to earn respect for what they’re, not because they’re my children, and next, charity work. Today she takes great pride in telling everyone about her children’s achievements. I want you to be like my mom; split your time into three circles: family, friends, and charity work; this way, you could enjoy the pleasures of both worlds,” I said.

“Sir, I must tell you that I’ve active and kicking parents, and they’re working on finding a suitable alliance for me; I’ll make sure to invite you to my wedding whenever that happens,” she said tersely.

“Madhu, I’m aware that you’ve refused to marry, and your mom is worried sick with your refusal and has asked my mom’s assistance in convincing you to marriage, and my mom’s job, I’ve taken on my shoulders,” I said, grinning.

“Sir, please mind your affairs, and allow me to do what I find good for me. If you continue to harass me this way, I'll not have any choice but to resign and go back to what I was doing or leave the country so you could never see me again," she said firmly.

"Madhu, your chances of working for another hospital or leaving the country don't exist, as I've the resources to enforce my decision," I said with a broad grin.

"Sir, you don't have the power to bring me back from any country I choose to reside. I would appreciate it if you stop bragging about your imaginary powers; you're not the government, and who do you think you're to dictate to me what I should or shouldn't do with my life," she said sternly.

"Madhu, from now on, you're my mentee and must take my suggestions as instructions to be followed strictly. Your refusal would result in spending increasing amounts of time in my company until I notice the changes I want to see as a permanent fixture of your personality. Please don't ever think you could migrate to another country, as our company's arms are too large, and it would be an easy task to get you on the next available flight from anywhere in the world. We don't have to use legal channels, just a few phone calls to the powerful politicians, and they frame you in anti-social activities, declare you *persona-non-grata*, and put you in a plane to arrive here safe and sound," I said with a loud chuckle.

Bullshit, I avoided even telling white lies, and this girl is making me say outrageous lies that could get me killed if Dad or Mom learns about it. But what to do? She's not giving me any choice but to show her my fictional powers.

"Okay, Sir, please do whatever you think you could to stop me from leading the life I believe is best suited to my likes. Daddy is after me to have my hospital, but not a complete charity institution; otherwise, he wouldn't be able to bear the recurring cash outflow for long. So now I'll ask him to start the hospital construction and settle for one-third for charity and the remaining paid patients. Tomorrow, I'll move out of your accommodation, which will restrict you from barging in uninvited, and in a year when my hospital is ready, you wouldn't be able to see me at all," she said curtly.

"Madhu, you're underestimating the power of our family. Forget about my family; if I call your dad asking him to refrain from the hospital project, he'll oblige me without asking for the reasons for the suggestion. If you move out of the accommodation, I'll come to see you at your home, and almost every day, I'll have dinner with your mom and dad," I said with a wide grin.

"Sir, I know I'm no match to you in anything; still, I suggest you do your best to achieve your objective, and I'll do my best to come out of your clutches," she said with the same firmness in her voice.

"Madhu, please keep it in mind; I'm not trying to impose anything upon you. I want to undo what I did a decade ago when I was immature and just out of adolescence with a firm belief in my ideal world. We all make mistakes, and I agree that I, too, made a colossal blunder and apologize for my stupidity, but it looks like you don't believe in forgiveness," I said.

"Sir, I strongly suggest you stop any further discussion on this subject and talk about something else," she said.

"Okay, suits me fine. Tell me which movie you watched in the recent past and how it was," I asked.

"Sir, I haven't seen any movie in a theater or at home for almost a decade, for no apparent reason except the dearth of spare time," she said.

I sensed she was softening, but the "Sir" had not gone; she responded to a very personal question, which made me happy.

"This weekend, on Saturday evening, I will organize dinner at my house, and after that, we will watch an old romantic feel-good movie. We've got a 50-seat theater in our house and an excellent collection of old and new Telugu, Hindi, and English movies. I occasionally watch movies, and that too when forced by my sisters or Mom; my sisters are crazy about movies, and they're the ones who keep on adding new and old movies to the collection," I said.

"Sorry, Sir, I cannot come; as I said earlier, I've no time to spare on such luxuries, nor am I interested in spending time in your company," she said.

"Madhu, I'll pick you up from your accommodation at 7:00, and please don't give me any excuses; there's nothing important on the weekend that your domestic help team cannot do," I said firmly.

"Sir, I don't understand your insistence. We're neither related nor friends or in a relationship, so why should I spend an evening with you and your family? Sorry, Sir, you have to excuse me, and I would highly appreciate it if you don't twist my arm," she snapped.

"Madhu, your refusal is not acceptable; just inform me whether to pick you up from your apartment or your parents' home and if 7:00 is too early, I could give you another half an hour," I said, laughing.

She didn't answer.

After dinner, I dropped her at her apartment building, and without a word of thanks for dinner, she said goodnight and left.

Saturday around 2:00, I phoned Madhu; after several rings, she answered, and upon hearing my hello, she said she'd a patient and would call when she had a free moment.

I knew she wouldn't return the call, so after half an hour, I went to her consultation room and entered with a light tap, as her receptionist had informed me that she was alone.

"Madhu, I've come to remind you that I'll pick you up at 7:00, and please tell me whether you'll be at your apartment or your parent's home," I said.

"Sir, I'm afraid I won't be able to attend. Mom told me to come home as soon as I could as some people are coming to see me for my alliance," she stated coldly.

"No issues, we will postpone it to next week," I said, leaving her room with an "All the best and have a wonderful weekend."

I knew she lied to me, but I decided to bring her home for dinner and a movie. Mom was organizing a massive feast in her honor.

At 7:00 sharp, I was at Venkateshwara Rao's palatial villa gate. When I informed the watchman that I had come to meet with Mrs. Mrunalini Rao, I was allowed to enter and guided to a visitor car parking area. Another domestic help took me to a large living hall and disappeared, saying he would inform Ma'am.

Madhu's mother came in a few minutes, and when I introduced myself, she greeted me with a big grin.

"It's a pleasure to meet you, and I'm delighted you arrived at the right time; dinner is almost ready, and I'd like you to join us and allow us to enjoy it in your company. Madhu arrived half an hour ago, and Madhu's father should be here shortly,' Aunty said earnestly.

"Aunty, I'd love to have dinner with you but didn't Madhu inform you that she's having dinner at our home?" I asked.

"Oh, she might have forgotten to mention, but I'm sure she's getting ready. Give me a couple of minutes to ask the servants for a drink and inform Madhu you're here," Aunty said and left the room.

After a few minutes, Madhu came in her night suit. She looked angry, evident from her blazing eyes, and said, "Why you're here, and why did you lie to Mom? Did I agree with you to have dinner with your family?"

"Mom has prepared a lavish dinner, and I've invited my sister to join us so we can have a good time together. I've come to pick you up, as I was sure you weren't busy; please go and get ready, and if you refuse, I'll seek assistance from your parents, who'll compel you to go with me," I said with a smile.

"Sir, I politely refused to come, but you insisted, so I had to find an excuse. I strongly suggest you leave before Mom comes, as I don't want to fight with her because of you," she said.

"Madhu, don't be stubborn; everyone is waiting for you, including my dad, who avoids dinner parties and only attends when a VVIP is coming or invited. Please go and get ready, but hurry, as Dad is very punctual in having his dinner at 8:00 sharp," I said.

"No, Sir, I'm not coming, and please don't emotionally blackmail me," she said.

Before responding, Madhu's mother entered the room with two servants pushing two trolleys full of fresh and dry fruits, snacks, and hot and cold drinks.

"Madhu, why you're not dressed up?" Madhu's Mom asked.

"She's unhappy with me and giving excuses for not coming. Even though I told her dad is waiting to have dinner with her, which is a rarity," I said.

"Madhu, are you okay?" asked her Mom.

"I'm fine, but I told Rama Sir a few days ago and today also that I wouldn't be able to make it as I've got a few pressing things to take care of," Madhu said.

"Aunty, she's making it up; today, she told me that some people are coming to see her for a possible alliance," I said.

"Madhu, I don't remember you ever lied to me or anyone; I'm disappointed. And, why do you want to avoid a dinner invite by Rama? Please go and get ready quickly," Aunty said.

"Mom, you know I don't like dinner parties or enjoy heavy night meals. So, Sir, please excuse me for this time, and I'll make it up with you some other day," Madhu said.

"Madhu, everyone will be upset if you don't show up for some flimsy reason. If you don't want to eat much, that's fine or let me know if you have any food preferences," I said.

"Madhu, go and get ready; you cannot behave this way. Just take a few bites and enjoy the movie," Aunty said.

She rose from her chair, looked at me with fire-spitting eyes, and walked out.

While waiting for Madhu, I had to answer a few dozen queries from her mother. Her questions were related to my stay in Australia and my current engagement, hobbies, etc. However, she smartly skirted asking about when I was getting married and whether Mom had found a girl for me or not.

In 15 minutes, Madhu came to the hall in her usual attire, a light purple color cotton salwar-kameez, very light makeup, and no jewelry except her diamond ear trinkets.

The moment our car sailed, Madhu said, "Sir, your mom discussed a decent boy for me with my mom. I suspected she's asking for my hand for you; it's now proved that whatever you're doing is only for this purpose. Let me tell you at the outset so that you won't be disappointed; I've decided to remain single, and even if God sends an angel from heaven, I'm not going to budge from my decision. And, like you, I'm also crazy: bestowed with a single-track mind that's inflexible and unyielding, and once I make a decision, I stick to it no matter what happens to me."

"Great, so you know the purpose of me chasing you. Oh, yes, I want to marry you, and I'll marry you. Mom knows I've selected you as my life partner, and she wanted to talk to your parents, but I stopped her. I don't believe in using force or twisting arms to achieve my objectives, so we'll come to your house only if you agree wholeheartedly to marry me," I said earnestly.

"Sir, my parents know I'll permanently leave the house if they pressure me to marry. So please note where I stand, and don't chase me to marry you," she said emphatically.

"Okay, dear Dr. Madhu, but can I ask you to be my friend and spend some time with me on the weekends or whenever you've got a free moment?" I asked.

"Sir, I'm not interested in having any relationship with you or anyone. My work is my worship. The only people I want to be associated with are my family members," she said curtly.

"Madhu, don't marry me, don't be my friend, but tolerate me until you become the person all your loved ones, including yours lovingly, want you to be," I said with a big grin.

"Sir, I'm the person that I want to be, and I'm not going to change because of you or anyone; if someone is not happy with how I look or how I dress, or my way of living, then that's their problem," she said.

"Madhu, you described my characteristics a short while ago, and I wholeheartedly agree that this is how I'm. Thus, engrave in your brilliant mind that this crazy man has chosen to be your shadow for the remainder of your life, irrespective of whether we marry or not. I suggest you accept this fact and first check me out as a friend, and if satisfied, you could take the next step of tying the knot," I said, laughing.

"Sir, please stop this discussion; I said what I had to say, and I won't change my stand even if you chase me as long as I'm alive," she said.

We were almost reaching home, so I decided to put off the discussion for the return journey.

Mom and my elder sister welcomed Madhu at the entrance, and I was asked to sit in the TV lounge with Dad and the kids. For almost half an hour, I heard loud laughs emanating from the ladies' side, but I could only recognize Mom and sister's voices; I didn't hear Madhu laughing or conversing, even with great concentration.

Mom prepared a sumptuous dinner, and every veg and non-veg dish you could think of was on the table. However, I noticed Madhu was hardly eating, even though my sister filled her plate with the best on the table. After dinner, we all went to the theater with our coffee mugs and watched an entertaining romantic Hindi movie, and at around midnight, I dropped Madhu at her home.

On our return journey, she said, "Sir, I would be highly obliged if you don't bother me in the future to come with you anywhere. Also, please keep in mind that I don't want to be your friend or your life partner; you may be a perfect person to have as a friend or spouse, but I neither have time for friends nor am I interested in marriage."

"Okay, fine, if you don't want to marry me, but what's wrong with me becoming your punching bag friend? You could call me 24/7 and talk to me about anything under the sun, your pleasures, pain, and frustration at work or home. I can be your chauffeur on the weekends, get the food you need, or drive you around, and I promise I'll not expect anything out of our friendship," I said.

"Sir, please don't forget that I've all the resources to do what I want; the only thing I don't have is the time for friends. So please don't drive me nuts with your suggestions," she said sternly.

"My dear Madhu, you can throw as many insults, abuses, curses as you want, but nothing would deter me from my decision to make you my wife," I said grinningly.

"Sir, why are you refusing to understand that I'll not marry you or anyone? Please don't waste your valuable time chasing a mirage," she said.

"Madhu, you do your best to stay firm on your decision, and I'll do my best to make you agree to marry me," I said.

x-x-x-x-x-x

Chapter Three

Madhu Priya

I, Madhumati Priya, was born in a middle-income household; my dad had a medium-size factory, manufacturing various industrial cleaning and descaling products. When I was seven years old, I woke up one night, hearing loud crying from Dad's room. I went to the room and found Mom and Dad crying, tears streaming down their faces, and Dad saying, "Honey, everything gutted down, nothing left, we're destroyed."

I asked Dad, "What happened, Dad? Why are both of you crying?"

"A tragedy occurred; you go back to your room. Tomorrow, Mom will tell you what happened," Dad said.

The next day I learned from Mom that, the previous evening, our factory had burned down to ashes due to negligent workers, who probably threw a cigarette near the concentrated liquid detergent barrels.

In the evening, I heard Dad telling Mom, "Mruna, the bank refused to give any assistance without collateral. We've got this house, factory land, and our savings, which is insufficient collateral to borrow the amount needed to rebuild the factory. Tomorrow I'm meeting with a tycoon, who's my prime customer. Only once did I meet him a couple of years ago; he asked me to see him if I ever needed any assistance. I don't have even an iota of hope to receive help, but I've no choice except to knock on every remotely possible door."

The next evening, Dad came smiling and told Mom, "Mruna, the tycoon I mentioned to you yesterday, went with me to our burned plant and gave me a check for 20 lakhs on the spot and asked me to advise him how much more I required after I exhaust the check money. I've only read and heard about angels, but today I met with one, and you know what? He asked me to buy all the latest and best machines, and there was no need to compromise on anything. And, when I told him I would visit his office tomorrow to give the house and factory land papers, he said there's no need for any documents."

Within eight months, our factory was up and running. Mom told me the factory's production had almost doubled compared to what it used to produce with the old machines. When I was 13, we moved to a massive six-bedroom villa with a swimming pool, gym, and beautiful lawn. Dad now had three factories, two manufacturing industrial cleaning and descaling products, and one manufacturing domestic use detergents and cleaning products. Money was pouring in, and Dad was spoiling me with anything I asked. When I was nine years old, I watched *ER*, the American TV series on the medical emergency room. I got so fascinated with doctors' and nurses' work that I decided to become a doctor. I asked Mom what I had to do to become a doctor; she said I must be a topper in all the school and college exams for the next 15 years, and only then could I become a good doctor. Upon securing excellent marks in the eighth-grade final exams, the Headmistress called me to her chamber. Naturally, I was frightened; a call from her office was never good news.

However, she congratulated me on my outstanding performance when I met her. Furthermore, she wished me continued success in my future academic endeavors, telling me that God had given me an "elephantine memory" and "analytical brilliance." Her encouraging comments made my day and boosted my confidence that I could become a doctor if I stayed focused on my studies. I had a younger brother, a bookworm, and a brilliant boy just one year my junior. From the age of seven, his only hobby was reading course books or some non-fiction books that hardly any kid of his age would like reading. Still, he read books like *The Flight of Apollo 11*, *Mama Built a Little Nest*, *Over and Under the Pond*, *The Story of Elizabeth Blackwell*, *The Story of Dr. Temple Grandin*, etc.

My duty was to take him to the park right in front of our house every day in the evening and make him play with other boys or just run with me, which was my passion. He would never go to the park on his own, but no one had to push him for studies, and in fact, Mom used to shout at him several times to stop reading and come to the dining table. He was consistently a class topper because of his intelligence and dedication to his academics. When I completed my first year of MBBS, he finished school. Dad took him to the US and admitted him into a Business Administration degree at Pennsylvania State University in Philadelphia.

Like any other rich girl my age, I also liked expensive dresses, jewelry, luxury cars, and high-end accessories. In addition, I enjoyed getting serviced by a team of domestic laborers, which gave me the feeling of living a king's life. However, even with lots of money in my pocket and too many rotten spoiled brat school pals, I never neglected my studies and rarely went out with them for a movie or lunch. All my girlfriends had boyfriends, and I was no exception, but there was no love involved, just friendship. He was a classmate of mine, and when I was in 9th grade, he kissed me; I instantly dumped him. He was a smoker with terrible bromhidrosis; he was lucky I didn't yak up my lunch on him. I vow never to have a boyfriend like him; to be my boyfriend, a boy must have healthy habits, be a gentleman and witty, and, last but not least, be a medical doctor. So, I decided to secure my medical degree and only then look for a life companion.

I secured my DM degree in Nephrology when I was 27 years. Then, as planned, I started my work with several charity hospitals.

These hospitals were small and far from each other, and shuttling between them to see just a few patients was tiresome and boring. So, one day I discussed the issue I was facing with Dad. He said, "Madhu, since you started working, I was debating whether to construct a small charity hospital for you but couldn't make a positive decision. Running the hospital could become challenging because it would become difficult to shoulder the recurring and continually increasing expenses. However, suppose you agree to make a semi-charity hospital and charge a nominal amount to cover the running cost, I could construct a 50-bed hospital with the needed equipment to treat all kidney ailments."

I asked Dad to give me time to think about his suggestion. I was a wealthy person on my own, being one of the directors and a partner in Dad's company from the age of 16, drawing a monthly salary and a share in profits. Even if I chip in my few crores, meeting ongoing and ever-increasing costs would be tough. So I decided to defer my hospital idea until I had enough funds to establish a significant trust to cover the running costs.

A few weeks after my decision, I saw the soon-to-be-opened Manju Charity Hospital advertisement seeking doctors in all disciplines. I thought it must be Rama's hospital, my first crush, or I should call it my first and last love. He impressed me; he must have just entered his twenties and was the only son of a billionaire, still dressed in unbranded jeans and polo-neck T-shirts, driving a Honda, and preaching how to achieve sustainable pleasures. I knew many rich boys and girls of my age and seniors who had destroyed their lives just because they'd a few extra doughs in their pockets, which they spent to revel in life and become school/college dropouts, alcoholics, addicts, satyriasis, and nymphomaniacs.

Interaction with Rama urged me to walk on the path he suggested and see whether it would provide the pleasures that could make me happy and content. It's not that I wasn't satisfied with my life or searching for Nirvana, but I wanted to see whether they could bring the pleasures he had talked about.

I identified a few orphanages and talked to them about whether I could visit them once a month; on a

Sunday, I would come with clothes, sweets, and gifts and spend some time with the kids. They appreciated my gesture but said I must call at least one day ahead to book the slot, as many NGOs and philanthropists come to spend time with the kids. Mom and Dad were genuinely pleased and encouraged me to provide all the needed assistance in my charity work.

On my first visit to an orphanage, as planned, I took clothes, chocolate boxes, storybooks, Lego architecture kits, colored pencil boxes, coloring books, and a few other similar items relevant to the children's age and gender.

I must always remain indebted to Rama for guiding me to a route that has given me nothing but an absolute pleasure. The elation trickled through your spine and veins when you got surrounded by children laughing with sheer joy and looking at you with gleaming eyes reflecting gratitude.

I told all the kids I would take responsibility for their higher education and jobs if they studied well.

I'm enjoying my charity work even to this date, and once in a while, Mom goes with me; else, I go alone.

Thus far, I have failed to remove Rama from my system, even though I never wanted to remember him. I desired to see him because I figured that if I saw his new persona as a married and content person, it would help me erase him from my heart and mind. However, even if I apply for the job, there's no assurance that I'll be called in for an interview because I don't have the required five years of experience. So, let's presume I get a call for the interview; is it inevitable that he'll be one of the interviewers?

I decided not to deliberate much, forward the resume, and pray to get an interview call and possibly see him. Within a week, I received an interview call that delighted me. Rama was among the four interviewers; his boyish visage has transformed into an adult man's hardened face, still slim, reflecting a well-maintained, exercised body. He looked dapper in formal clothes – a white full-sleeve shirt and light beige trousers; married life must've gone well with him. I gave him a cursory look and noticed he was checking me with curious protuberant eyes. I wondered why God didn't give me this man and make my life's journey an enjoyable walkthrough. Despite the fact that he crushed my ego and self-worth and hinted that I wanted to be friends for an ulterior motive, my love for him hasn't stonewashed to this day and will continue to be a lifelong burning ache till I die.

He didn't ask any questions for the duration of the entire interview. Finally, when the other three interviewers learned everything they wanted to know, he excused them and tried to be friendly by inquiring about my family. However, I gave him a cold and hard stare with a rebuke to ask questions pertinent to my job application only.

The bonehead may have thought all is forgotten and forgiven; no, Sir, everything is sorely fresh in the memory, and it won't be erased as long as I'm alive. After responding to his questions, I left him abruptly, without the minimum courtesy of saying goodbye and best wishes for the day. I'm sure he must've felt demeaned, which was the objective. I craved to see him, and that purpose was achieved, so there was no need to be courteous, nor was I interested in seeing him again or securing a job in his hospital.

In less than a couple of weeks, I received a job offer for the position of consultant nephrologist, which included a fantastic salary, furnished housing, a car allowance, and a few other benefits. A pleasant surprise, as working in a massive charity hospital with the latest equipment and excellent inpatient facilities was nothing but a dream. Apart from gaining the experience of working in a large hospital, I could possibly get a chance to learn how to manage the administrative side of running the hospital.

Currently, the hospitals where I was working were a nightmare – small and unclean, with no trained staff to assist, obsolete equipment, and fewer patients, and the worst thing was that every day I had to spend two to three hours traveling from one hospital to the next.

Dad was ecstatic when I told him I had received a job offer from the Manju Group's newly constructed charity hospital. And even Mom was happy, and both encouraged me to sign on the dotted lines.

Three days before the hospital opened, I moved into the accommodation assigned for my stay. Naturally, both Mom and Dad weren't happy with my decision and reluctantly agreed, as the daily shuttling was an inconvenient option. Mom accompanied me when I was shifting to the apartment and was amply pleased upon seeing the interior and said, "Madhu, I can guarantee you that this apartment was specially prepared for you. No one provides such a luxurious place to employees."

After Mom had gone, I went to look at the other apartments on my floor. All of them were vacant, and a few workers were busy putting the finishing touches. The flats were decently furnished for a comfortable living; however, they paled compared to my accommodation, a palace. It bugged me; what would I say to my neighbors when they visit? They would immediately assume that I got a sweet deal, which could be because I must be the sweetheart of someone higher up. My flat's interior decorator must've easily charged a few crores for such opulent fixtures and furniture, and no one could have approved such excessive spending except Rama. And if he did that, what was his motive? I failed to understand his intent. I decided to see him and called the hospital reception from the intercom to inquire where I could find Rama Rao, and I was informed that he was in his chamber.

The idiot had made a honeymoon suite, not staff accommodation. I went to his chamber and jumped on him, and instead of getting into a heated discussion, he calmly responded by saying he decided to make the flat for a comfortable living because I'm used to such comforts. I left his chamber with a bad taste in my mouth. He didn't give me an option: stay in the allocated accommodation or have no job.

I came to the flat exasperated, and after a bath, I sat on the balcony with a coffee cup and opened a few side panels. The hospital was on a hilltop surrounded by excellent greenery. Fresh air gushed in from the opened panels and filled my lungs, helping to slacken the body from the stresses. My parents' house was huge and had every luxury possible, but still, this flat was much more luxurious and comfortable, except for a missing swimming pool. The gym, study room, jacuzzi in the restroom of the master bedroom, TV lounge, comfortable leather settees all around the flat, and the kitchen was so amazing that a chef would give his right hand to have it.

During the luncheon of the hospital opening, some doctors gossiped about Rama being the most eligible bachelor in the country, heir to a multibillion-dollar outfit, a highly qualified professional, etc.

Considering his bachelorhood, does he have a motive behind spending such a massive amount to decorate the flat, or did he spend the money to provide the comforts I was accustomed to? Thinking of a motive was a joke because we hadn't spoken in almost a decade and then had a few minutes of tense question-answering at the job interview. Whatever had prompted him to be so generous was inconsequential to me. I had no desire to develop any bond other than an employer-employee relationship. And since I signed the employment agreement and moved into the flat, I should work for a few months, and if I find that the patient flow and work are not to my liking, I could quit.

Within two months, the patient inflow increased so much that I had to disperse them as fast as possible, which was frustrating. While pondering how to deal with this situation, I met Rama upon his request, and he expressed the same concern about the upsurge in my patients. He advised that I hire a junior doctor to assist me and conveyed the desire to visit me in the evening to check whether I was comfortable in the flat. I told him I was satisfied and that if I needed anything, I would inform him; still, he visited with a large red rose bouquet and a Swiss chocolate box. He apologized for his stupid behavior in the past and mentioned his interest in being friends. His visit perplexed me, and I couldn't figure out what he was trying to say with the chocolate, flowers, and profuse apologies.

Again, Rama came to my flat and took me to an Italian restaurant almost by force for dinner. He wanted me to become a regular person and divide my life into three circles: one circle for my charity work, the next for family life – get married and raise a family like our parents – and the last circle for friends. I was getting hints about what he was seeking, but it was too late. After my tiff with him, I still wanted him to be my friend and tried to establish at least a friendship bond for over a year. But he had brushed me aside like a piece of trash. He must be fantasizing if he believes I'll forget, forgive, and become his sweetheart.

I'll not marry him or anyone – period. In the last year alone, I had turned down quite a few decent proposals from wealthy business people, doctors, engineers, and civil servants. Both Mom and Dad were upset with my stupidity, but I was firm in my decision to remain single, and I threatened them that I would leave the house if they pressured me.

My medical services are only one side of my humanitarian work; I desire to establish an NGO for women's education and employment. I wanted to work on only one front, my humanitarian work; I didn't want to open another front for servicing a husband and children, which could become a full-time job.

Today, Rama took me to his house to have dinner with his family; on our way, I enlightened him that I'm aware he's attempting to marry me, which won't happen as I have taken a pledge to remain single. He said it was okay with him, and both of us would remain single, but asked me to make him my friend, a punching bag, and a chauffeur.

His family treated me like I was a fiancé of Rama, which was very annoying.

Rama became a nuisance; almost every alternate evening, he came for a cup of coffee, and during the weekend, he forced me to go with him for a bite. I threatened him to resign several times, and he said, I'm free to do whatever I need to do, but he wasn't going to stop his visits until I settled down with him or with someone. I knew resigning from the job would not resolve this issue; he would come to my house, and Mom and Dad would welcome him from the depths of their hearts. Even after banging my head for hours, I failed to find a solution to solve this irritating situation. Finally, one morning, while I was bathing, I got a bright idea of how I could keep him out of my life. Become a showoff with dazzling dresses, expensive accessories, and everything else that could turn him off to the extent that he would drop the idea of marrying me.

I hoped to earn his wrath if I became the person he hated the most, a rich showoff, arrogant and boorish.

Cool, let's try and see how it goes. I went online and ordered flashy and expensive branded outfits, accessories, makeup essentials, and fancy footwear. I called Mom and asked her to prepare a box containing expensive ornaments for dinner and daily wear.

Within the next four days, I got all the ordered items and was pleased with what I had bought. However, I kept my fingers crossed for Rama to go through the roof when he saw me in gaudy makeup, off-shoulder tops, and wearing stilettos heels.

As usual, Rama came to my clinic Saturday at noon and asked me to be ready at 7:30 to go out with him for dinner.

Oh, boy, I'd been looking forward to this. I left the hospital at five o'clock, took a power nap, showered, and began preparing to show a lot of skin while wearing expensive jewelry and elaborate makeup. First, I wore a pair of low-rise jeans, an off-shoulder blood-red crop top, and a red scarpin sandal. My flat tummy and belly button must give my dear Rama a push because the distance between my jeans and my top was more than eight inches. But, wait, there's more for your kicks, Rama boy. I then painted my cheeks, applied blood-red lipstick, affixed fake eyelashes, and painted the glued silken nails red to embellish my fingers. I was confident my top alone would be enough to put him annoyingly off, and he would be further mortified when I became the center of attraction for all the male diners. I finished my final touches at 7:20 and looked in the mirror. Holy shit, I looked gorgeous, not in the least slapper, which is what I was aiming for, probably because of my makeup expertise, courtesy of the professional makeup artists my mom had employed to teach me. There was no time for a makeover, and I hoped and prayed this alone should be enough to give Rama boy a heart attack.

The moment Rama saw me, he took a turn and looked at the doors of the other flats. I asked, "What happened? Did you see a ghost?"

"No, I wasn't hoping to see a beauteous, dazzling, alluring, enticing, and stunningly symmetrical gorgeous babe, so ensuring I thumped on the right door," Rama said innocently.

"Sir, flattery won't help you achieve whatever you aim for," I said.

"My dear doctor, I commented on what I saw without motives. But, first, allow me to tell you that you've made me very happy with your chameleon personality and excellent physique," Rama said.

"I'm not a chameleon; my working attire is because I treat the less fortunate, and I doll up when I go out to chic places to relax," I said.

"I'm glad to hear that you're coming with me to relax. A good start; I hope soon I'll hear 'I doll up when I'm going on a date," Rama said with a wide grin.

"Sir, I've never gone on a date with anyone and have no plans to do so in the future. However, having dinner at a decent restaurant is unwinding, not because of the person in toe," I explained.

"Dr. Madhu Priya, please don't value my company, but I would appreciate and will always remain indebted for the precious time you're sparing to have a bite with me," Rama said earnestly.

I didn't respond to his comments.

Instead of any famed ritzy eatery, he took me to a Japanese restaurant in a five-star hotel. I was sure he was feeling embarrassed with my dress and had he brought me to a popular restaurant bustling with diners, I would've become the focus of all the male eyeballs.

He asked me to order for both of us, and I ordered miso soup, sushi, and tempura, and for the main course, miso chicken. In addition, I ordered two glasses of red wine instead of our usual fresh orange juice.

While sipping the wine, he said, "Madhu, your scantily clad outfit won't turn me off to run away from you. You've failed badly, honey; you look breathtakingly beautiful, no exaggeration. I'm proud to be in your company, and I'm not saying this to please you."

"Sir, it's none of my concern how you're feeling about me; I'm coming with you because you could create more trouble for me if I refuse to go with you. But keep in mind, I don't have any feelings for you; neither your dinners nor your penance would help change my stance. I'm waiting for the day when I can resign and make sure I never see you for the rest of my life," I said reprovingly.

"This is not going to happen, Madhu. As you described, I, too, have a crazy single-track mind, and once I decide to have something, I go all out with all the might I can muster to attain my objectives. I've decided to marry you, and while I won't strongarm you into saying yes, I'll make sure you don't marry anyone else or leave my sight. And if you think your skin show will be enough to get rid of me, you're mistaken. I would accept you in any form because I've seen the inner person in you, fallen for the purity of your spirit," Rama said soberly.

"Sir, whatever has attracted you is inconsequential to me, as I decided long ago that I should die as a spinster. So, if you love me and care for my feelings, please leave me alone," I said.

"Dr. Madhu, that will not happen; I'm determined to spend the rest of my life in your company. Without you beside me, I would be incomplete, and life would become a meaningless journey," Rama said gloomily.

He appeared to be expressing his genuine feelings, but unfortunately, I was unwavering in my decision; no marriage. I wanted to marry and enjoy a normal life like my parents, but this man was responsible for my change of mind, and he now wanted me to like, love, and marry him; heck no. No, Rama boy, I'll not adjust the goalpost to fit you. It is not tit for tat; however, you should remember that I tried to be your friend/lover for over a year and lost my self-respect, self-worth, and self-confidence in my pursuit. Regrettably, instead of mellowing down in his company, his sight was causing jitters and brain signals that this person was unforgiving and could hurt me if I ever went close to him.

I'm dead against harboring feelings of revenge, getting even, or hatred, as it's against my character and Mom's teachings.

It's undebatable that once he turns his back on someone, he never reconsiders his stand or allows the person to offer forgiveness. Knowing this, on the off-chance that I make a fresh start by forgetting the past and marrying him, I must prepare myself to lose him for any slight that could happen inadvertently or otherwise. He's everything a woman wants to see in her man: educated, cultured, wealthy, and to top it all, great values with a golden heart that beats to serve humanity. Still, I'm better off without him in my life, considering the dark side of his character.

As usual, Rama came to my clinic the following Saturday afternoon and requested that I be ready to leave at 7:30 p.m. I agreed and told him we would go to a club where we could enjoy a visiting European band; the dress code for men is a black suit, bowtie, cummerbund, and a full-length cocktail gown for women.

I didn't mention that I planned to dance, as I was sure he hadn't learned any ballroom dances, and it would make him extremely unhappy when he saw me dancing with another man. An acclaimed dance master was hired by Mom when I was hardly 14 to teach me Kathak and all the ballroom dances, like the quickstep, foxtrot, tango, slow waltz, and Viennese waltz.

At the dot of 7:30, the doorbell announced Rama's arrival. When he saw me, he kept one hand on his heart and said, "OMG, I hope I won't have a heart attack, and even if I don't die, I assure you several will die an unnatural death at the club."

"Sir, your flattery won't make me happy, nor will it help soften my stand. Anyways, thank you for your compliment," I said.

My heart ached when I saw him. He looked like a Greek Aristo, a handsome hunk, tall, slim muscular body, whitish skin, sharp features, thick coal-black hair arranged in the side-parted executive cut. Without considering his personality traits, his physical magnificence was enough to make any girl go weak in the knees.

I wore a scarlet red off-shoulder gown woven with Norrfolks's synthetic diamonds, loose curly hair, and blood-red lipstick. I had brightened my neck with a single diamond string neckless and wore diamond ear tops and a diamond-studded watch. I wanted him to get annoyed with my skin display, expensive jewelry, and accessories. But I don't think it worked, as he demonstrated genuine happiness to see me elegantly dressed and bejeweled. I don't know what else I should do to make him annoyed so he could forget about me. I silently prayed and hoped he would get tormented seeing me dancing with another guy.

Rama came in a custom-made black Mercedes car, an armored vehicle with a glass partition for privacy and extended legroom. A chauffeur wearing a black suit opened the back door for me to sit, and Rama came from the other side and sat very close to me.

Without asking me, Rama gave the club name to the driver and said, "That's the only club where a European band is performing; am I wrong?"

"You're right; that's where we've to go," I said.

"Thank you for dressing so well; I never thought I would ever see you in any other dress than your usual salwar-kameez outfit. I'm not a poet who describes his lover's beauty in befitting words; however, allow me to tell you that you look like a fairy that has come flying from the skies. I've pinched myself a few times to ensure I'm not imagining that I'm sitting beside you. Of course, you could take it as flattery if you want to, but I'm expressing my true feelings," Rama said.

I felt extreme pain as though a dagger had pierced my heart. The country's most eligible bachelor considers himself lucky to be in my company, and I don't want to be with him or enjoy the evening.

He took my hands in his; I struggled to extricate myself, but his grip was too tight. I had no choice but to let him hold me and feel good. He then asked me to say anything, but I remained silent, and he said, "Madhu, tell me what I need to do to wed you, or at the very least make you my best pal."

"Sir, I've told you many times I've nothing against you, and it's just that I don't have time for friendship or socializing. I'm coming with you because you've not left any option for me to say no. You come to my flat and keep pushing the calling bell until I open it, and if I go to my parents' house, you come there, and my mom forces me to go with you. I'm in a difficult situation, but don't worry, soon I'll find a solution to resolve this impasse," I said.

"My dear Dr. Madhu, I don't know how I could live without you. My love for you is growing stronger every passing day, and since I didn't read much literary text, I'm failing to express the deep love I feel for you in poetic words. So please, Madhu, forget the past and be my companion for my entire life; I promise to keep you happy, to provide you whatever you want, as long as it's within my reach and means," Rama said.

Before I could respond to his sermon, he grabbed my face with his two hands, pulled me toward him, and took my lips in his mouth. I got cold; no body parts were moving, and his hold was body numbing and intoxicating. He freed me after taking his sweet time and said with a chuckle, "You were looking so beautiful that I was getting out of breath; to stabilize myself, first I took your hand in my hands, which didn't help much, then I thought to avoid dying out of choking, I must kiss you. It has greatly helped – thank you, and my apologies even if it was disgusting. You've saved a life, and you should feel proud that your resuscitation was timely assistance."

"Sir, this is the last time I'll come with you. Next time you'll have to kill me to take me out," I said curtly.

"My beloved Madhu, blame yourself for my despicable behavior. I could've died because of your enchanting beauty, and I've every right to save myself from departing at my prime. And, please stop calling me 'Sir'; I'm not your teacher; call me Rama only," Rama said with a loud laugh.

"Sir, please don't justify your debauched act with any pathetic narrative, and I'll not call you by your first name as you're my respected billionaire boss," I said, stressing "respected."

"All right, my love, please yourself and call me what makes you happy. You know, the end of the year is coming in a few weeks, and we're planning a large celebration at our house to ring in the new calendar year. Will you assist me in organizing a poolside party with delectable dishes and a BBQ?" Rama said, smiling.

"Sir, you have all the resources at your disposal to organize a party; I've already made plans for the new year, so don't count me in," I said.

"No issues, my love, but can I be a part of your celebrations?" Rama said.

"It's a women-only party at a farmhouse far from the city. We'd leave early in the morning and return the next evening. Please don't check with Mom; as far as she's concerned, I would be working at the hospital, handling emergency cases," I said.

"It's not okay with me, but I'll attempt to survive without you beside me to welcome the new year," Rama said gloomily.

We reached the club, and surprisingly the security didn't stop us at the gate; they probably knew the car and its owners. The main building entrance had a long queue of visitors and a few club staff allowing them after checking their invitation cards. When Rama's car stopped, two suited gentlemen opened our doors, greeted us, and asked us to follow them. They took us straight to the party hall through a different door and guided us toward a large table right after the dance floor.

The table was set for dinner with exquisite crockery and cutlery; in the middle, a bunch of red velvet roses looked mind-blowing. In addition, a breathtaking bouquet of mixed exotic flowers and a silver champagne pail stuffed with a Dom Pérignon Vintage Champagne bottle were kept on a side table. The hall was almost 80 percent full, with couples in the mentioned dress code. For buffet dinner, chafing dishes were lined on both the left and right sides of the hall, and a few smartly dressed waiters were standing behind the dishes to explain the contents of the dishes to the guests or provide the requested services.

Within a few minutes, after we sat, two waiters came with two trolleys of starters; roasted mushrooms, baked chicken spring rolls, garlic bread with toppings of olives and sliced baby tomatoes, prawn and ginger dumplings, and chicken and pine nut meatballs. While one waiter placed the dishes, the other took the champagne bottle, removed the muselet and the cork, and poured the pale yellowish liquid into the flute glasses. After the servers left, I said, "You must be a regular here and give heavy tips, resulting in this privileged treatment."

"My dear Madhu, this must be my 10th or 11th visit to this place, and this is the only time I've come here with great pleasure; my other visits were under the pressure of either my sisters or Mom. The reason for special treatment is that we own 85 percent of this facility. The remaining 15 percent is owned by five rich and famous persons of the city; among those five, your dad is one," Rama said.

Dad never mentioned to me that he had a stake in the club.

After a few minutes' pause, Rama asked, "Do you come here regularly?"

"I came here quite a few times before joining the medical college, but this is the first visit since then," I said.

"It's the best place in town to entertain your friends and business associates," he said and fetched a plastic card from his pocket and gave it to me – the club's VIP card with my name, photo, and lifetime validity printed.

It annoyed me, and I said, "Why you're giving me this card? I've got my card; I don't need this."

"We're issuing this VIP card to our doctors who consistently perform exceptionally well. This VIP card won't only allow you to use all the club's facilities, but you don't have to pay any bills for your food or drinks," Rama said.

"Who else got this card in our hospital?" I snapped with my eyeballs popping out in anger.

"You're the first to receive it," Rama said, grinning.

"Sir, keep this card with you; I don't need it," I said and pushed the card toward him.

"My dear Madhu, your old card is canceled. The new card is not needed to enter the facility; with a face recognition camera at the entrance, members are allowed in and serviced according to their membership terms," Rama said.

"Sir, these gestures won't help you achieve your aim," I said tersely.

"Are you good at ballroom dances, waltz, foxtrot, etc.?" Rama asked.

"Yes, I'm familiar with the ballroom dances and seeking a dance partner to enjoy the evening," I said, as I was sure this duffer would have never stepped on a dance floor.

"Great, let me talk to the manager to find a professional partner for you," Rama said and went to see the manager.

After a while, he came and said, "Done, a professional partner will dance with you, and in fact, you two will open the dancing session."

I said, "Thank you, I was dying to dance; it's been a long time since I was on the dance floor." I wanted him to be on fire while I hugged the casanova and danced to crush his ego.

The hall got full, and the doors were closed. Then, an event organizer came on the podium and announced, "Ladies and Gentlemen, please join me in giving a booming round of applause, welcoming the world-renowned musicians who traveled across the continents to entertain you." The hall exploded with claps, whistles, and screams, and once the noise settled, the announcer resumed his intro. "In the first session, the band will play a non-stop waltz music mix for an hour, and after a thirty-minute break, they will play popular Hollywood and a few Bollywood numbers till the closing time. I now ask that you please join me in giving a rousing round of applause to one of the directors of our club, Dr. Rama Rao, and his partner, Dr. Madhu

Priya, who will be entertaining us with their sleek dance moves. Those interested in joining the gorgeous couple should do so when they signal the audience to come onto the performance surface." Again the hall exploded with the roof-shattering sounds.

I got numb with the shocking announcement; I never thought I would be dancing alone in front of hundreds of eyeballs, watching critically every dance step of ours. I knew I didn't have the finesse to entertain the audience like the idiot event manager had announced and why the hell had this Rama duffer made this arrangement? I wanted to dance for a few minutes to put Rama boy on fire, but the situation had backfired.

"Sir, what's this? I was teasing you, and you've put me in a challenging position. I just know the basics of the waltz," I said.

"My dear Madhu, I can bet very few couples would be good at the dance; 70 percent of them won't come on the floor, and the remaining who would join us would be, at best mediocre. And you don't have to worry about any missing step; follow me, and you'll do fine," Rama said.

"Are you telling me you're so good that you could cover my mistakes?" I asked.

"I'm a sheer duffer when it comes to dancing; what we'd do is cover each other's back," Rama said with a chuckle.

"Sir, I'm praying, and you also do that, so we can come from the dance floor smiling," I said in a depressed voice.

He didn't respond to my comments due to the loud but soothing music the band had started playing. Finally, approximately after five minutes, Rama rose from the chair and took me to the dance floor, and the moment we stepped onto the floor, the hall reverberated with claps and whistles.

I put up a brave front with an ear-to-ear grin and prayed that I don't collapse with a nervous breakdown. Our dancing session started in a slow rhythm; Rama proved an exotic dancer as he quickly got into a fast tempo without missing any steps. All his steps, box, reverse, progressive, closed twinkle, were terrific, and I don't know how, but I matched him effortlessly. The hall was thundering with cheers, comforting sounds to the ear. After 10 minutes of dance, Rama signaled other couples to join, and within a couple of minutes, the dance floor became crowded with dancers.

"Sir, can we rest? My high heel is hurting," I said, even though no such thing was happening, but his closeness was intoxicating; my body felt relaxed and against my resolve, whispering to remain in his arms forever.

He stopped dancing, took my hand in his hand, and juggled through the dancers to reach our table. The table was empty of all the dishes, and the silverware was replaced.

I don't know why, but I blurted out, "Sir, you're an excellent dancer, which is surprising as I was under the impression that you're nothing but a bookworm."

"I was also pleasantly surprised; you're a fabulous dancer and much better than me. All the applause were for your smart moves; particularly the rise and fall step was too good," Rama said.

Two waiters came with two trolleys and started putting the main-course items on the table. A crisply dressed chef followed them, bowed with a good evening, and said, "Sir, when I was notified that you're coming, I chose to prepare roasted and grilled dishes personally and asked my trusted lieutenants to prepare authentic Hyderabadi cuisines. I hope you will enjoy the gastronomy." He then addressed me and said, "Ma'am, by looking at you, I could tell you eat like a bird, but please consider today your cheat day, and take at least a couple of bites from every dish on the table." He then removed the lids of all the dishes; holy mercy, a visual delight! Grilled lobster tail, grilled prawns, roasted whole baby chicken, roasted lamb cubes, roasted vegetables with halloumi cheese, assorted curries, biryani, and, last, assorted Indian breadbasket. He left after saying, "Sir, I'll be back with dessert and to take your feedback."

I said, "Sir, why did you order so much food? Even if I take one bite of each dish, my tummy will burst open."

"Madhu dear, I didn't order anything; I asked the manager to reserve a table for two and organize a decent dinner as my guest is a VVIP," Rama said smiling.

"Whatever you say cannot justify this much food, most of which would go to waste," I said.

"Don't worry about that, as all the leftover goes to an NGO," Rama said.

It was a king's dinner; to describe the food as delicious won't suffice, and I wasn't getting any better words to describe it.

"Sir, since this is our last meet outside of the hospital premises, I want to thank you for the dinners; unfortunately, I cannot reciprocate your magnanimity, for which I must say sorry," I said.

"My dear Dr. Madhu Priya, we're not friends that keep a tab on who did what and how to get even. You're my future wife, and the time you had given to me is much more valuable than the dinners' cost," Rama said soberly.

Thus far, everything has backfired; I dressed seductively, thinking it would put him off to the extent that he wouldn't want to see me again. Instead, he got pleased with my dress and happily took me out. I thought he was ignorant of social dances, and I would make him jealous by dancing with any floating hunk; instead, I ended up dancing with him, and he proved to be a fantastic dancer. He got so bitten by my beauty and appearance that he couldn't control himself and kissed me, and I failed to push him away. In fact, I got melted in his hold to the point that it felt good. I must keep away from him; if it continues, that day won't be far when I'll end up in his bed without marrying him.

Immediately after dinner, I said, "Sir, can we leave? I'm feeling a little weary and must rest."

We didn't converse much in the car, and while stepping out of the vehicle at the building entrance, I said goodnight and left without hearing his response.

The week went by in the usual hectic way. As expected, on Saturday afternoon, around 3:00, when I was about to leave for lunch, Rama entered the room with a loud knock on the door and said, "Tonight we're having our bite at your flat; I've ordered a French dinner that will come around 8:00."

"I'm going to my house, and I think I already told you I don't have time for you or your dinners," I said curtly.

"My dear Madhu Priya, the moment you walk out of the flat, I'll come to know, and I'll call your mom to tell her not to cook dinner; I'm bringing the food to have with her. Believe me; it will be music to her ears," Rama said with a loud laugh.

"Sir, why you're disturbing my peaceful life? Why can't you mind your own business and allow me to do the same? I'm doing my best not to resign; however, if you continue to harass me like this, I won't have any option but to quit," I said.

"Dear Dr. Madhu, allow me to assure you that you'll sit in the house as no other hospital could dare hire you even if you resign. And, if you stay in the comfort of your bungalow, then, hopefully, every day, my dinner will be with your parents. Let me assure you that they would love to host me and force you to join us," Rama said with a big grin.

"Sir, I regret the day I met you; you're an unforgiving, vengeful, and indecent person with whom maintaining any relationship is sheer foolishness," I said.

"My dear Madhu, your abuses won't deter me from marrying you. Say whatever you want, use all the powers at your disposal to keep me away from you, but I assure you that all your attempts would not yield the result you aspire to achieve. The only thing you could do is commit suicide, but since you're a fighter and not a coward, you wouldn't do that. Take my suggestion, continue your efforts that you're making by wearing skimpy dresses and attempting to dance with another gentleman to make me jealous or whatever you think could drive me crazy to the extent that I forgo the idea of marrying you. I'm deeply in love with you and decided that I would marry you or remain single. Madhu, I plead with you to bury the past, and I guarantee I'll always keep you content and happy. Like my father, who never interferes in my mother's decisions in or outside the house, I'll give you the same freedom. Please give me a chance to prove how much I love you and how much regard and esteem I've for you," Rama said.

"Sir, I'll not reconsider my decision to remain single, and you're free to do whatever you think would change my decision," I said.

"Sure, my dear, see you after 7:00, and bye for now," Rama said and left the room.

I don't know what to do with this man; he's the country's most eligible bachelor and chasing me to marry him; I must feel proud about it. However, my brain wasn't allowing me to have any relationship with him.

All his good qualities and richness have no meaning for me, even though everyone believes he's a catch and a very fortunate girl would get this precious gem. Recently, a few colleagues informed me he's very down to earth; anyone could walk to his chamber and tell him whatever they want. And he listens very patiently and does his best to resolve the issue satisfactorily. My heart was developing a soft corner for him and telling me to forgive him, but the brain wasn't willing to forget and forgive. It is dangerous to marry a person who couldn't condone one mistake. I definitely shouldn't test him for a second time and must never forget the saying, "If they do it once, they'll do it again." I should not let him trap me in his cobweb to denigrate and destroy my self-worth.

Without a man in my life, I'm content and have gotten used to a celibate life. Undoubtedly, his kiss stirred the dead emotions momentously. Still, I smothered the sensual craving with brute force and decided I shouldn't permit him to derive pleasures from my body in the future.

I had no clue how to stop his constant chasing, and it is true that even if I resigned, he could ensure I didn't get a job, even in charity hospitals. He could barge into my house and get a warm welcome from Mom and Dad, and I would be forced to go out with him or sit with him to have dinner. I tried to put him off with my skin show, but that didn't work; I thought of making him jealous by dancing with another person, which also failed. Since morning, I scratched my brain on finding a concrete way out to help offend him to the degree that he abandoned his decision to marry me. I couldn't come up with anything that would work; I won't go out with him, let him shout, use physical force, or do whatever he wanted, but I should stand firm. I believe he connected with my brain through telepathy, which guided him to organize dinner at the flat. Now, what choice I've got to avoid him; none. I thought not to have the food he would bring, but is it the solution to get rid of him for good; of course not, and even after lots of brainstorming, I failed to hit upon a tactical path that could end our interaction.

Two persons with a pile of corrugated boxes stood before my door when I reached the flat at 6:00. I asked them what the boxes were and who had sent them; they said they'd brought an audio sound system for installation on the flat's balcony, and they were from the technical support department and had no idea who had ordered them. I allowed them to come in, as I knew Rama had sent it, and if I stopped them from installation, he would come rushing and supervise the work.

They finished the installation in an hour and gave me the demonstration. It was a high-end sound system, perhaps the most expensive brand available in the market; six wireless jewel speakers were installed inconspicuously on the balcony's parapet walls, and the central system and a large subwoofer were placed on a free-standing glass cabinet. The audio amplifier receiver had an external storage device loaded with hundreds of popular Hindi, English, Telugu songs and evergreen symphonies. The techies uploaded the music system app on my phone and taught me how to switch on/off the system and upload, delete, or play songs. I switched on the equipment upon the techie's request and played Kenny G's "Going Home," which worked fine.

At 7:30 sharp, the calling bell announced Rama's presence at the entrance, and with a few minutes delay,

I opened the door, and he barged in, saying, "Hello Madhu, hope you liked the music system."

"Why did you send it? Please ask them to take it back; I don't have the time to enjoy the music, and neither do I prefer to spend my time on such pleasures," I said firmly.

"I sent it for my entertainment; I want to sit on the balcony when I come here. See my moon seated beneath the stars and soothing music flowing, or I would be holding the queen of my heart in my arms, enjoying a slow dance in circles," Rama said with an ear-to-ear grin.

"Sir, I cannot stop you from dreaming anything that you want to, but I would appreciate it if you take back your gadget and don't force me to dine with you at my flat or outside," I said harshly.

"My dear Madhu, you know well I've taken up the task to make you live a normal life like our parents: marry and raise children. I won't force you to marry me; however, I'll do everything possible to prove I would be your best choice. I assure you, if you wed me, I would always respect your decisions and give you the freedom to lead a life of your choice; as long as it is within the boundaries of decency and ethical values that my family and I firmly believe in and practice," Rama said in an even tone.

"Sir, I mentioned umpteen times that I've decided to remain single, so don't pressurize me to marry," I said.

Suddenly he grabbed my hand, took me to the balcony, and made me sit on a cane couch at the far end of the terrace. Then, he played a famous symphony by

Ludwig Van Beethoven using his mobile phone, walked to the wall where electrical switches were installed to open the windows and ceiling, and pressed a switch that made the windowpanes go opaque.

Humm, he's installed electrically powered switchable privacy panes; the idiot is nothing but persistent pain.

He came and sat opposite me and said, "Food will come in a while, and till that time can we dance, a slow dance, just holding each other and enjoying the feel and the evergreen music?"

"Sir, you can dance alone and have fun. Also, please feel free to bring a partner from outside; I'll go to my house," I said curtly.

He came to my couch, took both my hands in his hands, and pulled me with such force that I didn't have a choice but to stand; we were so close that our bodies were rubbing. He held my left hand in his left hand, placed his right hand around my waist, and started dancing. I had to follow his dance steps because of his tight grip on my body.

"Sir, please leave me; I don't want to dance; your hold is tight, and I'm feeling suffocated," I said.

Instead of losing the grip, he tightened so much that I had to raise my head to breathe, and the idiot took the opportunity and placed his lips on my lips. My body went limp in his hold, and I don't remember when my lips opened and how long he sucked them. He took his sweet time releasing me; I went to the couch, sat, and closed my eyes. My entire body was numb, and the only physical component that was functioning was my brain, but as far as I was concerned, it was malfunctioning as it was emitting pleasure hormones.

Before I could compose myself and talk to him, I heard the sound of the calling bell. Rama went to check and returned with two uniformed persons, most likely waiters of a posh restaurant. They brought a few boxes and two large plastic folding tables, and within a few minutes, they set up one table for a candlelight dinner, and on the other table, they kept the hot boxes and various other items. Crockery and cutlery they picked from the kitchen, but everything else they brought with them, including a free-standing champagne stand and an ice-filled bucket with a stuffed bottle of Bollinger.

Rama came to me, took my hand, and said, "Ma'am, dinner is ready, and the boys are waiting to serve."

I calmly followed him; I didn't want to create a scene in front of the servers.

It took almost an hour to finish the seven-course dinner; assorted tiny appetizers, salad mixed with tuna and boiled eggs, cheese platter, bisque soup, grilled salmon fish, for main course lobster thermidor, and crème brûlée dessert. I refused to drink the wine; Rama instructed the server not to open the bottle.

The music system continuously played various famous symphonies; it now played Mozart's classic symphony number 40 in G minor.

Nothing was working on this man, and day by day, he was getting bolder; if this scenario continued, then sooner than later, I would start enjoying his company, and we would become a lovey-dovey couple. Therefore, I must stop meeting him if I want to remain single.

"Would you care for a cup of coffee? I need one, as I want to sit for a while and talk to you," Rama said.

"I'll prepare, give me a few minutes," I said and went to the kitchen.

I thought it was an excellent opportunity to get into a serious discussion, and I must be forthright and convey my message firmly and be as offensive as possible.

I gave the coffee cup to Rama and sat opposite him on the shellback cane chair with my cup.

I began the conversation and said, "I saw you gazing at the sky. Were you counting the stars or planning to move there?"

"My beloved Madhu, the soothing effect of the sky is urging me to have our bedroom ceiling decorated with hidden sky-blue lights, paint the ceiling with patches of moving clouds, and spread ample twinkling stars in the background like the sky above our heads. Then, at night, when we're enveloped in each other's bodies, engaged in pillow talk while staring at the ceiling, it would provide us a relaxing and heartwarming upshot," Rama said with a grin.

"A fantasy, I would say. That day will never come as long as I'm physically fit with a functioning brain. Even if I change my mind and decide to marry, it wouldn't be you; you're not my type, nor do I like you as a person," I said curtly.

"Dear darling Madhu, whether I'm your type or not, I'm the only option you have if you decide to marry. Anyhow, enlighten me, queen of my heart, the areas of my personality that tell you I'm not the ideal person to marry. I'll work on them to meet your expectations," Rama said.

"I don't like too many things in your personality; what I hate the most is your rigid and inflexible nature. If I must marry, then a person with your character cannot be my husband," I said.

"My dear Dr. Madhu, I'm no more an MBBS student, which you remember. You're looking at a completely changed person; my stay in Mumbai and one year in Australia have transformed me significantly; before that, my approach toward life was only black and white, with no gray areas. Yes, I admit I made a mistake and abused you for hitting my car. I should have thought that no sane person could do such a foolish thing intentionally; you must've been in a rush or upset with someone or anything that didn't go well early in the morning that caused you to be immersed in your thoughts so much so that you damaged your expensive vehicle and my modest car," Rama said.

"You're right; it was a bad morning; the cumulation of upsetting events blocked my mind from focusing on where I was and what I was doing, which resulted in the accident. You decided to judge the book by its cover, humiliated me, and never bothered to think there could be compelling reasons for such a lapse on my part. Forgiving and forgetting are good acts that I practice, but when the stakes are high, it's better to play safe and not allow anyone to hurt you twice. You're asking me to take a chance with my life and marry you, a vengeful person; even a fool understands that a snake just sheds his skin, not his venom-producing ability or biting skill," I stated emphatically.

"Madhu, I don't know why you got so upset with a stupid boy's childish comments or irrational behavior. I'm ready to do anything you want that would give you the satisfaction that I would keep you happy and fulfilled as long as I'm alive," Rama said.

"For over a year, I tried to be your friend; I even changed my attire, thinking you could be a traditional person and prefer to see your girlfriend dressed in Eastern clothes. Almost every day, I stood in the corridors from where you would pass, thinking you could acknowledge and at least give a nod of recognition, but no such thing ever happened. Instead, you showed outrageous contempt for a minor slip on my part and never bothered to recognize me or even say a courteous hello. Now you want me to forget the humiliation, embarrassment, and affronts I had faced in front of my colleagues and friends, who knew that my makeover was to become your friend. On my back, they laughed at me and called me names. No way on earth you could compensate for my suffering; I'd rather kill myself than marry you," I said in an even tone.

"Madhu, I committed a blunder, and you endured; allow me to amend the slight on my part, which was only a puerile naivete. If you continue to chew on your horrid past, it will only serve to destroy your beautiful personality," Rama said grimly.

"You could attribute your act to whatever phase of life you were in; does it matter – no, never, and nothing could be condoned, buried, or put behind. Your dinners, flowers, and sweets won't thaw my hardened stance to remain single. Every year, millions of rupees are deposited into my bank account as my share of the factory profits and rentals of the commercial properties I own. I hardly spend more than a couple of millions from what I receive, so your multibillion-dollar empire, social standing, and a luxurious lifestyle are nothing more than carrots that I'm not interested in nibbling. On the off-chance that I at any point choose to wed, the odds of that occurrence are none to nothing; it would be purely for my happiness. So please take my advice, search for a beautiful, educated girl with an upscale family background and settle down and enjoy life with her, and don't waste your precious time chasing a boring doctor who knows nothing but diseases. I'm not seeking retribution for my humiliation, but your sight reminds me of how you degraded and humiliated me, making me shiver with rage and pain; if you want to see me happy, stay out of my life," I said firmly.

"I know you're a determined person and not a pushover softy. I'm also aware of the arduous task ahead of me to make you agree to marry me; unfortunately, I'm also not a weakling. Once I decide to achieve something, I throw my entire weight behind my aspiration, like a warrior on the battlefield who has to triumph or perish. So it's either you or no one. You do whatever you want to be away from me, and I'll do what I need to do, and trust me, I won't constrain you to marry me. The moment you wed anyone, I'll stop my pursuit, but till then, you don't have any choice but to stomach me," Rama said dispassionately.

"Fine, I'll find a washout parasite and wed him, which should burn you inside out roundly and soundly, and I'll be saved from the torment of your presence in my life," I said mercilessly.

"No issues, my love. Once you marry a loser, inform me to host a massive wedding dinner party. Then, in the presence of the who's who of the country, I'll put one bullet each in your and your loser husband's heads, and then one bullet in my head; this will earn permanent peace for both of us," Rama said with a chuckle.

"Oh, yes, this is a better solution, as it will save me from the persistent tortures," I said indignantly.

"Great, it's a deal. Now time to rest, so goodnight and goodbye," Rama said, walking toward the main door, and I followed him to make sure the door was closed properly. At the door, he suddenly turned and took me in his arms and said, "Madhu, don't torture yourself; you could hate me, abuse me, as much as you want, but stay happy and keep your parents happy," he said, kissed me on my forehead and left.

I returned to the balcony, sat in Rama's chair, and suddenly got emotional and cried uncontrollably. For more than five minutes, my wailing continued, and when the tears dried, I went to the washroom, cleaned myself, and again went to the balcony and occupied the same chair. Rama is a gem, blessed with everything one could only dream to have, a stunningly handsome, well-qualified medical doctor, dirt rich, and to top it all, a kindhearted and caring person. Even though he's bending over backward, to the extent of breaking his back, I can still not help bury the past and move on. If I ever decide to marry, I would never find a better person than Rama, who would give me anything and everything I would ask, on top of his love and care. But no matter how hard I try, I'll never be able to overlook or erase from memory my humiliation and the unceasingly infuriating gossip of my class fellows. I spent over a year of my life and did everything to become just his friend, and what he did crush my dignity, humiliated me, and made me feel like a worthless gold digger. If I decide to take a fresh start, what's the guarantee that I won't make a silly mistake, which he could take as inhuman behavior and turn his back on me for good? Dangerous man to marry; I would rather stay single and die in his love than face another humiliation of separation or divorce.

The following Saturday afternoon, Rama came to my clinic asking whether I would like to go out for dinner or if the flat was the best place to enjoy the evening. I said I must be excused, as I've some pressing work to attend to at home, and he said, "Okay, no problem, have a great weekend," and left. It surprised me as I expected him to press me to change all my engagements and spend the evening with him. So strange! Inexplicable, but deep down, I felt disappointed.

In the evening, when I reached home, I noticed Mom was busy in the kitchen with several servants. When I asked her what was going on, she replied that some VIPs were coming for dinner, and I should also be ready by 8:00.

I said, "Mom, tell me who's the guest, or else you must excuse me," I smelled the rat.

Mom said, "I've no idea about the guest; your dad said a business associate is coming."

At sharp 8:00, I came out of my room and heard Mom and Dad's voices, probably talking with the guests.

I got on fire when I entered the living room; Rama was sitting with Mom and Dad. I went and sat beside Dad and gave a grimacing look at the idiot, who said with an annoying grin, "Good to see you, Madhu; I thought you would be busy in your pressing work, and I would miss you at the dinner."

Mom left the room, informing us she would arrange the dinner table, and Dad also left, saying he would change and join in a few minutes.

"Don't you have any self-respect to show up here uninvited," I snarled.

"My dear Madhu, I asked your mom whether I could come with a Chinese or Spanish dinner, and she said, come minus your dinner, and whatever I would like to eat, it will be prepared by the in-house cooks, and she said she's thrilled and honored to have me for dinner," Rama said with a wicked ear-to-ear grin.

"You're not coming here again, or else I'll stay at the apartment, and you enjoy your dinners with Mom and Dad," I roared.

"That's what I want; you stay at the flat. I'll come with the dinner, and we'll wine and dine and dance. If you refuse, I'll meet you here. Dinner at your house is the last thing I want to enjoy; who's interested in the dinner anyways? I like to eat with you in seclusion and with a sweet kiss, which will keep me energized for the whole week," Rama said with a loud laugh.

"Why don't you understand that I don't like you or your company? Find someone who values your companionship, enjoys your dinners, and wholeheartedly offers you holistic energy doses," I said in the same angry tone.

"No, Madhu, no one else on earth could give me the pleasure I get in your company. It would be best if you decide to marry me right away; otherwise, till that time, you don't have a choice but to spend all weekend evenings with me," Rama said smilingly.

"This is too much, and you know what will happen to you if I kill myself with a note that I've snuffed because of your constant harassment? You'll spend a long time behind bars; do you want to go to jail for an ordinary girl who has nothing to offer to keep you happy? You'll find plenty of girls who are much more educated, beautiful, wealthy, cultured, sophisticated, and party animals who know well how to keep their man happy. In me, you wouldn't find any of those qualities; I'm a flat-out boring person who only enjoys reading and helping the destitute. Your infatuation will fizzle out within a few weeks of marriage; you'll find me a highly inept person when it comes to domestic chores or fulfilling your fantasies. So, Sir, I beg you to forget about me and choose a proper partner who could keep you and your family happy," I said with forceful certainty.

"Madhu, allow me to reiterate that it is you I would wed or remain single. Let me enlighten you that, thus far, I've met with hundreds of highly educated and beautiful girls who signified intense interest in courtship or permanent attachment. A few girls from decent wealthy families even offered co-habitation until I got comfortable with marriage. Unfortunately, none of the girls impressed me to the extent that I could decide to take the plunge. However, after meeting you, I was thinking about you only, and with careful soul-searching, I made up my mind that you're the girl I should marry. You subscribe to the same life I've chosen for myself, and you have everything that would make me proud as a peacock to have you as my life partner. Nothing will deter me even if you inflict physical harm, leave aside your insults, abuses, or humiliating comments of rejection. I've hurt you so severely that I deserve everything and anything you would throw at me, and you know what, every time you're humiliating me, my love toward you is increasing manifold. You're such an honest soul that you can't keep anything inside, making your personality more appealing. Madhu, whether you marry me or not, you'll always find me standing by your side to help you overcome any difficult situation or internal conflicts that bring anxiety and annoyance. I'm no God, but all the might at my disposal will be available for you whenever needed," Rama said soberly.

"Please understand, I'm not humiliating or throwing abuses at you; I'm only conveying my refusal to marry you, which you're refusing to accept. I decided to remain single, and I don't want you in my life as a friend, lover, or husband. If you love me so much and want to see me happy, then keep away and never bother to meet me," I said.

Before Rama could respond to my comments, Mom walked in and asked us to come to the dining room. The table was full of veg and non-veg dishes, and Mom fed Rama as if the idiot were her son-in-law. I got annoyed with the pampering he was getting; even Dad was telling him he's a poor eater; my foot, he was pigging out, complimenting Mom on the deliciousness of every dish so that she can feed more – smart ass. This scenario made me firm up my decision to keep him away from home, let him come to the flat, bring whatever food he wanted, and spare Mom from this labor.

I was breaking my head, thinking about how I could escape from his clutches. But unfortunately, running away wasn't an option, as I needed to stay with my parents until my brother completed his education and returned from the USA. Moreover, I didn't want to leave the hospital because it was the best place to work: state-of-the-art equipment, experienced assistants, superb inpatient facilities, and no wasted time traveling from one hospital to the next.

But, like everything in life, nothing comes without a price tag, and here I have to put up with this rogue; escape from him looked impossible.

Every time he left the flat, I spent at least 15 to 20 minutes sitting on the chair where he sat, filling my lungs with his perfume and howling aloud till the tears stopped. Life would've been a blessing to walk with him, hold his hand, and raise his children.

I was distressed by the conflicting views from the heart and brain; the heart was pressurizing to forgive and take the rope; in contrast, the brain vehemently opposed offering the second cheek. I was torn apart by my conflicting feelings; outwardly, he's a holy gem, but the pain and humiliation he inflicted made him a poisonous flower like the Pink Oleander.

In a recent conversation with Dad regarding the hospital project, he said, "First you marry, and I promise to construct at least a 50-bed hospital of your specialty, and to meet with the running costs, I'll establish a trust." I asked him to start work on the hospital front, and I would find a son-in-law for him the following year. The million-dollar question was how and where I could find the stupid son-in-law. Rama is a big no, and there was no one I knew other than the idiot. I didn't have a boyfriend, but for a few male class fellows under the acquaintanceships category and a small number of girls I knew well, all had got married and moved overseas. If I tell Mom to find a suitable alliance, she could put forward only one option – Rama. I have no choice but to dig the well myself if I need the water.

New Year was a few days away, and I told myself to make the coming year's resolution to find a husband in the first two quarters. Challenging, but if I want to be away from the pester by the name of Rama, then I must find a husband, even if it's a namesake and nothing but a loser. Honestly, I was getting addicted to his visits, the dinners, the dance, and the kisses, which were annoying and must be stopped.

The new year's night was on Thursday, a long weekend of three days, and Dad told us that we were invited to spend three days at one of his friends' farmhouses. I flatly refused to go, but Dad said it was a must; the host is his largest customer and insisted that I come with my family, and don't worry, there won't be any crowd, including us, only three families. I tried to convince Dad to go with Mom, but he disagreed and insisted I come with them; he said the host family was keenly interested in meeting with his nephrologist daughter.

The thought of spending three days with strangers, wearing a plastic smile for the entire duration, was depressing. Mom refused to help me and said, "You better convince your dad, as he'll not listen to me." It crossed my mind; that even Rama would've been a better choice; at least I could've spent three days hearing his pleas to forgive and marry him. He didn't call or even pay a visit to my clinic or flat, even though I was expecting him to invite me for the new year celebrations; had that happened, I would've put up a solid case to Dad for sparing me from this ordeal. Ditching Rama would've been the easiest thing, and even otherwise, spending an evening at the flat with the idiot was a much-preferred option compared to the irritation of spending three days with strangers.

On the 31st afternoon, we packed our bags with the necessary clothes and accessories and left for the farmhouse. Dad informed us that it would take around an hour, as it was 40 kilometers away, and the road was single-track, with too many unforeseen roadblocks of lamb, cow, and buffalo herds. As per the estimated time, the car stopped in front of a huge iron die-cast gate, the back of which was covered with an iron plate, with a half-moon board on top of the gate, mentioning in large metal alphabets "Manju Farms."

"Dad, you should have mentioned that we're going to Rama's family farmhouse, and I definitely wouldn't have come," I shrieked.

"Madhu, there was no way I could've refused the invitation of my angel. Had he asked me to close the factories for ten days and come, I would've done that without the slightest hesitation. So enjoy the next three days. I was informed they have many indoor and outdoor activities to keep everyone engaged," Dad said.

"Dad, I'll be on a bed of thorns for the whole length of our stay; I don't like Rama, and to put up with him for the next three days will be nothing but mental torture," I said.

"For my sake, Madhu, please be polite and cheerful; if you show any disrespect to anyone, I would be hugely disappointed," Dad said.

After a few minutes of waiting, no one came out, but the gate opened, and a security guard signaled us to move in. Our car slowly sailed on a wide concrete road. On both sides of the road, tall Ashoka trees were lined, and behind the trees, I saw various fruit-bearing trees: mango, guava, mulberries, fig, custard apple, papaya, wood apple, and a few others I failed to recognize. The farmhouse must have been spread over a few kilometers, as I couldn't see any boundary walls on either the left or the right side except hundreds of trees. We drove more than a kilometer to reach a large single-story tinted-blue glass building. Rama was standing at the building entrance, and the moment our car stopped, he came forward and opened the front door for Dad to come out. He guided us inside. We entered a vast hall, which must be 50 meters wide, but I couldn't see the length as it was partitioned after approximately 30 meters with an eight-foot-high frosted glass wall, leaving a ten-foot passage on either side of the wall.

Rama's parents, eldest sister with her husband, and a young girl and boy, both must be just in their teens, sat in the hall's center. They all rushed to greet us, and after the handshakes, hugs, and kisses on the cheeks, Rama's mother took my hand and made me sit beside her. Servers catered us a fresh fruit cocktail, and Rama's mother told me it was made from farm-grown fruits, and in the next three days, we would eat and drink most of the items grown or raised on the farmhouse. She must be telling me to impress me with what I would get if I married her son.

The hall turned into a chatterbox; women engaged in talking to women, and men talked to men, which went on for almost half an hour. It was an awkward situation; I was under the scanner of all the men and women, and even Rama's eyes frequently focused on me.

Rama's Dad stood from his sofa and said, "Let's rest, as a long night is awaiting; we will meet here at 8:00 in our dinner outfits," he then turned to Rama and asked him to take us to our room.

We followed Rama, who took us behind the partition wall of the hall from the right-side passage. There were six large doors, two on the left, two on the right, and two in the middle. He opened the second door on the right side and gestured for us to move in. We entered a spacious living hall decently furnished with leather sofa sets, a large glass top table in the center, and a few solid teakwood hand-carved coffee tables. The walls were decorated with various breathtaking sea and landscape oil paintings, and on one wall facing the large sofa was a wall-mounted TV, which must have been 65" or larger. A well-equipped kitchen at the end of the hall and a passage on the right led to the bedrooms.

Rama addressed Dad, "Uncle, you'll find everything you need, but please call me if you don't find what you want." He then guided Dad to the master bedroom and asked me to follow him to take me to my room. It was a large hall, and calling it a room was inappropriate; on one side, a king-size bed, and beside the bed, a sitting area with a four-seater leather sofa and a writing table and chair. On the right hand, attached to the front wall, was a frosted door that must be leading to the toilet and dresser, as I didn't see any cabinet or a mirror.

"Madhu, we've kept everything in the dresser area that you would be needing, and if you still need anything, please call me," Rama said and left the room.

I walked to the dresser area to empty the luggage trolley. It was a vast room, with a sizable three-door mirror wardrobe on the left, an open rack cabinet full of various size towels, bath gowns, a couple of free-standing cloth hanger stands, washbasins on half of the right side, and a dressing counter on the other half. I was shocked when I opened the first door of the cabinet and found three dinner gowns, several pairs of jeans and tops to go with the jeans, assorted jackets, formal dresses, bras, and panties, all my size. The cabinet's second portion was full of sportswear, tracksuits, shirts, shorts, swimsuits, sports bras, caps, headbands, sunscreen, and anti-chafing lotions. The last portion was the shoe rack, where several pairs of fancy high-heel sandals, pump shoes, and two pairs of sneakers, all my size. Finally, the dressing counter had several expensive perfumes and everything needed for makeup, lipsticks, eyeliners, color pallets, blushers, foundations, etc.

Son of a gun! How come he collected my body sizes, even for inners? He must've taken the sizes from Mom – no, he must've taken Mom to shop all the items.

After freshening up, I went to Mom's room; she was on the sofa reading a magazine, and Dad was snoring on the bed. I asked her to come to my room, as I didn't want to disturb Dad's sleep. After we sat on the couch of my room, I asked, "Mom, why did you give my body sizes to Rama without asking me?"

"Since when have I become answerable to you, Madhu? He wanted to buy a few dresses for you and asked me to accompany him; I couldn't refuse his request. He's a gem of a person and is dying to marry you, and it seems you're abusing and insulting him and have refused to marry him because of what had happened between you and him a decade ago. Your dad and I are distraught with you, and once we go from here, we've decided to have a serious conversation concerning your appalling behavior. It's high time you settle down, and there's no better choice than Rama in the entire world. Allow us to die in peace, give us grandchildren to play with, and spoil them with gifts and sweets. We know you're a straight girl and have no physical or psychological barrier that could prevent you from marrying. Unfortunately, since your fight with Rama, you've become like this. Rama has promised me that he'll always keep you happy and is willing to give you 50 percent of his shares in the Manju Group. Now please tell me what you would achieve by holding grudges and denying yourself the pleasures of married life," Mom said.

"Mom, did I ever say that I'm holding any grudge against Rama, and did I ever say I don't want to marry for any physical abnormality or my sexual preferences? A long time ago, I decided to dedicate my life to serving the needy, and I'm not going to change because a wealthy person is interested in marrying me. I have plenty of money in my bank account, which alone is enough to live a comfortable life as long as I'm alive. So why do I need someone's money, and why should I go against my decision to remain single? I've nothing against Rama; he may be a gem or a holy angel or dirt rich, but it won't influence my decision to stay single. Your son will fulfill your desire to play with your grandchildren; you just have to wait a while. Mom, please don't encourage Rama to come to our house or invite him in the future. If you'd told me we were coming here, I would never have come. Because of his nagging, I wanted to kiss off the job a long time ago; if it wasn't for the valuable experience I was gaining, I would have done so," I said somberly.

"Madhu, please tell me who's stopping you from doing your charity work. Rama told me he loved your dedication to serving the needy, and he would always encourage and support you in your endeavors. With his help, you could do much better than what you're doing currently. He's like you, Madhu; his primary aim in life is to help the underprivileged. Moreover, he's very decent and well-mannered; it will be a blessing to you from God to have him as your hubby," Mom said.

"Mom, don't use the emotional blackmail tactics; this won't work. I'm as firm as a rock in my resolve to remain single, and if you or anyone force me, I'll disappear for good. Remember, I wasn't waiting for Rama to come and marry me; if I wanted to marry, I wouldn't have rejected some of the proposals that no sane girl would've refused. I'm at peace and satisfied with my life; I firmly believe any change could result in massive unpleasant adjustments and diversion from my chosen path, which is unacceptable," I said.

"Why this uncompromising attitude, Madhu? I feel hurt. You know your father, and I get heartbroken when people gossip behind our backs about you. Please, Madhu, I strongly urge you to reconsider your decision; it's abnormal to remain single for no apparent reason.

God has given you so much; be grateful and enjoy your life with your work and a decent man. You're our blood, our loving child, and we're desperate to see you wed and give us babies to play with, and it will be a profound sorrow if we leave this world with unfulfilled desire," Mom said and started wailing loudly.

I went to her and hugged her, and instead of consoling her, I also started crying, and my cries became louder than Mom's cries. When our tears dried, I said, "Mom, I know he's the ideal person to marry, but give me some time. Whenever I see him, my blood boils, thinking about my humiliation and what he said about me. I promise you, within a year, I'll marry, if not Rama, then someone of my choice, but give me time. Mom, I'm not trying to make you happy, but it's a real promise that I'll be married within a year."

Mom hugged me and said, "Thank you, my love; you cannot imagine how happy your dad will be when I give him this news. And, please forgive Rama; he's a wonderful man, dying to marry you, and I noticed he's honest and trustworthy."

"Mom, I cannot promise to marry Rama, but I'll consider him, and let me tell you, it wouldn't be easy to decide in his favor. And, Mom, you don't know what he said to me and how he humiliated, insulted, and crushed my ego and self-worth," I said.

"Madhu, I'm sure he must've hurt you badly; however, I guarantee you'll find him a changed person. He's desperate to marry you, and I believe in this situation you could mold him the way you want him to, and remember he's putting on the table everything that he's to get a yes from you," Mom said,

"Mom, I believe every word you say; however, I've issues that aren't easy to overcome. But, rest assured, I don't want to disappoint you and Dad and will do what I can to keep both of you happy," I said.

We changed the topic and talked for a while about the vastness of the farmhouse. Then, Mom decided to take a rest and left.

I also stretched out on the bed and thought about why I had got into this wreck, why I had allowed my heart to screw me. The craving to see Rama boy got me into this mess, but now the question was how to come out of it. Despite his apologies, I don't want to marry the billionaire boy because of his inflexible and unforgiving nature. Even with his rock-solid assurances, what's the guarantee that he wouldn't hang me out to dry for a silly oversight? I don't know when my brain stopped functioning and when I went into a deep slumber.

Mom was sitting on the bed and rubbing my hand slowly and was telling me, "Wake up, honey, we're ready to go, and you're still sleeping."

I checked the wall clock; it was almost 8:00, and we were supposed to be in the hall by now, so I said, "Mom, you go, and I'll be with you as soon as I can." Mom looked stunning in her gold color Kanjeevaram saree, her regular hairstyle of a beautiful large low bun, and the makeup done to perfection with a light rosewood lipstick.

I quickly washed and opted to wear one of the three gowns. While looking at the gowns, I spotted a sticker on the fuchsia pink long-sleeved gown that said, "I would be delighted if I were to see you in this outfit." It was an Alexander McQueen gown with a V-neck and a bow made of pure silk, with acetate and silk lining. Rama boy must've paid a fortune for it, as I knew the designer is famous for being very expensive. Okay, dear, I'll put it on for you, but you'll be gazing at the moon out of your reach.

I was in the hall at 9:15; it was a changed place. On one side, DJ equipment was set up and at the center was a starlit LED dance floor; chafing dishes were lined on the left side wall, and leather sofas were placed in a half-moon shape in front of the dance floor. Except for me, everyone was seated with drinks on the coffee tables in front of the couches. Before I decided where to sit, Rama's Mom came, hugged and kissed me on the forehead, and said, "Darling, you're looking gorgeous; we all were waiting for you and must admit you've made it worth our wait by looking so beautiful." I mumbled, "Thank you, Aunty." She took my hand and walked to the other corner where her hubby was sitting; he greeted me and asked me to sit beside him. The treatment and stares of the host family members reflected that they'd taken me for granted as the would-be wife of Rama.

"Tomorrow, my wife and I will take you for a farmhouse tour. We will leave at noon; is that okay with you?" Nageshwar Rao Saab asked.

"Fine with me. Will Mom and Dad join us?" I asked.

"Your mom, dad, and all the others will spend the day with Rama, who'll first give them a guided tour of the farmhouse. Then, they planned to prepare biryani for lunch in the open. We will have the same biryani for our lunch, prepared from the aromatic basmati rice grown on the farm and the lamb meat of Karnataka's Bannur sheep raised here. In the evening, we will spend time together for a BBQ dinner at the pool," Rama's mother said.

Rama's elder sister appeared on the dance floor with a mic and announced, "Boys and girls, no exception here," to which everyone laughed aloud. "Our evening will begin with a slow waltz dance performance of approximately 10 minutes by my bro and our honorable chief guest, Dr. Madhu Priya. The next to come on stage will be my kids, and they'll dance to the fast numbers of Bollywood and Tollywood, and once they're exhausted, everyone is invited to burn the stage. "Please join me in offering a standing ovation to the first couple to enter the dance floor and dazzle us."

Everyone stood and applauded, and I felt weak in my knees because I had never expected to be cornered in this manner. A few moments later, Rama approached me and extended his hand to take me to the floor. Rama's Mom said, "Go, darling, have fun." I slowly raised my hand toward Rama, who grabbed the hand firmly, and we walked toward the floor under the loud sound of shrieks and whistles.

The initial steps for me were slightly shaky; however, Rama was very steady, and within a couple of minutes, we were all over the floor, and everyone was clapping on our sleek and effortless moves. We spent more than 10 minutes; Rama was going like a robot, and

I had to tell him enough. When we stopped, everyone stood and clapped, and Rama's Mom came on the floor, first kissing my forehead and then Rama's. She took me with her by holding my hand, and when we reached our seat, Rama's Dad stood and kissed me on the forehead and said, "First time I've seen two well-qualified doctors dancing the waltz so beautifully. I must admit both of you looked magnificent." I murmured, "Thank you, Uncle."

The new year arrived when everyone was on the floor with their champagne glasses in hand and stomachs full of food. The DJ stopped playing the music at one in the morning and announced the party was over.

The following morning, I told Dad I wanted to go with him and not with Uncle and Aunty. Dad said, "Madhu, they want to talk to you about your refusal to marry Rama. So go with them and inform them of your reasons for remaining unmarried. I've told them we had done everything to convince you but failed."

"Dad, Rama must've asked for their assistance since he failed in his attempts to make me agree. Dad, do you think my refusal will impact your friendship, or would it be okay if I tell them why I'm against marriage?" I asked.

"They know very well that we've been after you for the marriage for the past several years, but thus far, we didn't succeed. So I wished them good luck and asked them to exert as much pressure as possible to make you agree. Given all this, I don't think your refusal would have any dark shadow on our decades-old relationship," Dad said.

"Dad, you've put me in a tough situation; they're treating me so well that I don't want to say no, but I've no choice but to state my position, which I'm sure will sorely upset them," I growled.

"I wish and pray you would say a big yes to them. Not only us but everyone in this building will be thrilled with your yes. Please reconsider your stand, Madhu; married life will make you a complete person, and you'll get immense pleasure from having children. Since you and Vimi left the house, it's empty and dreary even though my wife and I are amply compatible companions," Dad said.

"Dad, I have promised Mom I would marry before the end of this year, so please relax," I said and walked out of the room.

I was in the hall at 12:00; Rama's parents were waiting for me; Aunty hugged and kissed my forehead and said, "You're looking like a teenage girl in your casuals," I murmured a thank you. I was in blue jeans and a silk top with red flowers printed on a yellow background and was wearing one of the sneakers I found in the cabinet.

A stretched bulletproof Mercedes car was waiting for us, and as the vehicle moved, Rama's Mom said, "I'll be your tour guide. The farmhouse is not for our entertainment alone; it is a hugely successful commercial venture. More than 90 percent of whatever we raise or grow here goes to the market.

"It is spread out over a six-kilometer radius, and roughly 80 employees stay inside the premises for the upkeep. We've hundreds of fruit-bearing trees, mainly mango, guava, papaya, fig, mulberry, blackberry, custard apple, etc. Apart from this, we grow rice, red gram, millet, and various vegetables.

"We've aquaculture ponds for fish and shrimp farming, a free-range chicken poultry farm, a sheep farm where we raise the Bannur sheep of Karnataka, and a Holstein cattle farm. The star money-making venture of this farmhouse is the horse stable. We buy the foal of proven thoroughbred parents and close relatives and train them for racing. Once they're ready for the race and around two years old, we sell them through auction, or if they have a massive potential of winning races, we keep them to participate in a primary race. If they win the race, several buyers will come forward and bid, which lets us make excellent money. The stable is spread over two kilometers and fortified with a water moat and high-voltage electric fence. The horse stable, lunging, and racetrack areas are highly protected and guarded round the clock by security staff and electronically. Raising and training thoroughbred horses necessitates having expensive horse handlers and trainers and the highest quality feed, and some of their diet components we had to import. These costs make it costly to raise thoroughbreds for racing and call for their 24/7 vigilance, especially against snakes and jealous intruders who could harm the animals.

"All of us are trained horse riders and have kept a few of them for our use. It's in our schedule to spend tomorrow morning on the back of our horses. Do you know how to ride a horse?"

"No, I've never sat on the back of a horse," I said with a grin.

"Don't worry; it's easy if you spend a few Sundays with our trainers, they'll make sure that you become an excellent rider.

"We will start our tour from the vegetable garden, which I like the most," Aunty said.

It took two hours to see whatever was in the farmhouse.

Two veterinary doctors, a few horse trainers, and jockeys stayed in the city; the rest of the staff had accommodation near the stable.

We also had a farmhouse spread over 10 acres of land, but it was tiny compared to this one. It had a four-bedroom house, and on five acres, we grow basmati rice, some pulses, and vegetables, and on the remaining land, we've fruit-bearing trees.

Upon our return, we had the delicious Bannur meat biryani lunch, and after that, I was asked to have a cup of coffee in their unit – time to confront the challenge of pushback to Rama's proposal. After a couple of coffee sips, Rama's Mom said, "Let me not beat around the bush and come to the subject, which you must've sensed very well: your refusal to marry my son. I've never seen tears in my son's eyes, at least not in the last couple of decades; however, just a few days ago, I saw his teary eyes, and he said it appears difficult to persuade you to agree to the marriage. Madhu, please tell us the reasons for refusing to marry him, and do you require any assurances that Rama and the rest of us will keep you happy? My husband and I've decided to have you as our daughter-in-law and promise to treat you better than our daughters. And it's not because our son is in love with you, but we found you a level-headed person with principles and virtues to which we subscribe and practice."

Rama's Dad interjected and said, "Before you say anything, allow me to tell you, I've come across very few people in my life who are like your father. He's a gem, a man of his word, honest, down-to-earth, and a philanthropist. The reports I've received about you tell me you're an improved version of your father. Your inner beauty is praiseworthy, which has made us decide to get you in our house as our daughter and not as our son's wife. Rama wanted to give you 50 percent of his shares in the Manju Group, and we've given him the go-ahead. If you still have some reservations, then please tell us."

I don't know what triggered me, but suddenly I started crying violently, holding my face in my palms. Rama's Mom came and sat beside me and took me in her arms; "What happened? Tell us, darling, together, we will find a solution to any issues you have," she said.

After a couple of minutes, my crying stopped, and I cleaned myself with the tissue papers I got from Aunty.

"Please tell us, honey; we could sort out anything bothering you. Even if you don't want to marry Rama, still you'll remain our daughter, so don't feel any pressure from us, and say whatever you need to; hold back nothing," Rama's father said.

"Sorry, I cried. I got emotional with your loving and caring comments. Allow me to brief you on what had transpired between Rama and me. I decided to become a medical doctor and marry a doctor at a young age. When I met with Rama, he impressed me so much that I wanted to be his friend first, and if he's not involved and things moved in a positive direction, I could tie the knot with him. When I expressed my desire to be his friend, he insulted, humiliated, called me a gold digger, and asked me to refrain from having any relationship with him. Still, I ignored his comments, thinking he was irate and I shouldn't take his insults seriously. I changed my appearance from a modern girl wearing jeans, tops, and skirts to an unassuming traditional girl wearing Indian outfits. For over a year, I stood in the college corridors where he would pass to get a gesture of recognition from him. No such thing happened, and when he left college, I decided never to marry and to dedicate my life to serving the weaker section of society. When I've become satisfied with what I'm doing and at peace with my life, he's chasing me to marry him and asking me to forget everything that happened between us. Aunty, it has become ingrained in my brain that he's a dangerous and vindictive person. After marriage, he could turn his back on me for good for any of my silly mistakes, which frightens me to my bones. My heart wants to forgive and move on, but the brain is firmly holding me back, saying people won't change their character, and the idiom I read a long time ago, 'Something I learned about people: If they do it once, they'll do it again,' haunts me. I'm torn between the opposing perspectives of my heart and my mind; I debated for endless hours to bring an end to this stand-off. Finally, I decided not to take a chance, as I survived one tsunami and may not become lucky to survive a second destructive wave. I've nothing against Rama, and to tell you the truth, you rarely come across such a gem of a person. During my previous and current interaction, I noticed he has something that very few men possess; calm as an ocean, a heart that beats for the poor's upliftment, down to earth, and never displays his strengths, whether his wealth, influential contacts, or professional skills. Because of him, I live a content and soul-satisfying life; he showed me the path to walk to find peace and lasting pleasures.

"Aunty, I don't need money; as you would know, I'm a one-third partner in my father's money-making business. Apart from this, I own prime commercial properties; Dad's company pays me a good monthly salary as a board member, and annually a substantial amount I receive toward the share of profits. So, thanks to my family, I've enough to live a comfortable life as long as I breathe. However, if I decide to marry, I would be disrupting my planned road maps to walk, and not only that, but I've to prepare myself to face an abrupt, devastating situation," I said.

"Madhu, please understand; Rama was hardly 20 years old when he met you in undesirable circumstances. Then, he rode on high moral grounds and viewed the world through his colored glasses, which may have influenced him to say and act in such an offensive manner. He's now transformed into a different person; particularly after meeting you, he participates in family conversations; at night, he drives me to his sister's house for coffee and table talk and takes his niece and nephew for a drive and ice cream on the weekends. It was unthinkable just a few months back; I had to squeeze hard to make him come with us to the farmhouse or a party hosted by our friends or business associates, or even in-house celebrations. But now he's forcing us to go out with him almost every weekend, asking everyone to have lunch at the farmhouse. I had quite a few long discussions with him regarding you. He's firmly told me he would marry you or remain single, and I shouldn't force or contact you and exert pressure on you to agree to the marriage. While coming here, we told him we'd talk to you to know your version for the refusal. My sweet baby, what you said is heartbreaking, and in all probabilities, I would've taken the same stand you took. However, clinging to bad memories means destroying your beautiful personality. Life's journey is never easy for anyone; you have a few insults and humiliations, but look at the bright side. You were guided to a path where you found the key to a content and soul-satisfying life. We all suffer at one point or another.

"Let me give you some insight into our journey; the first seven years of marriage were nothing but sleepless nights. My father was a wealthy businessman, and I was the first child of my parents, who had two more progenies, twin sons one year younger than me. I married your uncle immediately after my graduation when he was running a small generic drug manufacturing business. After marriage, Dad decided to inject money into your uncle's business to expand into generic and branded drugs. So a large factory with 80 lakh rupees was constructed to manufacture branded medicines, and 20 lakh rupees were invested into increasing the generic products business. And remember, in those days, one crore rupees was more than the present 100 crore rupees. The factory construction was completed, and machines were under installation and commissioning; when my mom and dad died in a car accident while traveling to Mahboobnagar, our native town. I was very close to Dad, just like a close friend, and after marriage, Mom, who used to hurl abuses at me all the time, became my best friend, a pillar of strength, and a 24/7 helpline. I was shattered, and if not for your uncle's love and care and hardly a-year-old Mohini's dependence on me, I would've gone mad or committed suicide. It took more than a couple of months for me to come out of my grief and take part in day-to-day life.

"We were to receive a check for 50 lakhs from Dad to buy the raw material, delivery vehicles, invest in marketing activities, and a few other necessary items needed to start the production and pay a few months' salaries to the workers. I approached my brothers to get the money, but they refused, saying Dad had already given me more than he should have. Eighty lakhs for the new factory, 20 lakhs for the up-gradation of the old factory, a luxuriously furnished villa in the city's prime area, two cars, and too much expensive jewelry. I wanted to challenge them in a court of law because I had some idea about Dad's wealth. However, your uncle stopped me; instead, he asked his dad for his share of properties and got a measly ten-lakh check as the full and final settlement of his share in the massive family property. His brothers were jealous that he got married to a wealthy girl and felt he shouldn't be given anything more than what he had already taken.

"We met with our bank manager and asked for a loan of 50 lakhs, and we got a 20-lakh loan and a ten-lakh overdraft facility for mortgaging all our properties. Our factory started, and so did our miseries. No distributor was interested in buying in bulk and paying in cash. The medical stores were unwilling to purchase the product unless we provided them with long-term unsecured credit, taking back the expired stock and offering a minimum of 40 percent as their cut on the set retail price. There was no other option but to accept their business terms if we wanted to be in business. All our capital was gone in the market within two years. The only consolation was that our credit amounts were small and thinly spread across hundreds of medical stores, so even if a few failed to pay, it wouldn't significantly impact business.

"The next few years were a terrible nightmare; we were robbing Peter to pay Paul, and this jugglery was causing sleepless nights. I often told your uncle to come out of the branded product business. He disagreed, saying, 'Manju, we're on a tiger ride; the moment we stop production, we may not recover a penny from the entire investment made for the factory building, machines, and the amounts due from the medical stores. Therefore, we must continue till we sink or succeed.'

"Because of our ultra-modern production machinery and top-quality raw material, we were producing highly effective drugs, and day by day, doctors preferred to prescribe our medicines. The business continuously increased, but we couldn't boost production due to a lack of money to pump into the market, and this went on for almost seven years. Finally, during one of our meetings with sales staff, we decided to take the bull by the horns; all new customers should pay in cash and reduce the open credit to the existing customers. For the next six months, business was slow but steady. Then things started moving favorably, mainly because of the doctors' confidence in our drugs over other manufacturers' medicines. Because of this scenario, medical stores began paying cash for their orders, which improved our cash flow, increased production, and helped us venture into new territories.

"When we were in our ninth year of operation, our company name had gained a reputation as a manufacturer of high-quality medications, resulting in steady demand from across the country. To cope with the demand, we constantly upgraded production lines and appointed hundreds of distributors to ensure our products were available throughout the country. Thus far, we've opened three new ultra-modern, fully automated factories across India and are selling our products across the globe. Today, our company has come among the top 10 pharmaceutical companies globally.

"However, if you ask us to relive the first seven years of our business, we'd prefer to take a bullet in our head than go through that hell. No amount of money or any worldly luxuries is worth the pain we've gone through. So don't think you're the only one who has faced a rough patch. Show your empathy, leave everything behind you, let bygones be bygones, and move on," Aunty said.

Uncle took the turn to talk and said, "Allow me to add, Madhu, no one can guarantee the future, but I assure you that we will ensure you're happy in our house as long as we're alive. Remember, if something terrible had to happen, it would happen; don't overthink about the future; it will only bring fear. Enjoy life with a loving partner, and don't allow any concerns to creep in, to frighten you. You're brave, beautiful, and with a heart of gold; I want you to produce babies like you who could carry your flag and make this world a better place for every human being. If you remain single, there won't be a torchbearer who could hold the fort, and all your good work will end once you're gone. Please don't think my words are just sweet talk to trap you into marrying my son. Neither your aunty nor I will ever trap anyone with our sweet talk, as it is against our principles and conscience. We'd be overjoyed if you wed my son, but we won't pressurize you."

Now it was my turn to comment. I said, "Please give me time till the end of the year, as I've promised my mom that during this year I'll marry. I've no obstacle to wed Rama if I overcome the fright creeping in me when I see him. I'll feel proud to be in your house as your daughter and the wife of your son, but please give me time to decide."

"Sure, my darling, but do your best to decide within the next 2–3 months, as day by day we're feeling very lonely in our house. My younger daughter is studying in the US. She didn't come for the new year even though we insisted that she come just for a few days. The elder daughter is a busy bee, office, kids, husband, and to find spare time to call me once a day is an arduous task for her. Your company will be fresh air in my life; my body will rejuvenate if you walk with me holding my hand," Aunty said.

"Yes, honey, I also need you right beside me to assist me in my exercises and diet and to protect me from your aunty, who badgers me on every slip and reminds me that I'm getting on in years, and it's high time I must hang up my boots," said Uncle, and we all laughed aloud.

Uncle continued, "Jokes aside, your presence in the house will give us the utmost pleasure and strength to our bodies to ward off the aging issues."

"I'll do my best to decide at the earliest. However, I'm a weak person and long ago realized that it takes time to overcome my fears and phobias, so please be supportive and understanding," I said.

"Honey, no one knows what the future will bring upon them. You know the law of Murphy, 'Anything that can go wrong will go wrong.' We've no control over our destiny; however, we must still attempt to protect ourselves from unforeseen casualties by setting up protective layers to minimize the impact of unpleasant happenings. We move around in an armored vehicle with an armed driver to silence any attacker, even though we don't have enemies. But you never know; an unhappy employee or a jealous competitor may like to inflict physical harm. We could attempt to control similar human-inflicted damages; other than that, there's nothing in our hands except facing all the undesirable scenarios with courage and dignity. I strongly advise you to marry Rama; he's a gem per your assessment, and for us, he's our fountain of pleasure," Aunty said.

"I understand what you're saying and will do my best to convey my decision as soon as possible," I said.

"Okay, let's stop this discussion. Tell me, are you a good swimmer?" Dad asked.

"I don't know whether I'm a good swimmer or bad, but I got trained by a girl who participated in the Asian Games," I said.

"Great, in the evening you come in your swimsuit and compete with me. The only person in our family who's a better swimmer than me is my son," Uncle said.

Aunty laughed aloud and said, "Your uncle has become senile; he's merely a moderately competent swimmer, but there's no way he could compete with a young girl trained by a pro."

"No, I'm sure he'll beat me. My swimming is okay, but I'm much better at three-meter springboard diving," I said.

"That's wonderful; our swimming pool has both; a 3M springboard and platform. I'm sure you would delight us with your skillful dives," Uncle said.

"Uncle, I've almost forgotten my diving skill; only once a week, I take a dip in the pool for a few lazy laps," I said.

"Your modesty tells me you're an excellent swimmer and diver. Let's check it out in the evening," Uncle said with a grin.

When we went to the swimming pool in the evening at seven, a popular Bollywood number was ear-splitting, and the smell of BBQ items was overpowering the other senses. The entire family, including Rama and his mom and dad, were swimming and playing with a ball. We were in our formals; everyone shouted at us to come in our swimsuits. We had to go back to our rooms; I wore my swimsuit, Dad had swimming shorts, and Mom refused to get into the water.

For three years, from the age of 12, I was under the training of my Asiad teacher. I used to click 100 meters freestyle in less than two minutes, and since I was passionate about learning diving, she taught me and ensured that I excelled in forward, backward, and reverse dives.

After 10 minutes of warmup exercise, I entered the pool and slowly swam from one corner to the other. I believe it was 25 meter long and 10 meters wide pool. While I was swimming at a slow pace, Rama's Dad came out of the pool, switched off the music, and asked for everyone's attention. When all were silent, he said, "Ladies and gentlemen; Madhu and I'll have a competition of four laps, and if she wins, she'll get a diamond neckless, and if I win, I'll get a bear hug. The competition will begin on the count of three, and my wife and daughter will record our timings. However, first, Rama will swim as fast as possible to set a record, and both of us will do our best to break it."

Rama was an excellent swimmer recording two minutes and 48 seconds for the four lapses. I thought it would be difficult to beat his time, as now I'm rusty; only on Sunday mornings, instead of jogging, I was spending time in the pool, and that too without pushing any boundaries.

About Rama's Dad, I was sure it would be difficult for him to complete the laps in less than three minutes.

I noticed Uncle was a good swimmer but no match. He was seven or eight meters behind in the first lap, and when I completed my fourth lap, he completed his third lap.

Rama's Mom came to me and said, "Darling, congratulations, you've won the diamond necklace. You've even beaten Rama's timings by completing the four lapses in 2:32. Look at my hubby, still another 10 meters away, which means more than four minutes."

"Aunty, considering Uncle's age, four minutes is a wonder; you should feel proud," I said.

"I am. God has blessed me with a loving, caring, and wonderful husband. Every day in my morning pooja, I pray for his health and wellbeing. However, teasing him gives me immense pleasure, particularly reminding him of his age, as he thinks and acts like a teenager," Aunty said, and we laughed.

When Uncle completed the last lap, everyone clapped. I was still in the pool, and he came to me and said, "You're an excellent swimmer, darling, and I'm sure faster than my son. Moreover, I'm positive you would captivate us with your diving skill. So, the pool is yours whenever you're ready, and remember only the first eight meters; the depth of the pool is 10 meters."

Again, everyone jumped into the pool, and the shouting and playing started. Rama came close to us and stood on my left side as Uncle stood on my right. Mom left, saying, "Both of you've been beaten hollow by my darling baby." Uncle also went, slowly swimming toward the other side of the pool.

"I was delighted to see you swim like a pro. Had you entered the pool with a couple of months of practice, you could get close to beating the Olympic record. I'm sure now we will witness some breathtaking, spectacular dives," Rama said with a smile.

"Your appreciation won't influence me to surrender to your wishes, so stop your unnecessary commendation," I said.

"My dear Madhu Priya, my respect for you is increasing with every passing day, and it's now certain that soon we will tie the knot. This afternoon while we were having our lunch, my entire family and your folks have collectively concluded that we're made for each other and must wed ASAP," Rama said with a big grin.

"Continue dreaming, Sir, but no such thing will occur, and your fantasies are destined to hurt you," I said and slowly reeled toward the other end. While I was making easy strokes toward the other end, everyone shouted, "Dive, Dive." So, I went to the diving board and stood at the edge for a few minutes, slowly bouncing to check the board's spring strength. Then, after asserting how much pressure to exert to get the needed height, I made a forward dive and entered the water like an iron rod, with a minimum water splash. Then, I went for a single somersault and a few more back and reversed dives. I could've gone for the twisted and double somersault dives, but I required at least a few days of practice to put on a flawless performance. All the time, while I was performing the dives, everyone was clapping, cheering, and shrieking. When I finished, Aunty came and, with a pat on my back, said, "My love, you're a wonder; no one I know can swim and dive like you." As usual, I murmured, "Thank you, Aunty."

I had enough of swimming and decided to change and come. When I returned, everyone was out of the pool, and while I was looking for a table to sit at, Uncle called and, with a hand gesture, asked me to join him. He was alone at the table, with no food except a glass of water.

"Our food will come when your aunty joins us; she's gone for a shower and change. Do you need a drink?" Uncle asked.

"Yes, I'll have a glass of fruit juice," I said.

Uncle called a waiter and asked him to bring a jug of mulberry juice. While I was sipping the tasty juice of freshly plucked mulberries, Aunty came with a gift box in her hand.

Uncle took the box from Aunty, gave it to me, and said, "Your gift, open it."

It was a heavy metal box, indicating it must be a costly gift.

I said, "No, I'll not accept it. The competition wasn't among equals. I thought of losing but decided against it as I wanted to beat Rama's timings. I didn't win to get this expensive gift."

Both Uncle and Aunty laughed aloud, and Aunty said, "Even if you had lost the competition, you would still have received this as your New Year's gift. But we're happy that you've earned it."

"Aunty, this is not fair; once I come to your house, you give me whatever you want, and I promise to accept all your gifts without any reservation, but now I cannot take it," I said.

"Give me a few minutes to continue our debate," Uncle said and asked one of the waiters to bring a couple of tables and chairs and club with our table and tell everyone to join us.

When my parents came, I asked Mom to sit beside me, Rama followed me and sat beside her mother, and Dad sat beside Uncle. The servers brought several assorted veg and non-veg BBQ items and fresh fruit juices.

Uncle addressed Dad and said, "Your daughter knew she would get a diamond necklace if she won the competition, but she's refusing to accept her winning prize."

"Dad, the moment I noticed Uncle's speed, I wanted to lose but decided against it, as Rama's timings became a challenge to beat. Moreover, I'm confident that the gift is an expensive piece of jewelry, not even in lakhs, so it doesn't make sense to accept such a pricey item for winning an unfair competition," I said.

"Madhu, my love, a deal is a deal, a commitment is a commitment, and you knew your strength and my weakness before the start of the competition. You've won, and you must accept your prize graciously. I never said you would get an expensive or inexpensive necklace, so your refusal on that ground or any other perceived excuse is unacceptable," Uncle said, smiling. Everyone, including Mom and Dad, clapped and said, "Please open your gift; we want to see it."

"Mom, I wanted you to help me; instead, you're supporting Uncle; I beg you to tell Uncle not to press me for accepting it," I said.

"Madhu, your uncle, is right; you competed and won, so accept it and thank him," Mom said.

"Mom, I'm sure it's pricey jewelry, which I don't deserve for winning an inequitable competition. Mom, please convince Uncle and Aunty to give me perfume or sunglasses or something to complete the formality of recognizing my win," I said.

"You convince your uncle; I'll not come to your rescue. Before entering the pool, you should have said that you won't accept any prize even if you win. You've won, for whatever reasons, period," Mom said.

"Open it, and say thank you to your uncle," Aunty said, and everyone started chorusing, "Open it, open it."

"Uncle, I'll open it, and if I find it too expensive, I'll not accept it. Is it a deal?" I asked.

"No, darling, it is not a deal. You accept your prize and make everyone happy. But, more importantly, allow me to enlighten you: the difference between expensive and inexpensive depends on how it impacts someone's pocket; I assure you that this piece of jewelry didn't burn my pockets," Uncle said with a grin.

"Uncle, can you not settle for a big thank you with a bear hug? And, I'll honor the promise I made earlier," I said pleadingly.

"No, my dear, the gift was bought for you, and you've no choice but to take it; of course, I'll accept your thank you and bear hug," Uncle said, laughing.

Mom said, "Come on, open it, and I assure you, you won't find a price tag, so assume it's inexpensive."

Everyone laughed and chanted, "Open it, open it."

Slowly, I tore the wrapper, and the moment I saw the box, I knew it must be a costly gift. It was a gold-plated metal box with a digital fingerprint lock. I looked at Aunty, and she said, "Press the upper portion of the lock, and it will open it, and when you want to register your fingerprints, follow the instruction given in the booklet."

I opened the box, and when I saw the necklace, my heart stopped beating from the blinding beauty of the diamond string and finger ring. It was a string of more than 50 pieces of 1-carat round brilliant-cut diamonds with a heart-shaped pendant encrusted with small diamonds and a larger-than-two-carats fancy intense green-blue cushion-cut diamond in the center. The finger ring at the bottom of the box was a blue diamond of the same size, encrusted with colorless half-carat diamonds. The jewelry set must be well above ten crores, as the two blue diamonds alone were surely above six crores, and as for the rest of the stones and the platinum, their cost couldn't be less than five crores. I gave Mom the box to look at and told her slowly in her ears, "Mom, please refuse the gift; it's very costly, must be plus ten crores."

Mom passed the box to Dad and said, "I believe my daughter is right; it is a highly pricey gift, and the occasion doesn't call for such generosity."

Dad also concurred and said, "I can guess an approximate cost of this necklace and ring, and support my wife that this is not the occasion to give my daughter such an expensive gift."

Uncle said, "You're right; this is not the winning prize; it's from the entire family to say sorry to Madhu for the pain inflicted by my son. Rama informed us that he profoundly regrets the imprudent behavior, which was absurd, and blames it on his infantile philosophy. Apart from all this, we've decided that Madhu is our third daughter, regardless of whether she becomes Rama's wife or not, and this we've informed Madhu. With our new bond, we've every right to give whatever we want, so please don't deprive us of our pleasure."

I looked at Mom; she whispered and said, "Please accept, say thank you, and touch the feet of Uncle and Aunty."

Rama was grinning, telling me, "I got you, babe." I knew it must have been his idea to give this ten crore-plus gift. Who on earth gives such an expensive gift unless they have ulterior motives? Don't worry, Rama boy; I'll find a way to return your pricey jewelry.

After the hugging, cheek-kissing, and feet touching, we had our BBQ dinner, and at around 8:30, Rama's sister and her children started dancing; the music volume increased to a deafening decibel. Then, suddenly, Dad rose from his chair and said, "I'm feeling a little lethargic, and prefer to take a rest, so please excuse me."

"I'll come with you," Rama said.

I got uneasy with Rama's offer; he must've noticed something that could have prompted him to accompany him. "I'll also come," I said and rose from the chair.

Rama said, "Fine, you go with Uncle, and I'll be with you in a while."

Mom also followed us. After reaching the room, Dad said, "Madhu, I'm fine, and your mom is with me, so you go and enjoy the evening."

"Please change and lie down, and once Rama is here, I'll go," I said.

Before Dad could come from the dresser room, Rama entered the flat with a medical toolkit and took out a stethoscope, infrared thermometer, oximeter, digital blood pressure monitor, and glucometer and placed them neatly on a side table.

"Why do you need to check, Dad?" I asked Rama.

"Not for any particular reason, just wanted to make sure his vitals are fine," Rama said.

When Dad arrived in his nightdress, Rama asked him to sit on his bed and told me to check the temperature, oxygen saturation, and sugar. Rama checked the heartbeat, BP and then looked at the somewhat swollen feet. I knew Dad had BP and diabetes for several years, but I had ensured that it was within the acceptable range. However, now the sugar was high, and I was sure his BP must also be spiked because of the new year celebration. Rama gestured me to follow him, and I left the room, telling Mom and Dad I would be back in a couple of minutes.

When we sat facing each other in the hall, he said, "The BP is high, and I saw that the glucometer reading is also high, but my concern is the heart murmur, which is asking me to run a thorough check; for that, I must take him to the hospital right away. You stay here with everyone, and I'll be back at the earliest," Rama said.

"I'll come with you; I must be with Dad; otherwise, he would be panicky and worried," I said.

"Fine, go and tell Uncle to get ready and I'll inform Mom and Dad," Rama said.

We were on our way to the hospital within a few minutes. I assured Dad that we were going to the hospital for a thorough examination and that he should not be concerned, but he looked uneasy and grim.

Upon reaching the hospital, Rama took Dad with him and asked an attendant to take us to his dad's office; he didn't allow me to come with him, even though I told him I wanted to be with Dad, but he said, "You need to be with Aunty, she's worried and sweating."

Uncle's office was large, lavishly furnished, and I could see a door beside his desk, probably to an anteroom that must've got a bed, dining area, and comfort room. Mom was under shock and must have been finding it difficult to digest the situation. I told Mom to relax, and that Dad was here only for a checkup, but it didn't console her. She wasn't stupid; she had a postgraduate degree in Maths and was a lecturer in a private college, and she stopped working when Dad started making loads of money.

There were several magazines on the table, but still, we sat without talking or reading. Mom looked tense and worried, even though I told her several times that there was nothing to worry about and that Dad was here only for a checkup. We were lost in our thoughts when a young boy entered the room, pushing a trolley with assorted soft drinks, snacks, and coffee and tea thermos. While going, he said, "If you need anything, please call reception and ask them to connect you to the canteen and place your order."

After almost two hours, Rama entered the room with a stern and tired look. He took the coffee from the trolley and sat opposite us.

"First, the good news, we did the angiography and didn't find any blockage. However, we found some issues with the heart; tomorrow morning, along with a couple of senior cardiologists, we will conduct a few more tests to identify the exact issue. We need to keep Uncle here, and I'll be with him to monitor his heart function. We've given him a mild sedative so he can sleep. Madhu, you go with Aunty to the flat, or if you want, I could arrange a room here, but I prefer you go to the flat and come in the morning," Rama said.

"Can we meet Dad?" I asked.

"Sure, allow me to finish the coffee," Rama said.

Dad was sleeping with several machines connected to his body in a spacious room. I checked the pulse, which was normal, and with Rama's cardiology stethoscope, I checked the heartbeat and noticed an abnormal sound, the heart murmur. It was a clear indication of mitral valve malfunction. It is a significant issue, as the valve must be repaired with surgery, or the patient should adopt healthy lifestyle changes, depending on the level of damage.

"Mom, you sit here, and I'll go out with Rama, as I needed to discuss with him Dad's condition and line of treatment," I said and gestured for Rama to come with me.

I said to Rama in the corridor, "Sir, I noticed the heart murmur, indicating the mitral valve issue. Please tell me what tests you're planning to do tomorrow. And thus far, with your ECG, echo, and the other tests you have carried out, what is your assessment?"

"My initial assessment, which could be very wrong, tells me that damage to the valve is not severe. It could be treated with regular follow-up, healthy lifestyle changes, and medication. Tomorrow, I plan to do a cardiac MRI, a 3D echocardiogram, and, if needed, cardiac catheterization. Once we establish the extent of the damage, we could decide to treat him with medication or surgery. Tomorrow I'll also talk to a couple of cardiologist friends working at Mayo Clinic in Florida to take their feedback. If the surgery is a better option, we'll take him to Mayo Clinic for a robot-assisted minimally invasive mitral valve repair. If you want to take a second opinion from some other cardiologist, please feel free to do that. He's your father, and you have every right to take a second opinion. Please tell me how I should proceed, and if you want to discuss it with your mom, please go and talk to her," Rama said.

"Sir, if my comments were offensive, then my apologies. I wasn't questioning your competence or doubting your assessment. Please do whatever is needed and make my dad healthy and fighting fit. One more thing, ask your staff to compile the treatment charges and send them to our insurance company; all of us have comprehensive worldwide medical cover," I said.

"I'm relieved to know your family has insurance cover, or else it could've dented my coffers," Rama said smiling.

"Sir, take this seriously and do as I'm telling you," I retorted.

"No issues. Would you like to discuss the situation with Aunty?" Rama asked.

"No need; I'll brief her at the flat. You're sure you want to stay with Dad; I could give you company if you wish to, or I could stay here, and you go to the flat with Mom and sleep there," I said.

"We will ask Aunty to stay here, and we two will go to the flat and sleep on the king-size bed," Rama said, smiling.

"Shut up. I'm serious; answer me," I said.

"Honey, I don't intend to be awake the whole night, just for an hour; I'll watch the monitors and then sleep on the guest bed," Rama said.

"Fine, can I have a couple of sleeping pills; Mom looks very tensed, and I don't think she would be able to sleep without a pill," I said.

"Okay, take Aunty and wait at the main entrance, and I'll be with you in a few minutes," Rama said.

When we reached the entrance gate, Rama was waiting for us. He handed me a small envelope and said, "My car is coming; I'll drop you at the flat."

"We will walk; it's hardly a few minutes' walk," I said.

"No, I'll drop you; you could come by walk or call me to send the driver to pick you up in the morning," Rama said.

The following day, when we reached the hospital, Dad wasn't in the room, and upon inquiring, we were informed that they'd taken him for MRI.

After around 45 minutes, Dad came in a wheelchair, looking pale as if someone had sucked blood from his body. I helped him lie on the bed and said, "Dad, you're fine; last night, I had a long discussion with Rama, and his initial diagnosis was very encouraging. First, there are no blocked arteries or any other issues of grave concern. Second, a slight malfunction of the heart valve is causing fatigue and swelling of the ankles, which needs to be fixed with proper diet and exercise."

"You're making me happy, right?" Dad asked.

"No, Dad, I'm not making you or Mom happy; it's a fact that you'll know from Rama in a while. I'm expecting him to be here soon, with all your reports," I said.

Dad took my hand in his hand and said, "Madhu, I think I wouldn't be able to handle the business for long, and I don't want to involve you either. So please ask Vimi to come back for good in the next couple of weeks and take over the reins."

"Dad, don't say such things, you're super-fine, and in a few days, you'll be in the office with the same zeal and dynamism. Yes, I'll call Vimi, but after we talk to Rama, which will allow me to give him a complete picture," I said.

Rama came within 15 minutes with several envelopes in his hand, which he handed me for review. He then addressed Dad and said, "Uncle, everything is fine with you, except sugar and cholesterol, which are a little high; one of the heart valves is slightly weak, but nothing is problematic. Could you tell me your daily routine – what time you sleep, how many hours you sleep, what time you go to the office and come back, how many days you work in a week, how much workload you handle, and whether you do any exercise? This information will assist me in understanding the reasons for the weakness of the valve and establish a line of treatment."

Dad gave Rama a long look before saying, "I wake up around 8:00 in the morning and leave for the factory around 9:00. I try to come home between 6:00 and 7:00 in the evening, but generally, it's only after 7:00 because of the workload. Lunchtime is not set; whenever I get the time, I take a break of 30 minutes. At 8:00, I take my dinner, and around 9:30, my wife and I take a thirty-minute stroll in our front yard and then spend two to three hours in front of the TV. I go to bed between 1:00 and 2:00 am, and before catching sleep, I read a business or financial magazine. Generally, I sleep around five to six hours. After lunch, occasionally, I take a 15- to thirty-minute power nap. I work six days a week, and on Sundays, I sleep late, wake up late and spend the day with Madhu and my wife. I used to smoke a cigar and take a couple of whiskey pegs every day after coming from the office, but more than five years ago, Madhu forced me to stop this ritual. So, unfortunately, now you won't find any bottles or cigars in our house; she's a bad girl, you know," Uncle said smiling.

"Sorry, Sir, but I must say you're a very polite person, and I'm not going to give my opinion about her as the slight chance I'm hoping against hope will also disappear," Rama said, and everyone laughed aloud.

"Thanks for the detailed input; I'll ask the dietician to give you a diet plan, and regarding exercise, Madhu will inform you. Every week you must come for a checkup. I'll give you some medicine to take when you find breathing difficulty, chest pain, or any kind of discomfort, and call me. You're not going to the factory starting today unless I give you the clearance. You'll be discharged in a couple of hours. Please ask Madhu or me if you've any questions," Rama said.

After Dad's breakfast, we went to Rama's clinic to have a bite with him at the canteen.

After breakfast, while having our tea, Rama said, "Aunty, Uncle's heart issue is mild, which generally happens due to high blood pressure. I've discussed the condition with my senior colleagues in this hospital and my cardiologist friends working at the Mayo Clinic in Florida. They've unanimously recommended avoiding surgery, as it's manageable with a strict heart-healthy diet, exercise, and maintaining recommended blood pressure and cholesterol levels. We need to reduce the work hours to five or six per day, as the more time he spends in the office, the more stress he would carry. My dad, too, has BP and diabetes, and my mom makes sure that he works five days a week and spends only six hours a day and occasionally eight hours. They both swim together, walk together, and sometimes play tennis with some family friends. It would be best if you do the same; make sure he never works more than six hours a day for five days a week, eats heart-healthy food, and regularly goes for a walk or swim. No rigorous exercises or running, only walking. And suggest you take Uncle for a second opinion, as that would give you the confidence that Uncle is fine," Rama said.

"My husband is getting treatment from his son, and I don't have to do anything except pray for his quick recovery. So please, next time, don't mention such things and hurt me," Mom said, and for the first time, I saw tears in her eyes; otherwise, I believe she probably got numb and flustered with the shock.

"Aunty, I'm sorry if I hurt you, but I thought I must put forward the second opinion suggestion being the treating medico," Rama said.

Rama dropped us off at our house late in the afternoon and told us he'd come with dinner around 8:00. Mom and I said we had people to cook, and there was no need to bring food, but he refused and said don't cook and left.

Dad was in shock and was hardly speaking, and I told Mom to be beside him and entertain him by watching any drama serial or movie.

After freshening up, I checked the time in Philadelphia; it was 5:30 in the morning, a good time to call Vimi, as he leaves for the office at 7:00.

Vimi answered the call in a sleepy voice; I briefed him about Dad's health issue and asked him to come immediately and for good. He said, "I'll come within a few days and discuss where I stand and what I intend to do."

"Vimi, do your best to say goodbye to the US and come. Our business is increasing year over year, and our last fiscal year turnover has exceeded 200 crores. Dad's health issue results from sedentary life, high BP, diabetes, and stressful sixty-hour-plus weekly work; if he continues to do that, then be prepared to face a disaster. Rama Saab has advised that he cannot work more than five to six hours a day and that too only four to five days a week. The limitation of work hours means the business would suffer, as he didn't groom anyone to share his responsibilities. And you know very well that I cannot help him, as I don't understand even business basics and still if I attempt to be helpful, I'm sure I would make a mess. Vimi, we need you here right away, so please don't disappoint us. Tell me if you've got a girlfriend holding you; otherwise, no excuses for not coming for good," I said.

"Akka, I'm not dating anyone, and I promise to find a solution to this situation when I come," Vim said.

"Sure, but I want you to be here within the next three to four days maximum," I said, and after further pounding to pack his bags for good and fly, I disconnected the line.

x-x-x-x-x-x

Chapter Four

Vimi

I'm Vadiraj Rao, son of Venkateshwara Rao, a wealthy industrialist. My mom, Mrunalini Rao, is an educated woman with a low boiling point, always shouting at my elder sister or me for something or the other. Dad is right opposite Mom, with a mild temperament and a man of few words.

From a very young age, I developed a passion for reading, and everyone used to wonder what was wrong with this lad and why I didn't play any games or mingle with other children. By nature, I could call myself an introvert, a bookworm, mostly buried either in reading the course books or fiction or non-fiction books on every topic under the sun. However, my elder sister Madhu was quite the opposite of me, extrovert, outgoing, always full of energy, and highly intelligent. I never saw her glued to books like me, but she was always a class topper.

Everything that got through my eyes used to print in my head with no endeavor whatsoever, and when needed, I could effortlessly recollect what I had read. Maths was my favorite subject, and I seldom got less than 100 percent marks on my exam papers. In other subjects, also I never secured less than 95 percent marks, even though I hardly used to put effort into ensuring a very high ranking.

I had a few classmates that I could put under my friends' category. After school, I occasionally conversed with them on the phone but never invited them to my house, went to their house, met outside for a movie, or accepted their invitation to attend their house events. I wasn't a popular guy among female classmates because of my reputation as a boring bookworm, and one could talk to me only about subject books or some other dull topic. Like other boys, I also wanted to have a girlfriend from tenth grade. However, I knew sparing the time for her meant ignoring my pleasure of reading books, so I decided to defer till I got bored with the books.

Dad was pouring into my ears from a tender age that if I had to take reins of his business empire, I must be an extrovert, visionary, motivational, a tough administrator, and so on. But, since he failed to see in me the desired traits, after completing my school, he admitted me into Pennsylvania State University in Philadelphia to get a degree in business administration and learn from my Yankee colleagues how to be outgoing, confident, and communicative.

From an early age, Akka was my sole companion; she helped me deal with everything that was stressing me out, or when I wanted to upgrade my recently bought electronics, etcetera. I wouldn't have survived in the US without Akka's daily doses of how I could combat the nostalgic bouts, the loneliness, the rumors flying behind my back about me being a jerk, gay, or something more humiliating. She used to strengthen me by asking me to continue on the journey of achieving everything

I aspired to achieve and not ever get distracted by the barking dogs.

After graduation and an MBA in Business Administration, I decided to enroll to obtain a Doctorate in Marketing Strategy and Consumer Behavior, as I wanted to expand Dad's business in consumer goods. While debating how to break the news of my further studies to my folks, a multinational company dealing in consumer goods approached me with a job offer. I declined, stating I wanted first to obtain the doctorate and then think of a job or go back to India.

The same company approached me again with a different offer; they wanted to pay me a monthly stipend until I completed the doctorate, provided I worked for them for a minimum of four years after getting the accreditation. I told them I needed a couple of weeks before responding to their offer.

A few days after my meeting with the representatives of the multinational, my Ph.D. supervisor asked me to meet him in the evening. At 5:00, I was in his chamber, and after the exchange of pleasantries, he said, "I believe Phillip-Merkel executives had met you. They visited me yesterday to discuss the job offered to you earlier in the week. Before meeting me, they also met with the Dean, who referred them to me. The Dean also called me and expressed his delight that one of our students is getting an unprecedented opportunity. He wanted me to make sure that you avail of it and make the University proud with your unrivaled success.

"I've informed the executives that the $50K annual stipend for four years is okay, but the $300K salary and

$200K in the variable are unacceptable; you don't pay such a lousy salary to a topper student of this institution. And, if they want me to convince you, they must at least double the offer, a $600K salary and $400K as a guaranteed minimum performance bonus. They've promised to get back to me in a few days. Vadi, if they show up with a revised offer close to what I had asked, I strongly suggest you accept, not for money alone. The valuable experience you would gain would greatly assist you in expanding your father's business."

"Thanks for asking the executives to up the offer; however, it would be an uphill battle to convince my parents to do the doctorate; leave aside work for four more years," I said smiling.

"I would be hugely disappointed if you don't do your doctorate, as this is a lifetime opportunity, and if you miss it, you'll regret it for the rest of your life," my mentor said.

"This is what I believe, and I'll do my best to convince my folks to allow me to get my doctorate, but I'm not sure I would be able to sell them the idea of working here for four years," I said.

"All the best, and I'll get back to you once I hear from Phillip reps," the mentor said.

I thanked him and left his chamber.

As the mentor said, I must convince Mom and Dad to permit me to do the Ph.D., or else going back without the doctorate would become a lifetime regret.

My mentor called me after four days, asking me to see him in the afternoon at 5:00, and when I met him, he gave me Phillip's contract to read. The highlights were a stipend of $50K per annum for a maximum of four years. Upon joining with a doctorate in hand, salary will be $600K per annum, a minimum of $400K guaranteed performance bonus, three weeks paid holiday, country club membership, a soft loan for a car and house purchase, worldwide medical insurance, and a few other benefits.

I asked for a couple of weeks to get back to him, and after getting his okay, I left with a mixed feeling of pride and trepidation. It would be wonderful to have a doctorate, and if I worked for four years with Phillip, it would be the cherry on the cake. The contentious question is how to bell the cat. I cannot talk to Dad; he'll be furious and may not say anything immediately, but through Mom, he'll send the message that I should come back immediately, no Ph.D. and no job – period! My trump card was Akka, but I shouldn't use her immediately; I decided to test the water through Mom.

I called Mom and briefed her on my plan of securing a doctorate and working for the multinational for four years. Mom went through the roof and said, "Vimi, this is not acceptable; we just wanted you to do your graduation in the US to enjoy hostel life and learn a few things lacking in your beautiful personality. However, instead of coming back after your degree, you pressured us to do an MBA, which was unnecessary; in our business, you don't have to possess such qualifications. But now you want to do a doctorate for four years and work for another four years, which means you're talking about an eight- or nine-year stay in the US. I don't accept this, and I'll not speak to your dad about it, as there's no point in upsetting him, and you know he's counting the days when you would come and offload some of his work. The factory is doing very well, and we just need your assistance to share some of the responsibilities of your dad."

"Mom, the company is paying me 50,000 dollars yearly till I complete the doctorate, and once I'm on board, they'll pay me more than a million dollars in salary and perks. Mom, our company earns seven to eight crores annually, which would equal my one-year salary. Even if I add our salaries as board members, we'd only talk about a maximum of 12 crores rupees. All my money is yours, Mom; I just need 20,000 dollars a year for my expenses. My interest in working for this prestigious company is the valuable experience I would gain, which will significantly assist me in expanding our business. You may not know Mom, but businesses tend to shrink if you don't constantly diversify and increase revenues, and to say we're doing well is only an illusion. Tomorrow, new technology or a better product will come, forcing us to close the business. Mom, Dad is very young, and he'll still be young and kicking when I return to take the company's reins. Mom, I don't want to upset you or Dad, but please, I beg you to allow me to avail myself of this opportunity. You know, Mom, the Dean of our University, and my Ph.D. mentor are all happy and encouraging me to take up the job, which is unprecedented in the history of the University," I said pleadingly.

Mom's stand got a little soft as she said, "Look, Vimi, I'm not happy, but I'll have a word with your dad when he's in a good mood and see how it goes."

"Mom, I love you; please do your best to convince Dad; if I don't avail this opportunity, I'll regret my stupidity for the rest of my life," I said.

"Enough of your pleading; I'll do what I can and let you know the outcome," Mom said and, as usual before disconnection, instructed me to eat well and sleep well.

After a couple of days, Mom called and said, "Sorry, my boy, your dad refused to accept any of your logic and asked me to tell you to come back immediately and assist him in running the business."

I expected to hear this from Mom and decided to use my trump card – Akka, my loving elder sister.

The next day, I called Akka and, after exchanging the usual pleasantries, explained the whole scenario and asked for her assistance in convincing Mom and Dad.

Akka said, "Vimi, I don't think I would be of much help; they're counting the days of your return, and now you're talking about another eight or nine years. So I don't think they would agree to your request, and I also believe you should come back."

I said, "Akka, touchwood, Dad is in good health, and there's no rush for me to join the business immediately. If I spend another seven or eight years, I'll come with valuable experience and a doctorate. My degrees and experience would for sure assist me in getting partners to invest, diversify, and expand the business to a level where we could go public and take the business to unimaginable heights. Please, Akka, help me to achieve my dreams. I would earn a million dollars per annum from the day I joined. I'll mail you my contract, and then you tell me whether to ignore it or grab it."

Akka said, "Vimi, I'll do my best, but you must be aware that sometimes it's challenging to convince Dad. So wish me good luck and pray, and I'll update you in a few days on the outcome of my discussion with the KING." We both laughed aloud, as whenever we needed something significant from Dad, we used to call him KING.

After a couple of days, Akka called and said, "I had to drain my energies to convince Dad and Mom to allow you to do your doctorate and work. Of course, Dad wasn't happy, but he got very pleased when he saw your employment contract and only then gave his consent."

I was over the moon with the fantastic news and said, "Akka, I wouldn't be able to pay you with anything except by being your slave for life and anything I own is yours."

"Stop the buttering, and make sure to visit us every six months, at least for a few days, or else I'll come there and put you in a plane to land here for good," Akka said, and we laughed aloud.

I'm now about to complete my first year of employment. During this short period, I impacted top executives as an excellent addition to the management pool. My first assignment was to study the production and distribution channel, recommend the areas that needed improvement, and determine whether there was room for cost-cutting.

I identified that the supply-chain division needed complete overhauling. Every warehouse was stocking goods based on anticipated sales projected by the area sales in-charge, resulting in overstocking or shortages. In addition, the production wasn't reflecting the changing market trends and demands, causing surplus stocks or shortages. I prepared a four-hundred-page case-study dossier; in essence, I recommended centralizing both operations under the supervision of senior executives.

My PowerPoint presentation and the case-study file were moved from my manager's desk to the CEO and the board members. A couple of weeks later, I was asked to attend a management meeting to corroborate the recommendations, as the suggestions looked unimplementable.

All the board members, the top management, and senior executives heading various departments attended the meeting. For six hours, I got grilled on every recommendation I made, and I'm sure they must've been pleased with the comments and the data I showed them from the company records.

Again, two weeks later, I was asked to attend another management meeting. I didn't find any board members, the CEO, and a few top-ranking executives in attendance this time. After the formality of the meet and greet, they asked me whether I could establish my recommended centralized operations by writing procedures on how it should function and then picking up the needed staff from the existing workforce to run the division.

I accepted the challenge. It took me almost eight weeks to document the functions of the division, procedures, and responsibilities of the executives in-charge. Then, I emailed the document to all the meeting attendees per their request. After a few days, an email came directly from the CEO asking me to pick the right staff from the existing workforce spread in 173 countries and make the divisions operational at the earliest.

Within the next few months, both divisions started functioning, and everyone noticed substantial improvement in the stock transfers and fewer complaints of non-availability of needed goods. And this resulted in improved sales, profitability, and a reduction in the headcount.

The next assignment was to look into any other operational area that needed improvement. Naturally, I thought of scanning the factories' functioning as it must've been cluttered with issues that no one would want to resolve as long as the business was profitable. However, while pondering which vertical to scan, I came across a memo of the warehousing head seeking permission to lease 15 more warehouses in various countries, with authorization to increase headcount by at least three hundred. I immediately decided to look into this segment. I asked the finance head to send me the last three years' expenses incurred for maintaining warehouses worldwide, with a cost breakdown of the lease of warehouses, human resources, shipping goods from factories to the warehouse, and delivery of goods to distributors. I then called two global logistics companies to visit me, mentioning we're looking into the possibilities of outsourcing the end-to-end operation of goods movement and stocking.

Within a month, I prepared a report on what's costing us to handle the goods movement and how much it would cost to outsource. Straightforward, 100-million-plus savings if the operation is outsourced; however, the logistic companies were unwilling to provide an irrevocable bank guarantee of half a billion dollars, which is the value of goods they'll have at any given time in their warehouses. I submitted the soft copy of the report to the CEO and asked him to call me to discuss my proposal.

CEO liked my suggestion and asked me to set up a meeting with the CEOs of both logistics companies. In two weeks, one company agreed to a 300 million bank guarantee and an insurance policy of half a billion dollars against fire and theft, provided we signed a contract for five years, renewable for a further period of five years. Board approved the proposal, and an agreement was drafted by the legal department and signed.

I was getting close to completing my first year of employment when the CEO's secretary called me to find out whether I would be free to meet with the CEO at 5:00 in the evening, and I agreed to come. Around 4:00, the CEO's secretary called me again and said she was emailing a revised employment contract, which I must review before meeting the CEO.

The revised employment contract offered a new position as 'Director Business Growth' with an increase in salary from $600K to $800K and an annual performance bonus of one million dollars in company shares at face value.

I had a long discussion with the CEO before accepting the new position. We settled for a $1,200K PA base salary and a two-million-dollar minimum PA performance bonus paid in company shares.

An exceptionally joyful day for me, not because I got a salary raise, but because my promotion to a senior position in such a short period was unprecedented in the over hundred-year history of the company. This was informed by HR when I was signing the new agreement. To celebrate my achievement with my family, I decided to go to Hyderabad in the coming few days.

I had some unfinished work, which could take around ten days, so I applied for leave considering my engagement. However, when I was to leave in two days, I received a call from Akka, who gave me the bad news of Dad's ill health.

x-x-x-x-x-x

Chapter Five

Nandini Rao

I, Nandini Rao, the younger daughter of the industrialist Nageshwar Rao and his wife Manjula Rao, have been studying in the US for the past five years and am now in my final MBA semester. We're in the first week of New Year, and today I'm traveling to my native place Hyderabad. Mom wanted me to come for the New Year to spend a few days, but she informed me so late that I didn't get any decent flight connection. She insisted I take a charter flight, but I refused and promised to come as soon as I got a seat on a commercial flight. I hate to travel thousands of miles in small business jets, the turbulence is worse in them because they weigh much less than large commercial planes, and when they shiver, your intestines come in your mouth.

I was in a cheerful mood, as after almost seven months, I was going home and intended to spend some wonderful time, particularly with my brother, who seems to have become a different person, as he's fallen in love. And it seems the love is one-way only because the girl refuses to marry him. What a joke, my handsome brother, a well-qualified cardiologist and heir to a multibillion-dollar empire, is getting rejected. I desperately wanted to meet with the girl who had the nerve to say no to my brother.

I sat in my business-class window seat and prayed I didn't get disturbed by the seat occupant next to me.

Most of the time, I met with men showing off their richness and talking about how much they travel, and then slowly, the inquiry comes, "Whether there's a possibility of meeting for lunch or dinner."

While I was lost in my wandering brainwaves, a young man in his mid- or late twenties, lean, whitish, perhaps five feet 10 or 11 inches tall, with a thick flock of jet-black hair in a stylish low-fade cut, dressed in dark blue jeans and a sky-blue round neck polo shirt stepped in and stood by my seat in the aisle. He slid his shoulder bag onto the luggage rack without glancing at me and pulled out a book. He was about to take the seat next to me when he looked at me, turned around, and walked to the hostess standing a few feet away. Then, in a hushed voice, he said to her he wanted to change his seat and got the response that the flight was full and only after take-off would she be able to find whether someone was willing to swap.

When I heard his request, I got pissed off; why this idiot wants to change the seat? Am I a monster or a ghost from a horror movie? The entire bloody University chased me, and I didn't entertain anyone, as I never wanted to break my promise to Mom that I would marry a person of her choice. And this man is not interested in sitting beside me; why? Finally, after standing for a while, he returned and sat; I looked at him to determine which breed of idiots he belonged to! His face looked familiar; I must've seen him before, but where and when cannot remember. I scratched every nerve of the right-brain hemisphere and even checked the left-brain hemisphere, but nothing came out. For sure, the face was familiar, and I've seen him somewhere, and in all likelihood, I rubbed him the wrong way, or something went awry between us, which could be why he doesn't want to sit next to me. Strange, very strange, as I don't remember ever fighting with anyone in the US; yes, I got upset with some fellow students but never got into an altercation. The curiosity was killing me, so I decided to initiate the conversation.

"Excuse me; I'm willing to swap if you want the window seat."

"I'm fine, thank you," he said hoarsely.

"Hello, I'm Nandini Rao, a student going to my native place, Hyderabad, for a short vacation," I said smilingly.

"Great, have fun," he said and, without introducing himself, opened the book he was holding, *How To Implement Lean Manufacturing* by Lonnie Wilson.

He must be an arrogant bastard; he didn't introduce himself, didn't look at me, and started reading the stupid book. He must be an heir to a piddly little manufacturing unit and a showoff, trying to impress people sitting around him by reading a book on manufacturing. Nevertheless, I decided not to give up until I found out whether I had met him earlier or had a cursory look somewhere on the street or in a shopping mall.

"Excuse me; I find your face familiar. Do you remember meeting me, or do we've a common friend who introduced us a few years ago?" I asked.

"Four years back, on May 19, at 12:40 pm, we shared a table at the New Delhi Restaurant on Chestnut Street, Philadelphia," he said and went back to his reading.

Holy shit, yes, I remember. Instead of eating at the hostel canteen, I wanted to have a good lunch at a decent Indian restaurant and sleep, as there were no classes in the afternoon. So I went to New Delhi Restaurant, and a girl at the entrance informed me that I needed to wait as there was no vacant table. Waiting could be at least 30 minutes; however, she could find a chair if I wanted to share the table. This situation annoyed me, and since I wanted to have a quick bite and hit the bed, I decided to share the table. She guided me to a table where this man was sitting. He tried to initiate a conversation, which annoyed me, and I snapped at him by saying, “Mind your own business and allow me to eat in peace.” He didn’t respond, took a few quick bites from his plate, and left, leaving behind a lot of unconsumed food.

His aversion to sitting next to me is understandable. However, I owe him an apology because it was impolite and unseemly of me to behave in such a rude manner. Neither my upbringing nor my family values permit me to act in such a conceited way with anyone.

I said, “My sincere apologies for the rude behavior that day, which had nothing to do with you. I was sleep-deprived and in a rush to have my food and go for a siesta, and when I didn’t find a table, I got annoyed.”

“It’s okay, Ma’am, and if you excuse me, I’ve to read a couple of books before I reach my destination,” he said and continued his reading.

For no apparent reason or motivation, I was bending over backward to please the son of a gun, but he was acting as if I’d murdered him or committed some other highly sinister act. His arrogancy really ticked me, so I decided to bug him just for the kick I would get by disturbing him.

"Are you a student like me or working?" I asked.

He gave me a menacing look and, in a hostile tone, said, "Didn't I tell you I've got to do some reading? So, Ma'am, I would highly appreciate it if you could mind your business and leave me alone to read in peace."

"Come on; you cannot say this to a young lady sitting beside you. It's a long-haul flight, and it's your responsibility to entertain me and make sure I don't get bored," I told him innocently, intent on bugging the asshole.

He looked at me for a while; this time, his muscles were relaxed, and I noticed a faint smile; and said, "You're a funny girl. I'm Vimi; tell me how I could entertain you and keep you happy till you reach Hyderabad."

I shrieked with fake pleasure and said, "You're from Hyderabad. That's a great pleasure to know. Tell me, are you a student in the US or working?"

"I'm working with Phillip-Merkel; it's a consumer goods manufacturer," Vimi said.

"I know Phillip-Merkel very well. It's a giant multinational, spread across the globe, and makers of quite a few popular food items we all consume daily. In which department do you work, and as what?" I asked

He took out his wallet, pulled out a business card, and gave me. A Phillip-Merkel card read Dr. Vadiraj Rao, Ph.D., Director – Business Growth.

My goodness: he is too young to have a doctorate and hold a senior position in a giant MNC like Philip Merkel – he must be an extremely brainy fellow. I extended my hand for a handshake and said, "It is a pleasure meeting you, Doctor. Recently, I heard an Indian student got a stipend for four years from Phillip-Merkel to do his doctorate and join them. Is that you, Doctor, that Merkel hired?"

Vimi took my extended hand in his hand and said, "Yes, Nandini, you're talking to that Doctor only. Did I entertain you enough, and can I go back to my reading?"

"Please call me Nini, my pet name, and thank you very much for talking to me; please continue your reading, as now I feel much better and exhilarated," I said with a big smile.

"Thank you, Nini," Vimi said with a grin.

We hardly talked for the rest of the journey, as Vimi was seriously busy reading and making notes on the book margins with a mechanical pencil. Most of the time, I either watched a movie or slept. Twice I noticed that he adjusted my blanket, that half fell on the floor; a caring and disciplined person, as the hostess, often brought champagne and other liquors, but he only requested water and coffee.

Speaking with him seemed like a good idea because I wanted to learn more about him and his family. But, although I felt the urge, I suppressed it out of fear that he would perceive it as an unwelcome intrusion into his personal space. Already, I had bugged him too much, and the conversation had become more drawn out after I learned who he was and what he was doing. In any case, I shouldn't disturb him further unless he initiates some sort of conversation.

I was seeking a person like him for a life partner. Before leaving for the US, I told Mom I needed my husband to be intelligent, disciplined, and hardworking, like Dad. It doesn't matter whether he works or has his own business, but he shouldn't be a sucker who wants to enjoy life with my money. Vimi boy fits the bill, but let's not rush; I should meet him in the US and ascertain whether he's married, engaged, or dating. If Mister Hottie is a bachelor, completely unattached, then I must find out his sexual orientation because if you've no girlfriend in the US, everyone firmly believes you're not straight.

After alighting at Hyderabad airport, we said our goodbyes without exchanging contact numbers; he didn't ask, and I was unwilling to beg for his company.

If he's single, he should come after me, or else I may not get the respect I deserve in our married life.

x-x-x-x-x-x

Chapter Six

Madhu Priya

Vimi came, and we all got relieved. We saw him almost daily on various video apps, but seeing him on a flat screen and in physical form was different. He had become more handsome and refined; it could be because of the corporate environment he was exposed to over the past year; the respect and money he was earning could have boosted his self-confidence, making him graceful and cultured.

In the evening, Rama came and left quickly after examining Dad, claiming his younger sister had come from abroad and was waiting to have dinner with him. Mom didn't like it as she had prepared a big meal, but excused him, on the condition that tomorrow he must come with his sister and have dinner with us. He agreed to it and left.

After dinner, we sat in the living room with our hot beverages.

Dad started the conversation and said, "Vimi, have you come for good, or do you've to go back?"

"Dad, I've come for just 10days. Because of contractual obligations, I cannot leave the US without completing the four-year employment contract, a legal document signed in the presence of lawyers. If I fail to complete the agreed period of employment, they have the right to sue me for compensatory and punitive damages. Apart from this, just before coming,

I got promoted to a senior executive position, which has never happened in the company's history, according to the HR department. After paying taxes, the new net salary and benefits would be more than 16 crore rupees. There's a huge possibility of earning even above the guaranteed income if I perform well above the expectations of board members and the CEO. I'm hopeful that this will happen. Give me a few moments; I'll bring the new agreement copy for your review," Vimi said and left the room.

We were all pleased to note that at such a young age, Vimi has progressed so well. And we collectively agreed that he should complete his contract.

Again, our brainstorming session started on how to curtail Dad's working hours to 25 per week for five days. Dad was adamant that there was no possibility of delegating some of his responsibilities, and if he had to continue to shoulder them, he must work six days a week for at least 48 hours per week. Even after two hours of our collective discussion, we failed to hammer out an effective solution acceptable to Dad. Mom suggested she go to the office with Dad and share some of his responsibilities, which we outright rejected. The house cannot be given into the hands of servants, or else we must be prepared to live in an unhygienic environment and eat food that would be nothing but slow poison. Finally, Mom came up with a solution to which Dad and Vimi agreed wholeheartedly, but I was against it. Mom suggested continuing our discussion tomorrow after dinner in the presence of Rama. I strongly opposed it, asking why Rama had to be involved in our family matters. They all said he's not only Dad's doctor but also a business person who would know how to handle such situations or guide us to people who could help.

The next day in the evening, Rama came sharp at 7:30 with a beautiful young girl. She must have been in her early twenties, slim, around 5'6" or a little more, with a chiseled dimple babyface, dainty nose, luminescent eyes, shapely figure, glossy fairer skin, and smiling face like her father. She was nothing but a drop-dead beauty. First, she came to me and hugged me like a bear and slowly whispered in my ear, "I don't know what has pleased me more, seeing your beauty or meeting with you; either way, I'm over the moon and cannot blame my bro for saying either you or no one."

"The feeling is mutual, Nandini; I feel like I'm meeting with my younger sister," I earnestly said.

Then, she went to Mom and Dad, took their blessings by touching their feet, and last shook hands with Vimi and said, "I'm pleasantly surprised to know you're the brother of Dr. Madhu Priya; anyhow, good to meet you again."

"Where did you meet my son, Nandini," asked Mom.

"We came here on the same flight and all the way sat next to each other. But you know he's such a bore; he read some damn books and made notes throughout the flight duration," she said, and everyone laughed aloud.

Mom said, "Yes, he's been a bookworm from childhood. We failed in all our attempts to keep him away from books, but if you want to try, our best wishes are with you."

Dad asked us to move to the living room; he probably wanted to rescue Nandini from Mom's further hints.

Mom said, "Let the men sit in the living room; we will occupy the TV lounge."

While sipping our fresh fruit cocktail, Mom asked, "Tell me, Nandini, what you're studying in the US."

"Aunty, please call me Nini, as that's my pet name. I'm in my final semester of MBA at the Pennsylvania State University," Nini said.

"After MBA, planning to come back or thinking of further studies to get a doctorate like my son?" Mom asked.

"Aunty, Mom will kill me even if I mention to stay for one more day after the MBA. She was heartbroken that I didn't obey her by coming back after securing my graduate degree in Business Administration," Nini said.

Mom left us saying, "Yes, you should come back and be with your parents, and please excuse me for a few minutes; I must check things in the kitchen."

"Madhu, I heard so much about you that I was dying to meet you, and whatever I learned was much less, and no wonder my mom and dad have made you their third daughter," Nini said.

"Nini, Aunty, and Uncle are marvelous human beings. I don't think I'll ever come across such an amazing couple. They're so decent, so down to earth, and disciplined that no one could believe that anyone who's so wealthy can possess such beautiful characteristics. It is a privilege knowing them and getting treated the way they treat me," I said.

"It seems you don't want to marry my bro because of a tiff you'd with him a decade ago. Is that true?" Nini asked.

I smiled and said, "Nini, I've decided about my future life and am content with it. If I marry, my charitable work will be disrupted, and my plans to have my NGO and other aspirations will be thrown out the window. Nonetheless, I'm under tremendous pressure from my mom and dad to settle down; I've promised to abide by their wish before the end of the year. Your brother has everything a girl would dream of having in her husband, but I've some reservations because of our past interaction. In any case, nothing is set in stone yet, and you never know what the future holds."

"I'm neither older than you nor a psychiatrist to lecture you on how to lead a happy life. However, I firmly believe that a girl is incomplete if she doesn't marry and raise kids. I love children so much that I want to have a complete cricket team, including the four extras sitting in the dugout," she said, and we laughed aloud.

"My best wishes are with you, Nini; tell me about yourself. Have you found your soulmate, or are you still on the hunt?" I asked.

"Before I was allowed to go to the United States for the first time, I had to promise Mom that I would marry someone of her choosing. But, lucky or unlucky,

I haven't found anyone yet who could have caused me to break my pledge. I believe the smarty-pants I'm looking for may not exist on planet Earth," she said, and we laughed for several seconds.

After dinner, everyone sat in the living room with their choice of hot beverages. I saw Mom signaling Vimi, probably to open the topic of discussion.

Vimi cleared his throat and said, "Rama, Sir, we seek your assistance in finding a solution to a challenging situation." He then informed him why he needed to work in the US for another three years and why Dad couldn't cut down the working hours.

Rama listened to Vimi without interruption and then said, "I believe Uncle is right; the moment he'll hand over some of the business-critical responsibilities to another person, he would open the door for malpractice and embezzlement, and so on. And, even if he hires several senior executives to have proper checks and balances, the additional overheads will kill the margins substantially and drag the profitability to unsatisfactory levels. Let me discuss the issue with Dad, and I'm sure he'll find an apt solution. One thing is absolute; Uncle cannot spend innumerable stressful hours conducting the business."

"Thank you, I'm banking on you; unfortunately, Vimi cannot come, Madhu cannot run the business, and I'm not allowed to go near the factory," Mom said.

"Aunty, don't be concerned; it's a trivial matter. Give us a few days to figure out how to get out of this stalemate," Rama said.

It was impressive and comforting how Rama made the issue so insignificant, and I believe Mom, Vimi, and Dad were relieved from the stress they were carrying.

The next afternoon, Rama came to my clinic and said, "Dad is working on resolving the issue, and in a couple of days, he's promised to find the solution. I wouldn't be able to come for a few days, as Nini keeps me engaged; you monitor Uncle and keep me informed."

I didn't see Rama for the next two days, and on the third day evening, Mom told me that tomorrow evening, we had to go to Rama's house for dinner.

"Mom, you have to excuse me; my presence is not essential as I know the purpose of the dinner. You would be discussing various options available to curtail Dad's working hours," I said.

"No excuse, honey, you have to come, and allow me to remind you that you're a partner in your dad's business, and your consent is a must for any proposed solution," Mom said smiling.

The next evening, we were at Rama's house just before 8:00; after dinner, we all sat in the living room with our preferred beverages.

"Vimi, it's an absolute pleasure to meet you and learn about your achievements. If I were in your shoes, I would also honor the agreement signed with the employer. But, unfortunately, now your dad is not in his best health and cannot continue to work the way he did before. So, with your dad's consent, my company accountants have scanned your company's financials for the past few years. And with that knowledge, I had intense discussions with my top aids, and we've come up with a few approaches to resolve this situation. But before I tell you what options we've, I want to know how you intend to handle this situation if it is left to you," Uncle said.

"Uncle, your accountants must've informed you that Dad's business is not standing on a solid footing, even though it's earning 10 crore plus gross profits and seven to eight crore net profit year over year. However, it's happening because of Dad's sound knowledge of the industry and handling of sales and purchase of raw materials by himself. These two departments are the company's backbone, generating at least four to six hours of work every day that Dad has been putting in for years.

"The unhealthy side of the business is that, if you measure the profitability being a manufacturing company, it earns razor-thin margins, just around five percent, because of the stiff competition from rival manufacturers. Another major downside is that hardly 10 customers give more than 60 percent of the business. You can picture what would happen to the company if these major customers stopped buying or the earnings took a further beating because of the new entrants who want your market share by dropping the prices. I'm confident that Dad knew all these pitfalls of his business too well. To protect his family's financial health, Dad invested most of the profits into buying commercial and agricultural properties instead of reinvesting into the company for expansion.

"To continue to run this business means you always walk on a fragile bridge whose pillars have the potential to collapse.

"I believe that taking the challenge of running Dad's business is only worthwhile if you've nothing better to do, and considering this, I think I shouldn't take the reins. However, even if I take up the task, I would be significantly underutilized. I'm only good in an MNC, as they've got the space to make effective use of my services, and not only that, but the money I earn in a year is much more than what Dad's company earns.

"If I take myself out of the picture, I believe we've three options to consider. First, find partners who could pump in massive amounts and expand the business pan India to make the company an industry leader, thus ensuring you remain in the business come what may. The second option is to hire qualified executives who could honestly and diligently run the business. The last option is to sell the company at the earliest. The first option is difficult to achieve as big investors shy away from manufacturers who earn insignificant margins. If we decide to go for the second option, we must prepare ourselves to face a further drop in margins and staff dishonesty, as there's no such thing that prevails in business called loyalty and honesty. Once, one of my professors said, if you want loyalty, go and buy a dog. According to him, to run a business, you don't look for honest and loyal staff; instead, you create an environment with no room for dishonesty. Unfortunately, small businesses cannot afford to invest sufficiently in a business setup that removes all opportunities for fraud. So we're left with the only option of selling the business to any party who comes forward with a reasonable offer," Vimi said.

"I'm impressed with your analysis, as my best financial wizards have come up with what you've recommended. They've informed that it's challenging to find wealthy investors to invest in and develop a small industry to make it huge. The second option is okay, but it is a pain to keep the executives in a straitjacket and settle for a one or two percent net profit, which is very poor considering the business volume and efforts you put in to run it. The option of selling the business is the best to go for, but finding a buyer instantaneously is not easy. However, I could attempt to find a customer as long as you all agree to sell," Uncle said.

Mom was first to consent and said, "My hubby is more important than the money, so from my side, a big yes."

Vimi was second to consent and said, "This is one of my suggested options, so I stand by it, and a yes from me."

"I'll go with Dad; whatever he says, I'll say the same," I said.

Dad paused before saying, "If my health is at stake, it would be foolish to gamble with it. So please, Nagesh Sir, find a customer and negotiate a reasonable price; my wife, children, and I will sign on the dotted lines."

"Vimi, for how long are you here, as I've to keep that in mind while I hunt a customer?" Uncle said.

"I'm here for the next few days only, and if you need, I could extend it for another four to five days maximum," Vimi said.

"I think that's enough; first, my accountants have to come up with a fair net present value of the business, and once I receive their feedback, I'll personally contact a few parties who might be interested in acquiring the business," Uncle said.

"Thanks," Dad said.

Nini took me to the living room and said, "I'm allergic to business talk in the house, so I brought you here; I'm sure you also find it boring. But still, allow me to ask, did the solution satisfy you, or did you agree to the proposal to keep everyone happy?"

"For me, not only in the house but anywhere, I find the business discussion highly unappealing. So I would've accepted any proposal to relieve Dad from taking stress," I said.

"Being a business administration student, I believe Vimi analyzed the business well and came up with a sensible solution. And it was unbelievable to hear Dad saying he'd impressed with your bro, as he never tells anyone that you've done abysmally or superbly," Nini said.

"Shall I give you his US number?" I said, laughing.

"I could've taken, but I've promised Mom to marry with her choice, and I'll not bring anyone from the US or anywhere else," Nini said with a long face.

"You want me to talk to Aunty? I said with a smile.

"Your bro is in the US for several years, and he must've got a partner or girlfriend, so no, thank you," Nini said.

"To my knowledge, he has none; he's very close to me, and I never heard him telling lies, at least not to me. So you decide, and I'm always available if you need my help," I said, smiling.

"Thank you for your help offer, but no thanks. I prefer Mom to find the Mr. Right," Nini said.

We reached home around 11:00 and decided to change and meet again in the living room to have lemonade and talk about our decision.

Once we sat, Dad said to Vimi, "Vimi, how did you learn so much about our business. To my knowledge, you never saw the balance sheets or account books."

"Dad, yesterday, I spent three hours with your chief accountant and scanned the financials and learned everything about the financial health of the business as well as about the responsibilities of senior staff, including yours. Dad, I must say, you've done an excellent job and made good money because of your sound knowledge of the industry and hard work. But now it is better to encash the business and rest," Vimi said.

"Since you scanned the accounts books and balance sheets, could you give me a wild figure on how much we should sell the business, including the factory land, equipment, and everything, for?" Dad asked.

"I believe the market value of the land could be around 200 million, and the machinery and equipment depreciated value as per the books is about 225 million. And, if we add a minimum of 600 million goodwill money or, say, the six-year profits, we're talking about 1,250 million rupees. Since we're in a rush to sell, we could settle for 800 or 900 million."

"I had a rough figure of 80 crores, and if I get that, I would be happy," Dad said.

"Dad, at the onset, allow me to tell you, I'll not take a penny from the sales proceeds. The complete money belongs to you and Akka. I'm earning a lot, and I hope to make decent money in the future also, and whenever you need anything from me, you need to instruct, not ask. I'm planning to buy a house in the next couple of months, and you all must come and stay with me as long as you want. And, Akka, you better marry Rama and spare Mom and Dad from your responsibility," Vimi remarked solemnly.

"Vimi, now I'm ready to marry; you find any man other than Rama," I said.

"Akka, I just met with Rama Sir a couple of times, and I can bet my life and say that you won't be able to find a better person than Rama in the entire world. I never expected you to behave in such an irrational way; what, Akka? You're in vengeance mode and fears – unbelievable. I was shocked to hear your apprehensions about Rama; tell me why your worldly vision has become so narrow. Who knows what the future holds for anyone; anything at any moment could go wrong, and your house of cards could come down like a dry leaf, Akka; Mom, Dad, and you're my ideal, and whatever I'm today is because of you people. I'm particularly indebted to you, Akka, as you lived a disciplined life from childhood. You had lots of money in your pocket, but you remained focused on your studies and kept a close eye on my studies, ensuring that I didn't get carried away and read fiction or non-fiction books instead of subject books. You also taught me how important it is to keep your body fit with regular exercise. So please, Akka, don't demonstrate that you're a weak person who can't conquer her anxieties," Vimi said.

"Vimi, you're right, and I also know that Rama is the best person to marry, but I don't know; whenever he comes close, I get petrified with fear that this man could turn his back on me for a silly oversight, and I would be licking my wounds of stupidity for the rest of my life," I said.

"Come on, Akka, you know very well that millions of divorces happen every day, and do you think they've stopped living because their spouse has ditched them? Life goes on, Akka, don't fear the future; if something unpleasant has to happen, it will happen, and no fence on earth could stop that devastation.

"Never forget that Rama's parents are gems; they're so down-to-earth and noble that you and I may not come across such amazing human beings in this lifetime. Dad worships Uncle, and we should also feel indebted to them and obey their wishes," Vimi said.

Whatever Vimi said was valid, yet it was challenging to overcome the deep sunken feelings of trepidation.

Rama was taking care of Dad, just like a son, and Mom was so happy with him that she would kill me if I even fantasized about having someone else as my better half.

"Vimi, I do realize whatever you said is true, but I need time to overcome my deep-set fears, and they're so overwhelming that unless I completely remove them from my system, I won't be able to enjoy life with Rama. Whatever you said about Rama's folks is not something anyone could contradict, they're gems, but you should also understand that I've to live with Rama and not with his parents. I need time to comprehend why I'm convinced that something would go wrong if I married him. Unless I become comfortable, I shouldn't wed, or else I'll ravage my life and also make Rama's life pathetic," I said.

Mom and Dad patiently heard our conversation without interruption or supporting Vimi's comments. Then I understood that this must be all a setup; yesterday, Mom went shopping with Vimi, and I believe Mom gave every detail of what had happened between Rama and me a decade ago and what's happening now. Mom must've shed loads of tears, which pumped Vimi, or else he was never so forceful in his conversation with me, but today I noticed a hint of aggression. So be it, but no one is implying anything derogatory. On the contrary, they are my well-wishers, and I should listen to their advice.

On the third day of our discussion with Uncle, Rama came to my clinic in the afternoon and said, "Tomorrow morning at 10:30, we've to be at Dad's office to meet with a potential buyer. Our car will pick you up at 10:00

from your home; I could've come to take you, but I have to do a few procedures in the morning, and I'll join you as soon as I can."

The next day just before 10:30, we reached Uncle's office. It was a huge 15-storied blue glass building, and in a dedicated elevator, we were taken directly to the top floor and guided to a meeting room, where Uncle was sitting with his two daughters. They rose to welcome us, and after the greetings, Uncle asked me to sit beside him. He opened the conversation and said, "A longtime friend of mine, an industrialist manufacturing various mass consumption products, is interested in buying the business. For the past two days, their accountants checked factory financials, and yesterday late afternoon he conveyed his interest in the purchase. He should be here to finalize the deal, and before his arrival, we should establish a minimum sales price. With the help of my finance executives, I've arrived at the minimum sales price that I'll tell you, but before that, I want to know what would be acceptable to you people."

Dad looked at Vimi, thinking he would want to answer, but he kept quiet, so he responded and said, "Nagesh Sir, I would be happy with 80 crores, but I'll let you decide, and whatever you say, we will gladly accept."

Uncle smiled and said, "That's a throwaway price. We're selling a profitable running business, for which we should get a decent amount. I've calculated 80 crores of goodwill money, plus 60 crores toward the land and building cost, 40 crores for the machinery, office furniture, fixtures, staff buses and delivery vans, and other moveable assets. So, I'll start with 180 crores and intend to settle for a minimum price of 120 crores."

"Anything you agree is fine with us," Dad said.

"One more thing, do you have any plans to invest the money or keep it in the bank," Uncle asked.

"Nagesh, Sir, we want to invest and would be indebted if you guide us to risk-free schemes where there won't be any possibility of losing the capital," Dad said.

"Our application for IPO is at the finance ministry, and we're hoping to receive the go-ahead in the coming six to eight months. Then, if it's okay with you, we will issue Manju Group's shares at face value. The moment we go public, I expect our share prices to shoot up manifold," Uncle said.

"We'd consider ourselves very fortunate if that happens, provided you wouldn't need to make a few trade-offs for selling us the shares," Dad said.

"No botheration whatsoever; before we become public, we can do whatever we want," Uncle said.

The discussion then switched toward Vimi, as Uncle asked him about his company's products. Vimi briefed him, and we all learned how massive his company is. While listening to Vimi, a red light on Uncle's intercom started flashing; he answered the call and announced the buyer was here.

Three guys in crisp business suits entered the meeting room. We all rose to greet them; Uncle introduced the plump guy as Harish Mirani, owner of several large industries manufacturing mass consumer goods, and the remaining two as the finance guys of his companies.

Before the horse-trading started, Rama also joined. Harish asked Uncle his expectations, and Uncle said, "We've calculated the selling price to be 180 crores."

"Nageshwar, Saab, it's way above our expectation and evaluation of a fair market price. But, allow me to tell you that we've arrived at 120 crores with due diligence, and that's what we're willing to pay, nothing more, nothing less. And, remember it's an all-cash transaction, no share swapping or guaranteed deferred payment in installments," Harish said.

"Harish Saab, please remember you're buying a profitable business, earning more than ten crores yearly. Considering the business profitability, the goodwill money itself will arrive at what you want to pay for the business and properties. No, Harish Saab, your offer is too low; you need to be realistic. I'm willing to come down but not anywhere close to the asking price," Uncle said.

The inconclusive discussion lasted more than 20 minutes. Uncle's stand was Harish was basing his offer on the book value of land and machinery, which is wrong, as it reflects the depreciated value instead of the current market value. And Harish's stand was it was unfair to consider the unsubstantiated market value. At last, Harish asked permission to deliberate among themselves and come to a final offer. And they were sent to a meeting room on a lower floor, and after 10 minutes or so, they returned and made a non-negotiable final offer of 140 crores. "I'll accept 142 crores; two crores should go to the factory employees," Uncle said.

"Do you think I could say no to you for two crores? No way, Saab. Please ask your staff to prepare the letter of intent, and I'll issue a five-crore check to confirm the deal. We will meet again the day after tomorrow in my office to sign the legal documentation," Harish said.

Uncle took the five-crore check that Harish gave and went out with Dad, probably instructing his finance people to prepare the letter of intent. In less than 15 minutes, they returned with a letter of intent, signed by Dad, witnessed by Uncle, and gave it to Harish, who signed and one of his accountants signed as witness.

After they left, Dad said, "Thanks is a small word, but that's what I know, so please accept my heartfelt thanks for your kind assistance, for which my family and I will always remain grateful."

"No need to thank me; I'm happy you're satisfied. Please prepare a note stating which employee should receive what amount from the two crores, and the percentage of shares each family member should receive," Uncle said to Dad, and he agreed to email him by this evening.

It was almost 2:00 in the afternoon, and Uncle took us to a nearby Chinese restaurant for lunch.

I observed two things during the meeting and at the restaurant: Rama's eyes were on me most of the time, and Vimi and Nini glanced at each other often. Rama's interest wasn't waning, a pain; something brewing between Nini and my brother, a delight. I must inform Mom of the development; she would be overjoyed.

When I mentioned to Mom what I noticed, she said, "I'm not blind, and you didn't speak about Rama, whose eyes were glued on you."

"Mom, you're hopeless. Tell me what you intend to do about Vimi," I said.

"I'll only talk to Vimi if you give me the green signal," Mom said with a smile.

"Mom, I've asked for time till the year-end, so, for now, forget about me and focus on Vimi; otherwise, he would come with a blonde next time," I said.

"Fine with me, whether he's interested in Nini or a blonde is not my worry. My worry is you, and unless you settle down, I'll be on a bed of thorns," Mom snarled.

"Mom, don't do this to me. I've promised you I would settle down before the end of the year, and you agreed to it, so why worry now? Please be patient and stay calm and happy," I said pleadingly.

In the next three days, everything was accomplished smoothly. Factory sale was completed per the law; the sales proceeds amount was deposited into the Manju Group bank account, and shares were issued to the beneficiaries as per the company's shareholding. Lastly, the factory staff received the two crores per Dad's instructions.

Before Vimi's scheduled travel date, Dad asked Vimi, "Vimi, can you extend your holidays for another week or ten days? Your and Madhu's presence in the house has become a source of energy, and whenever it's crossing my mind that you would soon leave, I'm getting uneasy and tense."

"Dad, I came for ten days but extended for four more days, so I must return within a day or two. In the next few weeks, I'll buy a house, and once I arrange for a cleaner and cook, I'll inform you to take the first available flight to come and stay with me. The change in the environment and rest will greatly assist you in recuperating and overcoming the stresses. Akka, it would be a great pleasure if you could also come; I know you would refuse, but I beg you to consider coming at least for a few days," Vimi said.

"Vimi, it's a brilliant idea; a change for Mom and Dad will significantly help them revitalize their energies, particularly Mom took a heavy beating because of Dad's health scare. And, yes, I'll come, but first, I'll send Mom and Dad, and when feasible, I'll come for a few days," I said.

"I cannot say about your mom, but I won't go unless I marry my daughter," Dad said.

"Dad, don't hold a gun on my head; I've promised you that I'll marry before the end of the year, then there's no point in resorting to this blackmail," I snarled.

"Dad, please come for a few months; you need this change to unwind and reclaim your energies," Vimi pleaded.

"You buy the house, send an invitation letter for the visit visa issuance; I'll organize their visas and put them on a plane. A new environment under their son's roof will help calm their tense nerves and rejuvenate their bodies," I said confidently.

As was customary, we sat in the living room with our drinks after dinner the following day. Mom began to sing praises for Rama. "He chose to become a doctor in defiance of his parent's wishes, who wanted him to pursue a degree in business management. Vimi, your dad, and I've agreed that we don't want to go anywhere without absolving ourselves of our responsibility toward Madhu. So, first, she must marry, then we will go to the US, and even we're thinking of a world cruise from east to west. If we must wait a year for her marriage, that's fine; we'll delay the trip."

I knew she was pumping Vimi to come heavily on me to marry Rama immediately. I didn't want to surrender to their pressure and make a hasty decision to weep in leisure. The question was why I should marry; what am I going to gain except a partner who has the potential to hurt and humiliate me? I had enough money to live a life of my liking, and was happy with what I was doing. I could adopt one or two children and enjoy life with them if needed. Celibacy is fine with me; I've successfully suppressed my biological desires, and there's no doubt in my mind that without a partner, one could lead a happy life. It's a false narrative that it's abnormal, and you're hiding your sexual preferences under the mask that you enjoy your unmarried life. All said and done, I had more than enough pressure from Mom and Dad, and the new force that joined the bandwagon was Uncle, Aunty, and Vimi, causing stress and massive and persistent pain.

And the less I talk about, Rama boy is much better; he's become a nuisance, and getting rid of him has become unattainable. Repenting the decision to have a look at Rama won't yield any good outcome either.

"Mom, Dad, and Vimi, please don't exert unnecessary pressure, and if you continue to do that, I'll just disappear one day. It would be best to respect my fears, preventing me from making a quick decision. I've taken it upon myself to work on my fears and wed when I would become comfortable with the thought that even if something undesirable happens, it won't devastate me to the extent I commit suicide," I growled.

No one replied to my outburst; instead, they merely gazed at me blankly.

After a while, Vimi asked me, "Akka, do you know if Nini has left for the US or is still here?"

"I do not know; I could check with Rama if you want. But why do you want to know?" I said, smiling.

"Just asked, with no specific reason," Vimi said.

"Give me a break, Vimi boy; tell me what you want, and I promise to help you. I've seen your eyes continually getting focused on Nini; not only me but other people in the meeting room and at lunch saw the constant focus you'd on one another," I said, chuckling aloud, and Mom and Dad joined me with a booming laugh.

"I'm not sure what it is, but I would be grateful if you could give me her US contact number. Please don't have any ideas; remember she's been in the US for the past several years, and to assume she's unattached is too much to ask," Vimi said sheepishly.

"Allow me to give the good news; she's unattached, and if you're interested, then all the best, not only from me but from Mom and Dad also," I said, and Mom supplemented with, "I love to have Nini as my daughter-in-law." Dad also said, "It would be a dream come true if you married Nini."

"Akka, please don't give any signals to anyone, as I'm not sure what I want, but I've developed a high regard for her, for being down to earth, instead of a rich rotten spoiled brat. You must have noticed that she touched Mom and Dad's feet when she came here, reflecting on her upbringing and values that aren't tarnished even with loaded pockets," Vimi said.

"Don't worry; whatever we've discussed will remain among the four of us only," I said.

The next evening, as usual, Rama came to check on Dad and joined us for dinner upon Mom's request. After dinner, we sat in the living room with our hot beverages.

Rama asked, "Has Vimi left, or still here?"

"He's gone shopping and to have farewell dinner with his friends. He's leaving early tomorrow morning. Is Nini still here or left?" I asked.

"She left two days ago," Rama said.

"I forgot to take her cell number; if you have it, give it to me," I said.

"Sure," Rama said and messaged me the number.

x-x-x-x-x-x

Chapter Seven

Vimi

After returning from Hyderabad, it took almost two weeks to catch up with the backlog. Finally, on the second Friday evening, I called Nini, and she promptly answered in a cheerful voice, saying, "Good to hear from you, Vimi. Tell me, what can I do for you?"

"Is it a good time to talk to you?" I asked.

"Yes, go ahead," Nini said.

"Tomorrow, can you have lunch with me and then be with me for a few hours for a city tour?" I asked.

"Lunch is fine, but a few hours is difficult, and only if you insist, I could spare two hours or a little more. But where do you want to take me?" Nini asked.

"I'll tell you during our lunch, and if you think you should be spared, then no issues; I'll drop you off after lunch. Please tell me what you want to eat, Indian, Chinese, Spanish, French, Italian, or seafood? I'm asking you so I can reserve a table, or else being a weekend, we may not get the table, or we may have to wait," I said.

"Let's go for seafood," Nini said.

"Fine, in a while, I'll confirm the time when I'll pick you up, and please send me your location," I said.

"Sure, and bye for now," Nini said and disconnected the line.

I reserved a table in an upscale, exclusive seafood restaurant and informed Nini that I would pick her up at 12:30 in the afternoon.

The next day I was in front of her hostel at the given time, and she didn't keep me waiting for long, just a few minutes. I stopped breathing when I saw her; she looked stunning in her floral beige silk top, ice-blue jeans, and black shades. I quickly came out of the car and opened the front passenger door for her, and she sat with a smiling thank you.

After steering the car toward the destination, I said, "I want to say something, provided you promise not to get offended."

"You could say anything, but please don't be hurtful," Nini said.

I laughed and said, "Ma'am, I cannot dream of upsetting you; leave aside hurting you. I wanted to tell you that you must take the blame if I get killed today." "Why would you be killed, and why would I've to take the blame?" Nini said, surprised, with raised eyebrows.

"Someone may get jealous of me for enjoying the company of the most beautiful girl on the planet and put a bullet in my head," I said with a chuckle.

"I felt terrified – you liar. I'm certain you said the same lines to each girl who went with you on a date," Nini said, laughing.

"You may not believe it, but it's a fact that this is the first time in my life that I'm taking a girl for lunch. Thus far, my passion has been reading books; I never wanted to waste a single minute on anything. Most of my school and college friends used to call me a mentally challenged person. But such comments never bothered me, as I was addicted to the immense pleasure of reading my textbooks, fiction or non-fiction books on any topic. If you come to my house in Hyderabad, you'll find not hundreds but thousands of books locked in a room that I read from my childhood. Mom is very possessive of those books, even though I often ask her to donate them," I said somberly.

"It's hard to believe, but I don't want to challenge it. However, I'm surprised that no girl tried to hook you at the university. Girls have become very bold even in Hyderabad, and if they find a handsome boy like you, they chase him," Nini said.

"A big thanks, the first time a girl called me handsome. A long time ago, I evaluated myself and observed that not only mentally but physically also, I'm challenged. When I was a fresher, a few girls initiated dialog to enter into some kind of relationship and gave up, tagging me as gay or weird. However, I never tried to refute my reputation, as that allowed me to remain focused on my studies, and whatever spare time I would get, I spent reading the books of my liking," I said with a laugh.

"I don't accept that you're holier-than-thou," Nini said with a loud laugh.

"I've no evidence to prove my innocence. How about you? Are you dating someone or engaged?" I asked.

"Unfortunately, while coming here, Mom agreed to send me with a few conditions. First, I would not date anyone, whether an Indian or otherwise, or bring a blond with me, and second, no one should know who I'm, and last, I must stay in a hostel like any other student. I came across a few decent boys chasing me but turned them down to uphold my promise. So very much single, not dating or engaged, and once I go back, Mom has promised to find a suitable alliance," Nini said.

Nini is unattached; wow, I was over the moon with the news and decided to express my interest. "Very happy to note; can you ask your mom to free you from the first condition," I said with a loud laugh.

"Sure, but let me first find an irresistible boy who could force me to seek permission," Nini said with an equally loud laugh.

"Don't worry about that; I could take responsibility for finding an educated, well-settled, fairly rich boy who could guarantee to keep you always happy and treat your wishes as his command. Trust me; it will be an easy job; you're so beautiful, and just by looking at you, a person like me feels inebriated, causing disorientation and haze," I said with a laugh.

"Look at you, claiming never had a girlfriend but keeping terrific pickup lines handy. And, thank you, but no thank you, I'll hunt, tame, and belt my dragon," Nini said, laughing. With her soft, mellow voice, I got the hint that she was also happy with my comments.

"Fine with me, but don't look very far and waste unnecessary time and effort. Instead, just look around you, and hopefully, you'll find a dragon already tamed with your beauty and brain and willing to get belted," I said with a chuckle.

"Thank you, I'll keep my eyes open," Nini said smilingly.

We had a fabulous lunch of shrimp soup and a grilled platter of tiger prawns, lobster, and salmon steaks served with superb dressings.

Then, while having coffee, I said, "Nini, I need to buy a house, and I've no clue what I should buy. So I want you to accompany me and select a place with all the amenities and comforts a woman needs to have. From here, we will go to meet a property dealer who'll show several mid-range ready-to-occupy houses. Is that okay with you, Ma'am?" I asked.

"Fine, but I'm not 'Ma'am;' tell me your budget, as that will assist in selecting what you afford," Nini said. "Willing to spend a million or more. Think as if you're going to live in that house and decide based on what would be your requirement. Then, take a call on which one you want to buy, and don't worry about the price," I said.

"Fine, how long do you think it would take to check the houses? I don't have an appointment; it's just my studies," Nini said.

"I've no clue how long it would take and how many houses we may have to see. If you want, I could postpone it to a convenient date when you would have ample time to spend, or you could refuse to help. All is okay and fine with me," I said.

"I'll sacrifice my study hours, provided you promise to assist me in a couple of subjects I want to excel in but find difficult," Nini said.

"It'll be my pleasure, always available for any assistance; you could call me 24/7. Can we move?" I asked.

The property dealer showed us houses from 800,000 to 3 million, and Nini selected two places; both were in a decent neighborhood, newly constructed and fully furnished. One was 900K, had four bedrooms, a TV lounge, living and dining halls, two garages, and a large backyard. The other house was fabulous in every aspect, an excellent neighborhood and hardly half a mile away from a beautiful and large lake. It had a huge front yard with an automatic entrance gate, 12 CCTV cameras installed in and outside the house, a burglar alarm connected to police headquarters, three-car garages, a boat parking shed, and a large mud room. The inside of the house was breathtaking, with four large bedrooms, all with a dresser and bath, a study room, a vast open area allocated for the TV lounge, living and dining halls, a powder room, and an indoor swimming pool with a gym. The backyard was over a thousand square yards with a high concrete fence wall. Half of the yard was a vegetable garden with exotic vegetables. The other half had several garden chairs and tables spread over a lush green velvet grass carpet with colorful sunshades tied to the walls and two large BBQ grills bolted to the ground. The asking price was 2.2 million.

I promised the property dealer to revert to him in a few days and left, and once in the car, I asked Nini, "So, which one do you want me to buy?"

"I'll go for the 900K house, which is within your budget, but if you want a luxurious dwelling with a gym and swimming pool to keep you healthy, then the 2.2 million property is the best; it's your call," Nini said.

"Okay, let me think and decide," I said.

I dropped her at the hostel around 7:00 and told her never to hesitate to call me for whatever assistance she needed.

The next day, I asked the property dealer to offer a reasonable price for the 2.2 million property as the amount seemed inflated.

He said he had already calculated the price, around 2 million. Then he informed the land price, construction cost to be about 1.2 million, and the furniture and fixtures could be 150K. So if you add the profit of 300,000 to 400,000 and the mortgage interest and other miscellaneous costs, it works out to approximately 2 million.

I informed him my budget was too tight, and if he could bring the price to 1.5 million, he would have a deal.

He promised to get back to me before the end of the day. My company agreed to a soft loan of two years' salary recoverable over five years to purchase a car and home. I had a little over 400K in my account, and considering the loan amount and my savings, I decided to go by Nini's liking.

In the evening, I received the property dealer's call informing me that the owner has come down to 1.6 million with great difficulty, and it's a take-it-or-leave-it price. I told him I would stick to my offer; however, I would pay the total amount in cash to compensate for his loss. A few minutes later, the dealer called to inform me that the owner had accepted the offer.

In a little over two weeks, the property was in my name. I called Nini to have lunch that coming Saturday, and she gladly accepted the invite. I decided not to waste my time chasing her; instead, I must propose to her. However, hearing a sorry from her is as high as the Himalayan peak; I'm no match for her in the money zone. She's very wealthy, and possibly her parents would prefer an equally rich and educated boy. And the other problem could be she or her parents may not like me to work here. They could press me to work for their company, which I don't want. Joining the father-in-law's company would be a disaster; even if I double the turnover and profits of their group, I won't earn the respect of my peers or society. Here I could demand the position and money, and when needed, I could join a new organization for better prospects. Another minor hitch was her quick temper, which I witnessed during our first encounter. But I believe it's okay, as I'm bestowed with a mild temperament; it takes a lot for anyone to make me angry. So one in the family is fine; I'm like Dad, and Nini is almost like Mom, a tigress in her youth, but now she's softened down a lot.

With the thought of rejection, I sank into a deep depression. I'm no match to Nini; she had already stated that she would hunt, tame, and belt her dragon, which signifies that I was not in the race. If I get rejected, life will become a horrible nightmare. She had occupied my heart, brain, and every nerve of my body so intensely that I had to put a superhuman effort into suppressing my aching to call her every night.

In a depressed mood, I called Akka to talk to her about how Dad was doing and anything I could do. Akka sensed something was wrong with me and asked me to tell her what was happening and why I sounded miserable.

I said, "Akka, this girl called Nini has become a massive pain."

"Why, what has happened?" Akka said worriedly.

"She's so intensely overpowered me that I cannot even sleep. I've no clue how I could overthrow her forceful entry into my body, nor do I know whether she would be interested in me," I said gloomily.

"Idiot, you scared me. She wouldn't have come with you for lunch if she had no interest in you. Take her out a few more times, choose an opportune moment, and propose to her. She won't find a better person than my bro, and I'm sure she would die out of pleasure once you bend on your knees," Akka said, laughing.

"Akka, there's another problem. I want to work here for Merkel, where I think I've got a better chance to grow, and I don't know whether Nini would like to stay here," I said.

"Find out everything before you propose to her. Come on, Vimi boy, it is easy for a person of your intelligence. I'm sure she already got a hint when you took her to select the house and must be waiting to hear the good news. I could bet anything; she must've already informed her mom about what's going on and most likely have got approval from her," Akka said.

"I hope you're right," I said.

After wishing me the best of luck, she disconnected the line.

As promised, I picked Nini up at the agreed time of 12:30 and took her to a Mexican restaurant for lunch. She ordered guacamole, chicken quesadillas, enchiladas, and red snapper vera cruzana. The food was delectable.

I took her to the house from the restaurant and informed her of the password for opening the main door. She was delighted that I had bought an excellent place and congratulated me.

We prepared coffee and sat with our mugs in the TV lounge.

"Got a good deal or ended up paying the asking price?" Nini asked.

"I got an excellent deal; paid 1.5 million in cash, as I got a soft loan from the company to buy a house and car."

"Great, so which car are you buying?" she asked.

"Your call. You decide which car you like the most, and I'll buy it," I said.

"I agreed to assist you with the house purchase because I believed a woman's perspective is essential. But when it comes to a car, you can choose whatever you prefer," Nini said.

"Nini, I need your help, as I'm a certified idiot for anything other than my work and books. While in Hyderabad, I never purchased clothes, footwear, sunglasses, or anything, except books, computers, and accessories. Akka and Mom were buying all my needs, and here I don't have anyone but you, so I need your help," I said.

"Do you have your laptop with you?" Nini asked.

"It's in the car; I'll bring it," I said.

"You didn't move in?" Nini asked.

"No, Ma'am, first I wanted you to step into the house. I've planned to move in late at night with my modest worldly possessions; eight boxes of books, one suitcase, and a backpack, which I should be able to load in my car," I said and went out to get the laptop.

I switched on the laptop and gave it to Nini. She asked me, "Tell me whether you like a four-wheeler or a sedan and what's your budget."

I said, "Nini, around 100K is okay, and if needed, a little more. You decide to buy a sedan or a four-wheeler; all is okay with me."

Nini surfed the internet for a while, and without saying anything, she came and sat beside me. Her closeness was electrifying, and her perfume was intoxicating.

She said, "In your position, you need to buy a decent car, and being a young man, I believe a four-wheeler would match you well. I suggest you go for a Range Rover," and showed me photos of a few models.

"Great, let's buy a Range Rover," I said.

"When do you want to buy it?" Nini asked.

"If you have time, we could go now," I said.

"I'll come, but if I miss my semester, I'll tell Mom you were the reason for my failure," Nini said with a chuckle.

"Fine with me, just check who the distributor is, what time they close, and how far they're from here, and in the meantime, I'll clean the coffee cups," I said.

Without any comments, she started punching the keys, and when I returned from the cleaning job, she was still pressing the keys.

After a while, she said, "There are several dealers in the state, and the nearest is around eight miles, and the next one is approximately 14 miles, and they're open till 6:00. And, to save us time at the dealers, I've selected Range Rover P525 Westminster, which is around 125K, and both the dealers have this model for immediate delivery. If we start right away, we could check both the dealers for a better price and the availability of preferred color," Nini said.

"Let's move," I said. And unintentionally took Nini's hand in my hand and walked toward the door. She didn't object, and I felt ecstatic.

While on the road, I asked Nini which car color she preferred. She said, "I believe a snow-white vehicle would best suit you."

I said, "Excellent; I like the color white."

We checked both the dealers and bought the car from the nearest dealer within two hours as I got a better cash discount. Delivery in 2–3 days, dealer informed.

On our way back, I asked Nini, "Would you care for a bite and coffee?" She agreed.

We went to a Starbucks and ordered a latte and chicken Caprese on ciabatta.

"Nini, tell me, if your future hubby would ask you to settle here as he's business or employment in this country, would you agree to that, or must you settle in Hyderabad and work as an executive in your dad's empire?" I asked.

"It's not necessary for me to stay in Hyderabad. I decided to marry a well-educated, hardworking, mannerly, soft-spoken person a long time ago. In addition to these traits, he must lead a disciplined, healthy lifestyle, take care of me, and not rely on my wealth. If I find such a dude, I would be very willing to wed him and go wherever he takes me," Nini said.

I thought one thing out of the window; she's ready to go wherever her husband takes her.

"What would you do if your mom and dad insist that your hubby should work for their company, as they need their daughter a stone's throw away?" I asked.

"I rather not comment on a hypothetical scenario, but I don't think Mom and Dad would say such a thing, as they have great faith in me for making the right choices. My elder sister's husband is also an industrialist. In his factory, they produce assorted edible oils and market them all over India. He's also a major importer of olive oil. His annual turnover could be easily close to 1,000 crores. After marriage, Dad offered him a merger option with our business and a permanent CEO position to run his business as before. A merger would've allowed him to give a sudden boost to expand his business and earn a lot more when compared to what he was earning, but he declined the offer. And, you know, Mom, Dad, and even my sister got delighted with his decision. Considering this, I don't think anyone would object if my future hubby decides to remain an independent person," Nini said earnestly.

"Good to hear, Nini, and let's change the topic. Is it possible for you to accompany me to receive the car and have dinner to celebrate the new toy?" I asked.

"It would be a pleasure to join you in your happy moments, but if I miss the semester, be ready to take the consequences. My mom will chew your bones, and to inflict the maximum pain, she'll do that very slowly," she said, and we laughed aloud.

"Don't worry about the exams; you still have plenty of time, and once I settle down, I'll spend all weekends with you to ensure you sail through smoothly," I said.

"Great, I'd love to take your assistance. It's your turn; you tell me what type of girl you're looking to marry. Maybe I could help you find what you need," Nini asked.

"I already found the girl; she's got everything I dreamed of; however, I don't think she would agree to marry me. She's too rich, and I'm just a business executive, and since there's no match in our social status, the probabilities of rejection are very high," I said.

"If you want, I could become your feeler, provided you let me know how well you know the babe; have you dated, or are you just friends or mere acquaintances?" Nini asked.

"Nini, I could say we know each other at this stage and nothing more. Thanks for your offer, but it's my battle, so I want to fight it, irrespective of the outcome of a win or a loss," I said.

"My good wishes are with you, and I don't think any girl would be so stupid to reject you because she's loaded with money. You don't spend your life with money; you need a loving, caring partner to make your life's journey happy and satisfying. Although I subscribe to this philosophy, maybe other people think differently and may think I'm stupid," Nini said.

"Thanks, Nini," I said, and since we had finished our coffee, we decided to leave.

As soon as I reached my pad, I called Akka, briefed her on today's conversation with Nini, and asked her how to proceed further.

"Dumbo, you've won her over; go ahead and buy a quality finger-ring and get down on your knees and propose to her," Akka said.

"Akka, I'll not propose to her without her parent's consent. Instead, I'll call Mom to speak with Nini's Mom, and only after getting a green signal from them would I propose to her. Her parents are very wealthy, and we don't know what they'd planned for their daughter," I said.

"Fine, go ahead and tell Mom everything and ask her to speak with Nini's mother," Akka said.

I then called Mom and briefed her on my intent to propose to Nini, provided her parents were okay with taking me as their son-in-law. Mom was delighted to hear I intended to marry Nini and promised to speak with Nini's Mom and get back to me in a day or two.

Mom called the next evening and said, "Good news and bad news. They're happy to take you as their son-in-law, and have complete knowledge of what is happening between you two. Nini is thrilled and highly impressed with you and ascertained that you're the most suitable person to marry. And her mom has given Nini a green signal to go ahead and accept if Vimi proposes to her. Now the bad news is she won't give her daughter unless she gets their daughter. Thus, the ball is in your court; you need to convince your Akka to marry Rama at the earliest," Mom said with a chuckle.

I thanked Mom and disconnected the line.

It's indeed a piece of good news and bad news. To make Akka agree to anything against her liking is next to impossible. After beating my head to the wall till I went to bed, I couldn't firm up anything tangible to resolve this problematic scenario. Finally, I decided that first, I should propose to Nini, and once this hurdle was out of the way, Nini and I could think of a plan of action to make Akka agree to the marriage.

After two days, around 4:00 in the afternoon, I picked Nini up in a cab, and we went to collect the car, which was ready for delivery. Upon signing various documents, I got the car key, a bulky folder containing the car manual, and several other documents.

I gave the key to Nini to drive. She said, "No, you drive; it's your car."

Without responding to her comments, I went and sat on the passenger seat and gestured for her to drive.

"You're too much. Don't blame me if your expensive car gets damaged due to my lousy driving skills," she said and smoothly moved the car. Once on the road, she asked, "Where are we going?"

I gave her the name of the recently opened shopping mall, which housed many renowned national and international fashion and jewelry stores.

She was an excellent driver and possibly better than me. We reached the mall in roughly half an hour, and I took her straight to the Tiffany Jewelry shop. I told her, "I want to buy an engagement finger-ring for my girlfriend, whose fingers are almost the same as yours, and I would be highly obliged if you select a decent solitaire for the engagement; anything around 100K is fine." Nini gave a quizzical look but didn't say anything. A young lady greeted us, and I told her what we wanted.

She showed us 50 or more pieces, and Nini fell for a three-carat brilliant-cut round diamond embedded in six prongs 18K rose gold – a stellar piece of jewelry. The ring cost was a little over $100K, which I paid, and we came out of the mall, and this time Nini forced me to drive the car. I took her to my house; once inside, I asked her to sit on a sofa, brought a tripod phone stand, kept my phone on it, focused on her, and switched on the video recorder. She sat still without saying anything, looking at me with curious eyes.

I went to my knees and said, "Ms. Nandini Rao, I haven't read romance books or poetry to express my desire poetically or romantically. And, to put it plainly, I've fallen in love with your beauty, intelligence, and unpretentious lifestyle. I believe I would be a paralytic person without you beside me in my life journey. If you hold my hands to grow old with me, I'll consider myself the luckiest and most blessed man till I take my last breath. I love being in love with you, and I promise to be there for you in your good times and bad, and I'll do everything to ensure your happiness and contentment. I realize I'm yearning for something tantamount to asking for the moon, but I don't want to live in regret of not attempting to catch hold of the moon. I'm prepared to hear a denial; it would crush my heart, but since your happiness is fundamental, I would still extend my good wishes for a blessed life of good health and happiness. So, Nini, I must ask, will you please marry me?" I said, took out the ring, and looked at her expectantly to offer her hand.

"Yes, Dr. Vadiraj Rao, I'll marry you and adore rearing your children, getting old with you, and dying in your arms," she said with a smile on her face, eyes welled with tears; she gently extended her hand.

"Much thanks to you," I said and pushed the ring on her finger, kissed her hand, and stood in front of her.

She got up, gave a tight hug, kissed me on both cheeks, and said, "I'm in seventh heaven, Vimi; you've everything I dreamed of from my teens, and thank you for choosing me to be your better half."

We forwarded the engagement recording to all our family members and received congratulatory messages and video calls within a few minutes, which kept us busy for almost an hour.

Once through with all the incoming calls, I took Nini to a recently opened Indian restaurant that earned a name for its delicious biryani and kebabs. The restaurant looked remarkable, with excellent interiors, dim lights, and Jagjit Chitra ghazals playing softly.

All the occupied tables had two or three flickering electronic candle lights, giving a soothing effect. We were guided to a corner table, and Nini ordered biryani and a kebab platter. While devouring the tasty food, I told Nini, "Now the biggest challenge is how to convince Akka for the marriage. Your mom said my daughter would only go when I get the replacement. Can you be of any help in handling this incredibly tricky task?"

"I'll talk to her, but don't worry about it; Bro has taken a vow to marry her in the next few months," Nini said.

"I'm pressuring my parents to come here for a few months since Dad is still stressed, and I'm hoping that he'll be able to relax once he's here," I said.

"Brilliant idea; can we dash off to Hyderabad, just for a few days, to take blessings of all elders, and while returning, we will take your parents with us?" Nini said.

"No, Nini, at this stage, your studies are critical; you've already wasted quite a few precious hours because of me," I said.

"You're a bad man, but I must agree I got carried away. Tell me why you were sure I would say yes to your proposal and spent more than $100k on the ring purchase?" Nini asked.

"I wasn't sure at all, but when I saw that you didn't refuse to help me with my home and car purchases and seemed happy in my company, I decided not to waste time dreading rejection, and I must cross the bridge of fire," I said grinning.

"Excellent observation, Vimi; you rightly said I was glowing with pleasure in your company and, day by day, getting fond of you. When you were in Hyderabad, you impressed both Mom and Dad; especially Dad, who said, take my word, this boy will go places, and I'll not be surprised if he would run an American conglomerate one day, earning millions of dollars. And Vimi dear, from the day you took me to purchase the house, I was expecting this to happen, and this I mentioned to Mom and got her green signal," Nini said joyously.

The next evening, Nini called and said, "Mom has promised to come with Dad for a few days to give their blessings in person."

Chapter Eight

Madhu Priya

Rama was coming almost every third day to check Dad, and one evening when he finished his checkup, Mom pressed Rama to have dinner with us, which he accepted without fuss. And after dinner, as usual, we sat in the living room with our hot beverages and entered into the routine casual conversation. Mostly, Dad and Rama talked about the current political and financial scenario.

I believe Mom got bored with their conversation and interjected saying, "Rama, Vimi is pressing us to come to the US at the earliest, as he believes a change will do wonders for his dad. But you know the travel time is so long that it terrifies me when I think of how I could handle any emergency. Moreover, Madhu is unwilling to accompany us, so I've no idea whether we should take up the challenge or give up the idea of traveling on our own."

"I'll arrange everything. Tell me when you want to go, and do you have US visit visas?" Rama asked.

"Vimi has finalized the house purchase and may take possession in two or three weeks. So, you could say we've got a month to schedule the travel, and we don't have the visas," Mom said.

"Okay, first, I'll arrange the visit visas, and for that, I want you to fill out the online application, take a printout, and give it to me with passports. Madhu, it's better if you too apply for your visa, so you could travel anytime without waiting for the visa process," Rama said.

"Thanks; I'll give you all three passports with the duly filled printout of applications in a couple of days. What about the travel? Do you think we won't have any trouble, or shall I ask Vimi to come to take us?" Mom asked.

"I'll arrange everything; no need for Vimi to come, one or two of our executives travel to the US almost every week, and I'll book your flight with one of them, and they'll ensure you reach the destination safely," Rama said.

"Thanks is a small word for your help Rama; I'm indebted," Mom said.

"No need to thank or be grateful; whether this girl of yours marries me or not, I'll always be your son," Rama said.

Mom said, "You're my son and will always remain that, and for this girl, I suggest you kidnap her and take her to your farmhouse, and we will join you with Pandits to perform the marriage rituals." Everyone had a hearty laugh, and I grinned in annoyance.

Rama boy is working hard to win my heart; I thought, why is it not acceptable to my brain to put the past behind and enjoy life with a loving, caring, and educated man? But, somehow, my fear was so overwhelming that I was failing to put the past behind me.

After Rama left, I expressed my displeasure to Mom for asking for Rama's unnecessary help, as I could've handled everything effortlessly.

Mom said curtly, "I know what I was doing, and I don't have to seek anyone's permission to say what I want to say."

"Mom, please understand that we may have to repay the favors one day, and if you don't oblige, the relationship will be ruined beyond repair. For this reason, I strongly suggest we maintain a cordial relationship and keep a distance, so tomorrow, if I turn my back on them, you don't feel embarrassed that you used Rama," I said.

"Madhu, your attitude is confusing. On the one hand, you're saying that you don't want to marry Rama because he's a vengeful person; on the other hand, you're displaying your highly vindictive nature by refusing to bury the past. What others are seeing is that you're no different from Rama. At least that boy is remorseful, admits to his slightness, and does what he can to make you forget the past. But you wanted to punish him for his immature demeanor. Your behavior is appalling, and we're ashamed of you," Mom snarled.

The moment Mom started blasting, Dad left the room. Nowadays, he was hardly speaking; all of us tried to cheer him up, but the shock was so much that he was yet to overcome it. As a doctor, I was aware of this scenario; when a healthy person suddenly faces a dreadful disease, the first phase is denial, and then the patient goes into a state of shock for some time before coming to terms with the ailment.

My mom and dad were too precious to me, and seeing them unhappy was terrible, especially if I was the root cause of their unhappiness. So I went to Mom, hugged her, and said, "Mom, please give me a little time, and I promise to make you happy. I don't believe in any form of revenge; I'm facing anxiety and nervousness, which I must overcome before saying yes. Just a few months, Mom, your daughter is a weak person, and her fears and anxieties are frightening her, so please, be supportive."

"You have no idea, Madhu, what I'm going through. Your dad's worrisome health condition and your aversion to the wedding are driving me nuts. I used to think I didn't get frightened or nervous easily and that I could deal with any situation without wrecking my nerves. However, it was a misapprehension. I'm regularly getting panic attacks, unable to sleep, unable to eat, and living in constant fear of how I could handle if something nasty happens to my hubby. At this moment, Rama is my only hope; he could keep my hubby healthy and free me from this pathetic situation I'm in, and if you refuse to marry him, then I must prepare to lose him and my hubby," she said and started crying.

I took her in my arms and said, "Mom, I never want my family to be unhappy because of me. But, please just give me at least two or three months to say yes. I know my fears are feeble, but every night I'm getting terrible and frightening dreams that must be stopped before I can say yes. So, please, Mom, be patient and allow me to overpower these stupid thoughts that I know are unfounded. Even if something goes wrong in the future, I believe I'm competent enough to deal with that adverse situation."

Whatever you say, however, remember that pleasing other people often requires compromising your comforts, preferences, and aspirations. Your charity work exemplifies your core value of putting other people's pleasure ahead of your own. Giving to others should start at home, so please provide us with the joy we dearly seek. Take my word, sweetheart, that Rama is a bar of pure gold and will never let you down," Mom said pleadingly. "Okay, Mom," I said in a cheerful voice, and then we talked for a while about Vimi's engagement, which was heartening for all of us, and even Rama's family was very happy.

In hardly a few days, Rama gave Mom and Dad their passports with ten years of US visit visa stamps. Regarding my passport, he said it could take a few days or weeks as I'm young and unmarried, and they need to ensure that I'll return.

Mom and Dad left for the US within a month, and I moved to hospital accommodation. One day before the departure of Mom and Dad, Aunty came to our house and asked me whether I would like to move into their house. I declined the offer saying it would become inconvenient as I want to stay close to my patients. Aunty didn't press me but said daily she'll send lunch and dinner, and for breakfast, she would fill the fridge with all the required items, and I just needed to toast the bread and prepare the eggs as per my liking.

The next day around two in the afternoon, Rama called and said, "I'll have lunch with you; call me before you go to the flat."

Around 3:00, I called Rama and informed him that I was leaving for the flat, but there was no food, and I planned to have a sandwich.

"I'll be with you in a few minutes, and the food is at your door," Rama said.

A guy with two large bags was at the door; he followed me inside the flat, took out several small hot boxes, arranged them on the dining table, and left.

Rama took 20 minutes to come, and when he saw me reading a journal, he said, "How sweet, but in the future, don't wait for me as even if I want, I won't be able to be on time."

"How could I eat without the permission of the one who bought the food," I said.

"Don't be so formal, darling. Let's eat; the food is getting cold," Rama said.

While eating, I said, "Too much food, enough for two or three days, even if we eat twice a day. Would you please tell Aunty to send only one veg and one non-veg curry and some rice and bread?"

"Sure, do you need anything apart from what you said, like a bowl of fresh fruits, a sweet dish, or any specific dessert?" Rama asked.

"A bowl of fresh fruits would be fine," I said.

"Sure, my love," Rama said.

We finished our lunch as soon as possible and rushed back to the hospital.

For the next few weeks, every day, Rama had lunch with me and, on the weekend evenings, came with dinner from some popular restaurant and, after the food, forced me to dance. His kissing was increasing; it had started with one kiss, but now it had gone to three to four kisses. And the idiot in me was enjoying them instead of pushing him away or asking him to refrain from fulfilling his lewd desires.

He took me to his farmhouse on Sunday mornings to teach me horse riding. On my first visit, the trainer lectured me for half an hour on how to mount and dismount, adjust the stirrups, sit, the importance of wearing a helmet and horse-riding gear, greeting the horse, and so many do's and don'ts. Rama assigned a young filly, a big brown English thoroughbred named Grace, for my riding. Initially, it was frightening even to mount, and for the first two weeks, the horse trainer was holding the reins and walking while I was just sitting on the back, fearing for my life. Finally, in the third week, the trainer asked me to hold the reins and guide the horse. In my fifth week, I became comfortable and started enjoying the ride, and I spent at least an hour on the back of Grace. The trainer showed me the five-horse gaits and how I could master them. I began with a walk and then moved to trot; even though it was enough for me, the trainer must be under the instructions of Rama, so he pressurized me to learn all the gaits, including the gallop. I fell in love with Grace and was looking forward to my visit to meet with her.

One day during my telecon with Vimi, he mentioned his plans to take Mom and Dad for a complete checkup, as both looked lethargic and not in the best of health. He also said that his workload had increased because the management increasingly involved him in almost every operational activity. He worked 10 to 14 hours each day to cope with the workload.

The next day, during our lunch, I told Rama about my conversation with Vimi, and he asked me to tell Vimi not to worry and that in a few days, he would tell me where to take Mom and Dad for the checkup.

The following Saturday, Rama called and said, "Be ready at 7:30 to go out for dinner; the dress code is casual."

As asked, I was ready at the dot, dressed in dark blue jeans, a white silk top, blueprinted silk scarf, and rubber clogs. I was getting fond of his company every passing day and looking forward to spending time with him. My heart was constantly telling me not to be an unpleasant vindictive person. But the stupid brain was unwilling to forget the past suffering and cautioned me not to trust unless I wanted to face humiliation, ridicule, and become a laughing stock. The pressure I was getting from Mom was unbearable; Mom always stood by me for anything I asked for; even when I decided to stay at the hospital accommodation, she agreed to it and forced Dad to respect my decision. I prayed to God to help me overcome the past and accept Rama.

The calling bell announced Rama's arrival. He looked dapper in his faded jeans and light-blue round-neck t-shirt. He came in his armored Mercedes with the chauffeur, which was strange, as generally, he used to come in the BMW minus the driver.

Instead of going to a restaurant, the car took us to the airport's private terminal to board private and chartered planes. At the entrance, a guy greeted and guided us to an immigration booth; the officer at the counter stood from his chair and welcomed us. Rama fetched two passports from his pocket and gave them to the officer, who entered the details in his computer and returned them.

"Where are we going, Rama?" I asked.

"I'll tell you once we board the plane; just relax and have fun," Rama said.

We had to pass through an electronic security gate, the next step toward our journey to an unknown destination. An air hostess wearing a Manju Group badge greeted at the other side of the gate and guided us toward the exit gate to board a Gulfstream jet parked on the apron with the Manju Group name and logo printed on its body. In the cabin, two pilots welcomed us, and the air hostess who brought us to the plane guided us to the seating area. The interior was striking; there were two rows of six luxurious seats on each side, probably suitable for sleeping, and a shining door on the back of the chairs, likely leading to another seating area.

The air hostess said, "Sir, where would you prefer to sit? And what would you like to drink?"

"We'll sit in the bedroom and give us any fresh fruit juice," Rama said, and she opened the door, which had two large flatbed queen-size beds on the left and the right side, two luxurious chairs opposite each other. Rama asked me to sit on one chair and belt myself. So I sat on the door-facing chair, and Rama sat opposite me.

I thought about what kind of surprise Rama boy was trying to give me and whether he was taking me for dinner or some other exotic place to enjoy the night in revelry. Whatever, I should not be inquisitive; let him tell.

As the air hostess informed us, within a few minutes, we were airborne. When the plane reached a reasonable altitude, the captain's announcement came, and he said, "Again, I welcome you on board. Our journey to Philadelphia will take around 18 hours to cover the distance of 13,000-kilometer with a stopover at Amsterdam. We will fly at an altitude of around 39,000 feet and cruise at an aerial speed of 800 kilometers an hour. The weather conditions are excellent, and I don't expect any turbulence; however, stay belted and enjoy the flight."

Son of a gun; he's taking me to the US without informing me. Now I have to waste a lot of time shopping for essentials. And what about my inpatients?

"Sir, you should have informed me that we're going to the US; I could've prepared for the trip and organized everything," I said irately.

"Honey, I've organized everything. Two suitcases full of your clothes and everything you would need are in the cargo hold, except for your laptop, which you don't need while not working. Your assistant will take care of your patients, and when needed, she can seek help from the two highly acclaimed nephrologists in the Manju Hospital," Rama said.

"Thank you, but still, I believe you should have informed me. At least I would've carried my plastic money. It would be best in the future if you don't take me for granted; always remember I've got a life of my own," I retorted.

Noted; for your information, yesterday morning, Vimi called me, and it was a distress call, as he noticed a substantial decline in Uncle's health. It seems uncle is panting just after taking a few steps, his legs and abdomen swelled, and he's complaining of fatigue. So I decided to fly immediately and spare you from the stress you would carry till we're airborne. We'll pick up Uncle, Aunty, Vimi, and Nini from the Philadelphia airport, fly to Florida, and from the airport go straight to Mayo Clinic for Uncle's treatment and a thorough checkup of Aunty," Rama said.

Suddenly my eyes welled with tears and rolled down my cheeks. I don't know what hit me more, my mom and dad's health or Rama's gesture of helping my folks. Rama came to me, unlatched my seatbelt, took my hands in his hand, and pulled me. I stood but didn't look at him, and he cleaned my eyes and cheeks with tissue paper, hugged me, and said, "Please don't cry. Uncle will be fine, and you know that very well. I've arranged everything; my friends are waiting at the Mayo Clinic, and rest assured, he'll be seen and treated by highly acclaimed doctors."

"Thank you," I murmured.

He again hugged me, and I don't remember what had happened to me; I put my head on his chest and closed my eyes. He slowly rubbed my back and, after a while, said, "Time to have our dinner; the crew has promised to make us delighted with their choice of food," Rama said and released me, calling the air hostess and ordering dinner.

Dad was in the hospital for ten days; they repaired the valve with keyhole surgery. Vimi and Nini left on the second day of the surgery; both were under pressure for their work and studies. Finally, Dad was discharged on the morning of the 11th day. Mom's test reports were good, except for the cholesterol, which was slightly higher. We left for Philadelphia on a commercial flight; as Rama's plane returned to Hyderabad the next day, it dropped us in Florida. Vimi received us at the airport, and Rama asked him to drop him at any good hotel nearby his house, but Mom said he must stay at home, and as I expected, he didn't contest.

After dinner, we sat with our hot drinks in the living room, and Mom asked Rama, "For how long do you plan to stay, Rama?"

"I've asked Dad to send the plane tomorrow night so that I can leave the day-after-tomorrow noon or in the evening. If Madhu wants to stay for a few more days, that's fine with me," Rama said.

I said, "Mom, I'll go with Rama and come to see you in a couple of months or when convenient."

"Sure, go with Rama," Mom said.

"Tomorrow, I intend to explore New York; my office is arranging a sightseeing tour. Everyone is welcome to come," Rama said.

"I can't come as I've got to look after your uncle, so you take Vimi, Nini, and Madhu," Mom said.

"I can't come, and I don't think Nini will join. So, Rama Sir, you take Madhu with you," Vimi said.

"I want to stay with Mom and Dad. Sir, you go alone or ask your office to arrange a guide or a companion," I said, snapping.

"Madhu, there's no need for you to stay at home to look after us; you go with Rama," Mom crisply proclaimed.

The following day, a stretched limousine picked us up at 9:00 in the morning. A chirpy young Caucasian welcomed us into the limo and briefed us on the tour details – starting with a boat ride to the Statue of Liberty and ending the day by having dinner at 'The View' revolving restaurant on the 48th floor of the Marriott Marquis.

It has been more than a month since we returned from the US. Rama took me to his farmhouse every Sunday for horse riding, swimming, and a BBQ supper.

I became good at horse riding and gelled well with Grace. Before riding her, I always spent at least 15 to 20 minutes caressing and feeding her favorite food of carrots and apples, and sometimes I played with her by asking her to jog with me. Soon, I moved from walk and trot to canter and slow gallop. Rama was very encouraging and told me he hadn't seen anyone who learned to gallop in such a short period, and even the trainer said the same. I thought it wasn't me but Grace, who loved to take my commands and give me the pleasure as if I mastered the gaits. Now I don't know how I could quit riding or not seeing Grace;

her neighing sounds of joy upon seeing me became intoxicating and a stress buster.

We were only using the horse race track for our horse riding, which prompted me to ask Rama why we weren't taking the horses to the other areas of the farmhouse. He informed that occasionally they find snakes, and the possibilities are high of horses going berserk when they see the reptile; they could run fast in any direction or buckle and rear. In both cases, the rider could fall or be thrown violently.

Twice or thrice a week, Nini called to say hello and reminded me that if I wanted to see Vimi and her happy, I should marry her bro, the best eligible bachelor in the world. My fears toward Rama were lessening, particularly the weekly visits to meet and ride Grace considerably helped; his parent's love and affection was another major force in expunging the fears. However, my brain was still not comfortable with the thought of taking the plunge, but from flat refusal, it was now in contemplation mode. I believe I had arrived at a stage where a strong push from my parents and Rama's parents could result in surrender.

Whenever Rama left the flat, I sat on his chair, wept, and cursed myself for not forgetting the past and marrying him. Even though I was intelligent enough to understand that anything could happen to anyone at any moment, to have fears of Rama's abandoning me was childish. What's the guarantee that a person of my choice would not ditch me or philander? So why worry about a hypothetical scenario, and even if he does that, what difference would it make, except I would feel hurt?

Still, no one could stop me from continuing my journey of serving humanity.

This nagging dilemma of whether or not to accept Rama's proposal was becoming unbearable for me, and I was enraged at my inability to make a decision.

To come out of this stalemate, I decided not to act or behave like a weakling; I must be what I'm: confident, valiant, and intelligent. However, first, I must calm myself down and have faith that I'll make the right decision, and once I do that, I must stand by it come what may.

One day while picking my brains, I concluded that the only way to make the best-suited decision for my future life, I must go away from this environment to a place where I could spend some time in secludedness. Dad didn't take us even on a short holiday for the past several years because of his business pressures. At the same time, I was busy with my studies and never yearned for a holiday. A few weeks or a month off to a serene and nerve-invigorating place would allow me to sit in peace and decide what's best for me without the pressure of any loved ones. And for that, I mustn't go to a place where Rama could trace me and no big cities of the concrete jungle; instead, it must be a place of the natural beauty of mountains, lakes, rivers, waterfalls, and thick forests. After spending almost two weeks searching for a country of my liking, I settled on going to Gaborone, the capital of Botswana, which had a population of little over a couple of lakhs with a low crime rate. Excellent place to spend at least a few weeks, as well it would be tricky for Rama boy to trace me instantaneously and disturb my holidays.

While returning from the US, I took my passport from Rama, not for any particular reason, but why he should keep it. So one evening, I went to a travel agency that organizes visit visas to Botswana and South Africa and gave them the necessary documents and passport to get the visas at the earliest.

I got the visas within two weeks and booked a seat on a five-day Chennai bus tour scheduled to depart on Saturday evening. Then booked a flight from Chennai to Colombo and from there to Abu Dhabi by Air Lanka. From Abu Dhabi to Johannesburg by Etihad Airways, by Greyhound bus from Johannesburg to Durban, and from Durban to Gaborone by Air Botswana. It would take a lot of time and effort for Rama boy to trace my whereabouts, and I wanted to see how resourceful he was in tracking me down.

On Saturday late afternoon, I called Rama and told him, “It’s the time of the month, and I want to rest and sleep, so please don’t disturb or send food; I’ve enough food in the fridge to eat if I need.”

The bus was scheduled to depart at 10:00 at night, so I left at 8:00 in a cab and asked the driver to drop me at the railway station, which he did and left. After ensuring the cab had gone, I waited for a few more minutes; I then walked to a bylane that led to the main road and took a taxi to the bus stand.

Before the scheduled travel date, I withdrew a large sum in cash from my bank and opened an account with the Bank of Baroda, which had a branch in Gaborone. Then, with the assistance of the bank manager established internet banking and transferred a small sum to the Bank of Baroda (Botswana) Limited that I could collect by showing my passport. I also bought a 20,000-dollar bank travel card and some currency and instructed the bank manager that he shouldn't inform anyone of my whereabouts. I did all this so I didn't have to use the credit or debit cards that would reveal my whereabouts.

I reached Gaborone, exhausted not because of the travel alone; the waiting at different airports was the culprit. Nevertheless, Gaborone was a pleasant surprise, with wide streets, well-planned and clean residential areas, large green parks, and breathtaking greenery. I was pleased with my hotel, Hilton Garden Inn, located in the city's heart, with superb amenities.

The following day, I contacted a messenger service company in the US to convey and receive messages confidentially from my family. My first message was to Vimi, informing him that I was on a world tour and they need not worry about me. After that, almost every alternate day, I sent messages about my well-being and how I was having a whale of a time roaming the streets of world-famous cities. Vimi responded to my messages promptly and ended them by asking me to call him, promising he wouldn't reveal my whereabouts to anyone. Once, he informed me that Mom was mad at me and threatened that she would never speak to me if I did not call her immediately.

It was almost three weeks since I had come to Gaborone, and during the first two weeks, I had seen the entire city and its surroundings, been to Khama Rhino Sanctuary, and seen both the black and white rhinos. I had also gone to Mokolodi Park and watched giraffes, zebra, red hartebeest, sable, and gemsbok, which coexists with the indigenous fauna such as kudu, impala, hyena, and leopard. Then, finally, I traveled around the Northern Tuli Game Reserve, made up of savannah plains, riverine forests, open marshland, dramatic outcrops of sandstone, and too many elephants.

I didn't want to talk to anyone; I wanted my body and mind to feel relaxed and think about marriage and everything else when I would feel I was at ease to ponder and decide.

After I finished the sightseeing trips and got bored with the daily jogging, weightlifting, swimming, and meditation, I decided to visit a few hospitals to see how big they were and what services they offered.

While searching the internet for this purpose, I came across a German charity hospital, Bamalete Luther Hospital, located in the scenic town of Ramotswa, approximately 40 kilometers from my hotel. Best to start the day with Bamalete and then visit the other hospitals, I decided.

After breakfast the following morning, I took a cab and went to Bamalete. It was a large two-story building, and at the entrance, I saw a board mentioning the services they were offering, which weren't ample except covering the major conditions. Inside was an impressive sight, a vast reception area with a few photos of political leaders of the country; beneath the photos, the hospital's name was written in the aluminum alphabet. The brown granite tiles were shining, and the smell of phenol indicated that the area had been cleaned just a while ago. I asked the welcoming young reception girl that I wanted to meet with the hospital in-charge and inform the person that a medical doctor wanted to meet.

The receptionist spoke on the intercom with someone and guided me to a room where a wrinkled old Caucasian lady, who must be in her mid- or late seventies, was busy keying data from a file to the desktop computer.

She introduced herself as Ms. Ilana Kloss, in charge of the hospital and a non-practicing surgeon. She was very warm and welcoming, and when she learned I'm a nephrologist and holidaying in the country, she was pleased. She took me for a hospital round, showed me various wards and facilities, and said they're getting enough funding to run the hospital but not for expansion. They have a little over 100 beds, which is not enough. However, they're in touch with a few philanthropic organizations and expecting to receive soon anything between 10 to 20 million dollars, which would allow them to increase the beds, upgrade the aging equipment, and buy the needed new machinery.

When I mentioned that I work for a charity hospital, she asked me several questions: why I've decided to treat the less fortunate at a young age, how I take care of subsistence costs, and whether I've got a partner.

I informed her everything she wanted to know, and she listened with great interest. When I asked about her journey, she said, "First, let's go for lunch, and then we will spend some more time in my office with a cup of coffee and learn more about each other."

It was 12:10 pm and a little early for me to have lunch, but I couldn't refuse her invitation. I developed an instant affection toward her, probably because of her age, the agility she displayed, and her warm hospitality.

It was a neatly maintained self-service canteen. The food was a mix of Rwandan and German delicacies; overall, all the preparations were satisfactory to my taste buds. During our bite, Ilana said that the hospital provides breakfast and lunch to all staff and accommodation to non-native staff. The staff housing was a little away from downtown, in serene surroundings, with a clubhouse, jogging track, and a gym. They hired the workers only if they wanted to serve the ailing and never took anyone on board that sought employment.

After lunch, we returned to her office with coffee paper cups in our hands. While sipping the coffee, she said, "Honey, you really wanted to know about my close to 80 years of journey in this immortal world?"

"Yes, I'd like to know everything there's to know about you and your family. However, my primary interest is learning when and why you chose to serve humanity, provided it doesn't bring up any painful memories or apprehensions," I said.

"Darling, my tears have dried, and there's no fear left of hurt, physical or emotional, as I'm waiting to go into my grave, and if someone expedites that process, I would be grateful. I can tell you every step of my journey, which I haven't shared with anyone, but you wouldn't find it ear-pleasing or heartwarming. So to hear me out, you need to give me ample time, as I want to tell you everything from my birth to this date," Ilana said.

"Learning about your journey would become the highlight of my trip to this beautiful country, so please tell me, and I've as much time as you want to hear you out with utmost attentiveness and pleasure," I said earnestly.

"If you insist, honey, I'll gladly do so, as long as you have the heart to listen to human brutality and misery, but now it's time for me to return home. I work from 6:00 in the morning until lunch, around 12:00. Do you mind coming with me to my home where we could be together as long as you're tired of listening to this blabbermouth? Besides, I feel like I got my one and only stillborn daughter back, and that feeling is pushing me to ask you to spend some time with me," Ilana said sheepishly.

"I'll be pleased if you take me to your home, and I must say I'm honored that I reminded you of your daughter," I said.

"Thank you, darling; let's go," Ilana said and rose from the chair.

Ilana had a Toyota RAV4; it must have been a few years old, but its shining body and cleaned tires announced it was very well maintained. An aged Botswana driver opened the car door for us and, when seated, asked Ilana, "Ma'am, to home or some other place?"

"Eric, take us home," Ilana said.

It hardly took 10 minutes to reach the accommodation compound; a board displayed 'Staff Accommodation – Bamalete Luther Hospital' at the closed gate. After a couple of honks, a uniformed guard opened the gate, and slowly the car sailed inside. I could see on my left two rows of single-story buildings, on the right side several small cottages, and in the middle volleyball, badminton, tennis courts, and encircling the courts a walking track.

Ilana said, "Cottages are for doctors and a few senior nurses and administrative staff and those who have their families. We've studio apartments for the rest of the workers in the two buildings on my right side."

The car stopped at a far-end cottage. The facility was maintained immaculately; a broad and clean cement road on both sides, a small wooden boundary wall in front of each cottage, and a large plastic trash bucket covered with a lid placed adjacent to the wooden gate. The front lawn had evenly cut green grass, and the wooden entrance door was well-polished. The summer weather and the lovely surroundings gave a soothing effect, and the arid air filled the lungs without making the body uncomfortable.

The inside of the cottage was a view to cherish, a large hall, on one side TV lounge, and on the other side dining area. Every piece of furniture and fixture was made of gleaming wood; furniture, painting frames, wall hangings, side table lamps, and all else I could see was only wooden.

Ilana asked me to sit in the TV lounge while she changed and returned with a drink. The sofas were comfortable because of the thick foam cushions; otherwise, sitting on wooden furniture becomes painful.

Ilana entered the hall in a blue pajama and blue floral round neck top, with two coffee mugs in her hand. She sat opposite my sofa and said, "So Madhu, you want to know about my parents, how I grew up, where I studied, my professional and personal life, and anything in between till this date."

"I'd love to hear, as long as reciting your past doesn't bring back memories that you've forgotten, and recollecting them could bring grief and despair," I said earnestly.

"Madhu, I never opened up my past to anyone, including my close friends. But, since you reminded me of my daughter, who I believe could've been like you, gorgeous, talented, and with a heart of gold that feels the pain of the less fortunate, I decided to open my wounds," Ilana said.

I rose from my sofa and went to her and sat on the floor holding her legs, and said, "You're my second mother, and from now on, I'll call you Mom only, and I'll always be there for you as long as I'm alive."

"Thank you, Madhu," Ilana said and placed her wrinkled fingers on my head and slowly massaged my skull.

I said, "Mom, please tell me good things about your past, as opening up the wounds could hurt you. We all know forgiveness is divine, so it's better not to remember the unfortunate events and let them be bygones." Suddenly my heart jumped and said, "Look who's talking about forgiveness and bygones," I silently retorted, "I'm working on it – shut up."

"Madhu, go and sit on the sofa; you'll be uncomfortable on the floor after a few minutes," Ilana said.

"When I become uncomfortable, I'll go; it's giving me pleasure to sit here," I said sincerely.

"Okay fine. Now let me tell you everything from my birth to this date, what I've been through and why I've not married," Ilana said and, with a pause, started narrating her life journey.

I was born in 1933 to a wealthy Jew family in Berlin; my birth was after four brothers, and after my birth, Mom didn't produce another brother or sister for my fun. My father was a fresh and dry fruit wholesaler. We lived in an affluent neighborhood in a palatial villa. Before a couple of years of my birth, animosity against Jews increased by the day, and the only discussion elder Jews had in the synagogue was what to do to avert this situation. Mom once told me that in 1934, with the help of one of his influential friends, my father cleverly changed our identities to reflect German citizenship and Christianity as our religion. Persecution of Jews gained momentum in my birth year, but it didn't come to the doors of wealthy Jews, and according to Mom, Dad had said many a time that dare no one touch us since our documentation and money will ward off even the mighty Gestapo.

Most of the younger Jews or seniors who didn't have much to lose were migrating. But it was unthinkable to move; for people like my dad, who had a profitable running business, properties, and plenty of money in the bank. When I was ten years old, I overheard Mom and Dad's fights; Mom was desperately pleading with Dad to migrate, and he was refusing. Every night, they were fighting, Mom constantly reminding Dad we've enough cash and gold, and we could quickly establish a business in any other country where our lives were safe. Even my two elder brothers joined Mom and pressed Dad to move to the UK or another country where no antisemitism existed. But Dad didn't change his stance, though the news was filtering down that the Gestapo was picking even elder Jews and sending them to labor camps. According to Dad, the Military needed labor for the construction and was taking poor peasants, and they would never come to big cities like Berlin to hurt or arrest the wealthy Jews.

All Jews almost stopped going to synagogue, but still, elders were meeting in secret places and discussing the happenings. Soon the poor Jews started disappearing from the big cities. Either they were migrating, or the Military or Gestapo had picked them. One night Dad and Mom had a big fight; Mom called the sons, and even I was allowed to sit and listen. Mom insisted on packing the bags and going to a place where we could be safe, but Dad was unwilling to concede to Mom's pleading.

My elder brother, 21 years old, said, "Dad, our money wouldn't save us; it's better if we go to any Latin American country or the US. A few of my friends have investigated the possibility of leaving the country without any risk. They found a German who would take them to Hamburg and get a labor job in any docking vessel going to North or South America. The amount he's charging is fair, so my friends and a few families have decided to avail of his services and leave in the next two days.

I suggest we all go and if you don't want to come, please give me whatever gold and money you could provide, which would help me establish a business."

Mom interjected and said to Dad, "Let all the four boys go, and give them whatever money and Gold you could give."

"How we could stay here without our children; you're trying to break my back," Dad growled.

Mom asked my younger brothers, "Tell me do you want to go with your elder brother or stay here and get killed?"

The youngest brother, who was 14 years but looked much older because of his build, said, "I want to go as there's no future for us in this country."

We all looked much older than our age, I was barely 11 years, but I would easily pass as a 16-year-old teenager. Our above-average growth could be because of our heavily built Mom and Dad and the food intake: fresh fruits, dry fruits, cheese, meat, and seafood.

The other two brothers also decided to go with the elder brother and strived to convince me to go with them. I declined, saying I needed to stay with Mom and Dad and protect them, and they laughed at me, saying if I could save myself, it would be nothing short of a miracle, not to mention protecting our parents from any danger.

I snapped at them and said, "They're free to go to hell, but don't ask me to accompany them." Mom and Dad took my side and said, "Let her stay with us; hopefully, nothing will happen to any of us."

Dad conceded to the pressure of Mom and my brothers and said, "Tomorrow, he would bring four cheap handbags and put as many gold coins and US dollars as possible in the base of the bags. Be vigilant; take good care of your bags as that would allow you to survive anywhere in the world. I'll also give you a couple of thousand dollars that you stuff in the hidden pockets of your jackets. This money will be enough to cover all your expenses until you reach your destination."

The following day, Dad brought four different used leather handbags; they were sturdy, not very big, but capable of holding quite a lot of weight. Mom, Dad, and my brothers worked late at night and managed to open the base of the bags neatly and placed 100 gold coins, equivalent to a couple of kilos and 5,000 dollars, in each bag.

I overheard Dad telling Mom, "Are you happy now for taking my babies away from me? You've made me weak and vulnerable, and I don't think I would survive without my children for long." Dad started crying, and Mom joined him, and the wailing went on for quite a while. Then Mom said, "Ba•al *(Husband in Hebrew)*, you're telling a mother that I'm happy by sending my babies away. No, it's killing me, but I must take this poisonous pill for the greater good."

As planned, after two days, my brothers left, and to this date, I haven't seen or heard from them. In late 1943, Dad handed over his business to one of his senior employees, an honest, hardworking German Christian. He almost stopped going out of the house, as the Gestapo was picking every Jew and sending them to labor camps.

I reached puberty in the mid-1944 and turned into a beautiful young girl. In the first week of January 1945, Dad decided to stay with a retired police officer friend who promised to host and protect us for a large sum. The German military was losing everywhere, and the Russian and allied forces captured almost all the lost territories. In the last week of April, around mid-noon, we heard loud noises of several men; Dad said, "Both of you stay here until I return," and left the room, closing from outside.

Within a few minutes after dad went out, we heard gunfire and cries of pain; four Gestapo officers entered our room after a while. Mother stood before me and said, "What you want, we're Christians and law-abiding citizens."

"Shut up, you old Jew bitch. We've killed everyone in this house, and now it is your turn," the officer said and pulled out his revolver, came close to us, and fired at Mom's head, who fell to the ground with a loud noise.

My screams of fear and anger grew with tears rolling down like a waterfall. The same officer who killed Mom said, "If you don't stop screaming, I'll put a bullet in your head too." He then turned to the other officers, instructed them to wait at the door for their turn, and asked me to undress.

I started shivering from the fear and used all my strength to tell him to kill me, but I wouldn't allow him to rape me. He may have sensed that it wouldn't be an easy task for him to handle me without assistance; he called the other officers and asked them to undress and strap me to the bed with hands and legs spread. Three adults versus a child of hardly 13 wasn't a match. They raped me beside my mother's dead body, and except for crying in pain, I couldn't do anything, and when the third man entered my body, I lost consciousness.

I woke up in a makeshift hospital run by the Russian Military with a dry mouth and pain in the abdomen and vagina. There were several beds in the small room, but, except for me, there was no other patient visible, and near the door, on a small table and chair, a nurse who must have been between 35 and 40 years of age was reading a book. She came to me when she heard the creaking sound of bed as I attempted to turn and said, "Glad to see you awake; you must be thirsty, let me get a glass of orange juice for you, and then I'll sit and talk to you."

She returned with orange juice, sat on the bed, and helped me drink. Then, she took my hand in her hand and asked me whether I spoke English or only German. In a faint voice, I said, "I speak English also, but you must speak slowly." "Don't worry, my English is also bad, but I'm sure we'd be able to understand each other very well. I'm Irina Strokous, Russian military staff nurse, and what's your name?" I informed her of my name.

"Ilana, we found you in a house with several dead bodies. You're alive even though you were brutally raped by a few inhuman, vicious animals and left you bleeding; they probably thought you would die, and there was no need to waste a bullet on you. Luckily, when our men were passing through the street in front of your house, a good Samaritan informed them that a few hours back, Gestapo entered your house and probably killed everyone as he heard gunshots. Our guys found every person in the house was shot dead, except you, in a critical condition. Our doctors worked very hard to save you, and thanks to their timely care, you're now fine. It would take at least ten days to recuperate fully, but you're out of danger," Irina said.

"Thank you, but you should have allowed me to die," I said faintly and started crying.

"Don't say such things, and don't cry. You deserve to enjoy life, put everything behind you, and make a fresh start. Please tell me about yourself and your family and whether you have any close relatives with whom you could stay?" Irina said.

"My father was a Hungarian Jew who migrated to Germany when he was hardly 14 years old and worked for a small fruit vendor. When he was in his fifth year of employment, the owner died. He didn't have any children, and it wasn't possible for his aged wife to run the business, so she sold the shop to my dad for whatever money he had. With his dedication, hard work, and honesty, he developed the business and became one of the country's largest fresh and dry fruit merchants. He married a Hungarian immigrant Jew girl when he was 24 years old.

"I had four elder brothers, who all left a couple of years ago and probably went to America, but I don't know, as since they left, we never heard from them. When things became difficult for the Jews to remain in business, Dad handed it over to one of his honest employees to run it and take 50 percent of the profits. This January, Dad decided to move to the house of a retired police officer friend willing to host and protect us for a considerable amount of money. Unfortunately, I believe he and his family were also massacred, along with my parents. Now I don't know where to go and what to do with my life," I said and started crying.

"Do you know who knew you were staying with this police officer, and you're a Jew?" Irina asked.

"No one knew except the German employee, Justin Hamann, running Dad's business. He was coming at least twice a week to take Dad's signature on checks, as Dad didn't give him check-signing authority. Since my brothers left, Dad kept me informed of everything that was happening on the business front, and most of the days after school, I went to the company to acquire knowledge of our business. Dad maintained an excellent cash balance in the bank as a buffer to cover contingencies, like delays in receiving payments from the debtors or placing substantial orders due to unexpectedly high demand. Without money support, the business could collapse, and Dad told me Justin had no money to run the business, so there was no way he would slaughter his golden goose and possibly destroy his life. Apart from this, he's around 60, a loner, and stays with his ailing mother.

"My hunch is that either our host or Dad may have suffered from a brain fart during one of their bottle-hitting nights, which a domestic help may have heard and reported to the Gestapo. The other scenario could be one of Dad's business rivals would've got the knowledge from someone," I said.

She didn't ask any further questions but asked me to rest and said she would meet me at dinner. After that, Irina spent at least a couple of hours with me every day, mostly talking about war-related issues. Daily, she took me for a walk and made sure I ate healthily to help me recover as quickly as possible. When I questioned her about her family during one of our chats, she answered, "Almost every close relative died a natural death or war has perished them. And barely three weeks ago, my husband, an officer in the Russian infantry, was killed by enemy gunfire. I'm traumatized by this scenario and don't want to return to Russia, where I've no friends or family left except for a parent's dilapidated house. I feel it would be better to start a new life in a new country where I could earn decent money and live peacefully.

"I'm a certified nurse, so finding work anywhere in the world is simple. I intend to go to the United Kingdom since they desperately need nurses, as most nursing personnel died during the war. But it is risky because if I get caught, my military will kill me, and I don't have money to bribe the guards, cover the travel cost and stay in a B&B for a few days. I still have a few weeks to arrange the cash; otherwise, I must go back or jump the boundary wall without thinking of the consequences."

"If you give me 10 or 15 days, I'm sure I could give you whatever money you need, and I beg you to take me with you as I also don't want to stay here, where I lost my parents and where I got raped just beside the dead body of my mom," I said pleadingly.

"Honey, it would be a pleasure to take you with me, and I promise to take care of you till my last breath. I got married very late, and in the 11 years of my married life, I had four miscarriages, and I believe my pre-menopause started as, for the past three months, I missed my periods, which meant no babies of mine. So, please be my baby and come with me, and I'll look after you and make sure you continue your studies and go to a medical college and become a doctor," Irina said earnestly.

I hugged her with tears rolling down my cheeks and said, "Thank you, Mom."

"My sweet baby, you don't have to express gratitude, and in fact, I should be grateful that you're allowing me to be your guardian, which will give a purpose to my life," Irina said and held me tight in her arms. I felt the same warmth and comfort that I used to get from my mother's cuddle.

After a couple of minutes, Irina released me from her hold and said, "Tomorrow morning, a doctor will check you and hopefully sign for your discharge. Furthermore, I've taken permission for you to stay with me until you become physically fit to go out and find a foster house. We're in a school building, using it as a makeshift hospital and for the storage of the arsenal; it is under military police guard with orders to shoot any unauthorized intruders. Getting out of this building and coming in is impossible without a pass issued by authorized personnel. Once we're out in the open, instead of searching for your new accommodation, we'd go to your home, fruit shop, bank, or wherever you want to arrange 2,000 dollars, 1,000 for the bribe, another 1,000 for travel, and around two or three weeks' stay in a B&B."

"Hopefully, arranging the money won't be any problem," I said. I knew Dad had plenty of money in his bank account. Also, there's one suitcase in our bedroom that Dad brought a few months ago, which both Dad and Mom guarded with an eagle eye, and I was confident that it contained either gold or US dollars. Even if I didn't find the suitcase, I was optimistic that I could get the required amount from the bank because I had met with the bank manager several times, a good friend of Dad who was very cordial to us. I could pressure him to give me at least a loan if he did not allow me to withdraw.

The following day I was discharged; Irina took me to her room and asked me to rest as I still needed to recover fully. The room had two single steel beds covered with soft fiber cotton mattresses, white cotton bed sheets, and no bedside tables or lamps, and I could see a handbag beneath Irina's bed. Aside from the two cots and Irina's personal effects, there was nothing in the room to engage in; no books, magazines, or even a radio. It was a punishment to be confined to this hole in the wall in the name of a room, but I had no choice but to rest, which I did by throwing myself on the bed and closing my eyes, believing my body was getting rest. Every morning and evening, Irina assisted me in doing several exercises and jogging to ensure that my energy levels were optimal to undertake a possibly dangerous sea and land journey of days. During her absence, I was doing push-ups, squats, and sit-ups in the room and soon realized that this was the best way to kill time and be physically strong. Inside a week, I trusted that I could fight with a bull and was sufficiently fit to walk miles without hearing the cries of muscles and bones for mercy.

On the eighth evening, Irina said, "Honey, good news, I got the passes to go out with you to hunt for a foster home. The best part is that we don't have to go with a military escort, as the officers believe I'm trustworthy and only interested in helping the kid."

The following day, we left early in the morning and reached home in under an hour via train and bus. The main gate was locked, but the wicket gate opened when we pushed it. Even after shouting whether anyone was inside, no response came. So, after waiting a few minutes, we decided to go to my room. The room door was opened, and still, the blood smell was in the room. My bed had a large patch of bloodstain, and even on the floor, I could see my mom's bloodstains. The suitcase beneath Dad's bed was there, but it had a small brass padlock. I looked for the key but couldn't find it anywhere, and as a last resort, I checked Dad's jacket and found a tiny key in the inside pocket. The key worked, and when I opened the suitcase, it was a shocking sight. Six plastic boxes containing gold coins could easily be more than 10 kilograms and stacks of 20 US dollar bills.

I asked Irina to count the currency as I wanted to pack my belongings. Before I could finish packing, I heard Irina saying, "Holy shit, it's 30,000 fucking dollars; you could buy the whole world with this gold and currency."

She locked the suitcase, gave me the key, and said, "Hurry, we must leave before anyone comes, or else we may have to deal with an unpleasant situation."

When we came out, Irina suggested we go to Central Railway station, rent a locker, and dump the suitcases, as roaming around with it could be nothing but asking for trouble. Her suggestion was excellent, so we took a bus and went to Berlin Hauptbahnhof, and with my identity document that I had collected from the house, I rented a large locker for one week and stored the suitcases. Before leaving the house, I took out one bundle of 2,000 dollars and gave it to Irina. She refused to take the money, but I said, "I want you to pay all the bills, and we've lots of expenses to cover till we reach England." I had to thrust the bundle into her inner jacket pocket, which she unwillingly accepted.

From the railway station, we headed to Dad's place of business. Justin greeted us warmly and expressed his pleasure in seeing me alive, especially when the authorities informed him that all the house occupants had been found dead. Then, after thanking Irina for looking after me, he said, "Ilana, let me update you on the business. We immediately need finances to pay the suppliers and staff if we want to continue to operate. I know we've got a substantial amount in the bank, but I'm not authorized to withdraw, and neither are any children except your parents. The bank has informed me that you and your brothers are beneficiaries in the event of your parent's death. As per the written instruction of your father, the bank should distribute the funds equally once the children reach adulthood. If a kid visits the bank as an adult, they should pay only one-fifth of the held funds and keep the remaining funds until other siblings show up. If any amount remains unclaimed in the bank account after 50 years, it should be donated to a Jew NGO.

Given this scenario, we didn't have a choice but to sell the company, and we were fortunate that we were able to find a buyer who was willing to pay a reasonable price. I've talked to a lawyer who had agreed to organize the sale under the bank's supervision. Initially, the bank refused to be a party to this transaction, but yesterday they agreed when they understood the situation. The legal sales paperwork will be completed in a couple of days, and once ready, the bank will sign on behalf of the deceased, collect the sale proceeds, and pay the dues to suppliers and employees. The balance amount will be credited into the company's account. Would you like to witness the signing of the sales agreement?"

I said, "From here, I'll go to the bank and find out whether they need me to be present and a few other things."

After spending a few more minutes with Justin, discussing his and my plans for the future, we left for the bank. The bank manager was pleased to see me alive, reiterated what Justin had informed us, and asked whether he could help me in any way.

I informed the manager what had happened to me and how I got saved by the Russian Military. Then I asked him whether there was a way I could get 20,000 UK pounds, as I intend to go to the UK to settle down because this place is causing anxiety attacks and nightmares. He agreed to give me an interest-based loan of 10,000 UK pounds against my share of the inheritance I would receive upon reaching adulthood. I asked for more, but he didn't agree to my request citing bank rules. Finally, after signing various loan documents, I requested him to transfer the amount to their UK branch or any other UK bank to collect the money by showing my identity documents. He said he could do that and transfer the funds to Barclays Bank through a bank in any other country, which is time-consuming, and it could take a couple of months or more for me to receive the amount.

After receiving the funds' transfer slip, I asked the manager whether he knew anyone who could take us safely to the UK. He said he knew a Croatian who could be of help. He had a travel company as a front, but his main business was the trafficking of young girls from all European countries. Now he's seventy-plus, confined to his home, but I'm sure he knows people who could help. I'll give you a letter requesting his assistance, and if he can help you, he'll, just as I've helped him several times by bending the bank regulations."

I thanked him and requested that he give me the letter and his address.

Once we were out of the bank, Irina told me, "You're smart, Ilana, and I'm impressed that you've secured us from an adverse situation if we get robbed or lose the suitcase – thank you."

We met with Stipe Cukrov, the Croatian; he must be pushing 70 and was frail and coughing.

After reading the letter, he said, no issues, he'll send us to a man who'll take us safely to Hamburg and put us on a commercial vessel sailing to London port. "The transporter fee was 1,000 US dollars, but I'll ask him to charge you only 500 dollars; is that okay with you?" he asked. We said it was okay with us, and then he said we don't need any papers, but just in case of an unexpected check, you must carry documents of any country and be on the ship as kitchen help. When he learned Irina did not have any papers, he asked us to go and see a man with his letter to make the papers and then come to see him. The following day, we went to the man who had a photo studio. After going through Stipe's letter, he said it would take a few hours as first he needed to take Irina's photo and then prepare the citizenship document. His fee was 500 dollars, but we could pay anything since we came with his mentor's letter. We roamed the streets, bought clothes for either of us, dropped them at the railway station locker, and went to the photo studio. Irina's German citizenship documents were ready, identical to my papers. It was impossible for any person even to guess them as fakes. We paid him 200 dollars, and he accepted with a smile and thank you.

We then went to Stipe, who gave us a letter addressed to one Patrik Cvetko and the address of his shop. It was a small grocery shop, and on the cash counter, a bald and obese man was sitting with a magazine. When he said he was Patrik, we gave him Stipe's letter, and after reading it, he asked us for our papers. He reviewed them casually and asked when we wanted to go. When we said ASAP, he said the latest he would take us after two days, as some more people are coming tomorrow and the following day. His charges usually are 1,000 dollars per person, but Stipe had asked him to charge us 500 each. He had no problem taking less; however, if he had to wait for the ship's arrival, he would charge 20 dollars per day per person. We agreed to pay all his charges, and he asked us to come after two days, and he needed the money before letting us board his bus.

Without paying a bribe to guards, we came out with passes on our departure date, took a bus to the central rail station, collected our suitcases, and went to Patrick's shop by cab. Patrick took us to a road behind his shop and asked us to board a parked beat-up 12-seater bus, but before that, he took the agreed amount of 1,000 dollars from us. Eight young boys boarded the bus, and once they settled, the bus sailed toward its destination. Within 20 minutes, we were on a highway leading to Hamburg, and without any stop or bus breakdown, we reached the journey's end in approximately five hours. We stayed in a cheap hotel near the seaport for three days before boarding a British cargo ship as assistants to the cook, and the young boys got on the vessel as cargo handlers. I saw the vessel captain taking money from

Patrick, which was a relief; the captain and some more workers on the ship knew the purpose of our traveling to London.

After five days at sea, we arrived at the London commercial dock, where the captain gave us passes to visit the city for a three-day break. Toward the end of our voyage, when we were only a few hours away from docking, we asked the cook whether he knew where we could find inexpensive lodging. He informed us that central London was swarming with American soldiers, and finding a single room in a hotel or B&B was exceedingly challenging. However, he knows someone who could arrange a room in a house for less money than the B&B would charge. We obtained the address of the real estate agent, who was primarily dealing with the sailors with whatever they required, including lodging.

The real-estate dealer informed us that the accommodation was on Baker Street. It was on the back of a mansion, and the owner charged three pounds per week, including breakfast for single occupancy and four pounds per week for two persons. It was still cheaper when compared with a small hotel room. We agreed to see the rooms, and we will take them; if they're to our liking.

While walking toward Baker street, we noticed very few houses were in their original condition, either razed to the ground or cracked due to German bombings. Finally, we walked to an area where many large mansions were in their original condition.

He took us to a mansion with a 'For-sale' signboard at the gate. The broker informed us that the owners are an elderly couple who wanted to relocate to a nursing home, but they'd been unable to find a buyer for long due to the war.

The units were old but well maintained, so we agreed to take one unit for two weeks. The broker took us to the owners, who were possibly in the late seventies. After taking the dollar equivalent to eight UKP, they checked our papers and gave us the key.

The following day, Irina and I went to the Immigration Department seeking permanent residence in England and were interviewed, or, better to say, grilled, for over two hours by an older man who was rather impolite. They brought a Russian-speaking guy to ensure that Irina was a Russian, brought a Jew to speak with me in Hebrew, and then got a medical doctor to confirm Irina's claim of being a qualified and trained nurse. After the probing was over, we had to wait at the reception for more than 30 minutes, and then an elderly lady came and took us to a room where a plump middle-aged lady was sitting. She rose from the chair, shook hands with Irina and me, and said, "Ilana, I'm pleased to inform you that we've decided to grant British nationality to you and your guardian Irina. Please wait a while in the waiting hall, and we will give you temporary papers confirming your details and nationality. Proper documents will be mailed to you when you give us your photographs."

We returned to our room, happy and content, and decided to go to the nearest branch of Barclays Bank the following day to open an account and collect the transferred amount.

The next day we opened two accounts, one for me and one for Irina. We got a little over 21,000 UK Pounds for 28,000 dollars, and I deposited 2,000 pounds in Irina's account and the remaining pounds and gold I deposited in my account. The bank was unwilling to open my account as a minor, but they agreed when we explained what I had gone through and proved that I was educated enough to handle my account independently. However, they still put a rider that I could draw only a limited amount, and for withdrawal of a large amount, I must meet with the manager with my guardian. Irina wasn't happy with my gesture, as she wanted only 100 pounds to be deposited in her account, refundable upon receiving her salary. Regarding the amount transferred from Berlin, the attending lady officer informed us that it could take 45 days to three months.

Within the next few days, I got admission to a private school. Irina got an operating room nurse job in a government hospital because of her extensive experience. The bus was the medium of transportation for us, and we nearly settled, except for a dwelling, as living in a single room, with bare walls was painful for me.

In the evening, Ilana prepared food for dinner and lunch, never allowed me to enter the kitchen, and wanted me to focus on my studies. One day while having our dinner, I said, "Can we move to a bigger place as this one-room accommodation is not comfortable for a permanent stay."

"For the past few days, I was also thinking about the same. This house is for sale, and it's not only at a decent location, but you could get a regular income to cover the monthly grocery expenses. I believe you should buy this property, and since it's a desperate sale, I'm sure you would get a killer deal. Moreover, there's one more advantage to buying this property; besides the six units, sizable open space is available, which we could use to construct another ten spacious units with better amenities. I would grab this opportunity if I were you, as money sitting in the bank will only devalue," Irina said.

"You're an experienced person and my mom, so whatever you think is right. I'll go by your suggestion; just tell me how to move forward." I asked.

"Negotiating with an old couple could make us uneasy, and at the same time, throwing our money is also bad. So I suggest, tomorrow we meet with Mike, the real estate guy, and ask him to show us some decent properties, which would give us a fair idea of the prices and then put a reasonable offer for this house," Irina said.

The real estate guy showed us several properties, but nothing close to the mansion's beauty and location, and the prices were between 2,000 and 5,000 pounds. Considering this and Mike's insistence that we buy the mansion, we told him we could go for it if he could get us a good deal.

Mike said, "The owners had two sons, and both of them died in the First World War; since they're not in the best of health and no one is there to look after them except me, they want to move to a nursing home at the earliest. They have been trying to sell it for 8,000

GBP for two years now, but no one has even made a counteroffer. I'll check with them and get back to you, but rest assured, the property is worth even 8,000 pounds."

They agreed to sell for 6,000 pounds with all the furniture, fixtures, and even kitchen equipment and utensils, and within a few days, I had the property in my name, and in a week, the owners moved out to a nursing home.

I pushed Irina often to find a man and settle down, but she wasn't interested, as all her past relationships left a bitter taste in her mouth. It seems all of them were smokers and heavy drinkers, and after getting high, they physically abused her. And the man she married was okay but a miser. Still, she tolerated him but had fought almost every day as he kept his money safe in a bank instead of at least part-shouldering the house running costs. Finally, she was at peace when both of them had to join the military and part ways; after a long time, she had tasted the life of single status and decided to continue to enjoy her freedom as long as she was alive.

I was in my third month without menses; I didn't understand why, so I asked Irina, and she said, most likely, you're pregnant. So the following day, I went with Irina to the hospital for a checkup, and the test confirmed that I was carrying. The next four months were a nightmare. I was uneasy most of the time, failing to go to school and neglecting to catch up with my studies at home. Then, one night when I was in my seventh month, I suddenly developed acute abdominal pain, and we rushed to the hospital; while the doctors were checking, the placenta ruptured, and I delivered a still baby girl. After the miscarriage, I decided to focus on my studies and devote maximum time to becoming a surgeon, per Irina's wishes. She had developed extreme respect for the professionalism and skills of British surgeons.

Thanks to Irina, I became a medical surgeon with an FRCS degree from England's Royal College of Surgeons. My first job was in a government hospital. For over three years, I worked in the same hospital, and one day Irina said, "You must set up your clinic, and daycare unit for minor surgeries, at Harley Street. We've enough money to buy an old clinic and renovate it or buy a floor in a good building and furnish it according to our requirements. You could go to any private hospital for major surgeries and pay them for using their facilities. If you're unfamiliar with Harley Street, allow me to educate you: wealthy individuals worldwide flock to Harley Street for medical treatment. Too many talented doctors in every discipline who want to earn lots of money have established their clinics and daycare units on Harley Street. Think about it, and if you give me the go-ahead, I'll organize everything."

The idea of having my clinic was very appealing. Moreover, my gold and property value had increased manifold, which meant I had enough money to gamble. So I gave the go-ahead. Irina found a Daycare Surgical unit for sale; the surgeon was above 65 and desperate to take retirement in Cyprus's warm weather, where he had a luxurious sea-facing bungalow. He was selling the building and the clinic; however, his asking price was very high but not unreasonable, considering a profitable running practice.

He also wanted to help the buyer by working until the patients were comfortable with the new surgeon. Irina smartly negotiated a reasonable price, less than 25 percent of the asking price, and I bought it.

Within a few weeks of purchase, I started working in the clinic. The receptionist pushed the patients toward me, informing them I was a young, dynamic surgeon with impressive qualifications and commendable skills. I forced Irina to resign and join me, which she did, and it proved an excellent decision, as she was methodical and believed in perfection.

My patient inflow went through the roof in less than a year, and even after hiring two assistant surgeons, I had to spend almost six hours in the operation theater. Irina's health was admirable; she ran in the clinic from morning to evening and spent the evening in the kitchen for at least one or two hours; even though I insisted on hiring a cook, she refused. She was nearing 60, but everyone would pass her for 45. Like her, I refused to marry or enter into some form of relationship because of an unpleasant occurrence. While doing my internship, I was dating Bob, a senior doctor who got smitten with my beauty or whatever he saw in me. He took me for dinner a few times but never invited me to his pad or expressed any desire. Then, one weekend he asked me to have dinner at his apartment. My feelings toward him were mixed, so I discussed them with Irina, as I was sure the dinner wouldn't end with drinks and food. She said, "Go, girl, have fun, and there's nothing wrong with checking his virile abilities, but come back no matter how late, as I won't sleep until you return."

Bob had mentioned that he was living in a two-bedroom apartment, sharing with another doctor, who would attend the dinner with his girlfriend. At the suggested time, I was at his pad and met with his friend, whom I often saw in our hospital corridors; his girlfriend was also a doctor working in another hospital. We had a few glasses of red wine and then had our Mexican food dinner brought from an eatery. After dinner, everyone had a peg of brandy and talked for a few minutes about work, the two armistices Germans signed in France and Berlin, etc. Then, his friend said goodnight to us and went to his room with his girlfriend. My host said, "Can I show you my bedroom?" I agreed and went with him to his room, and instead of showing me the room that had nothing to show, he closed the door, took me in his arms, and kissed me. We kissed passionately for a few minutes, then he said, "Is it okay to make love?" And I nodded. He stepped back, removed his clothes, and walked toward me naked, and I don't remember what had happened to me; I started shouting no, no, no, my whole body shivered uncontrollably with a panic attack, and I fell to the ground unconscious.

I had no idea how long I was unconscious, but I woke up on my host's bed wrapped in a blanket; the three doctors watched me with worried faces. Then finally, my friend asked me how I was feeling. I looked at them for a while and said, "I believe I'm fine now."

My host's friend and the girl left the room, saying they would be back in a moment with a hot cup of coffee.

"Do you have the strength to explain why you got frightened and so furiously reacted, even though I took your consent?" Bob asked.

"When I was young, I had a bad experience with an animal disguised as a sweet young boy, and I believe I should see a psychiatrist to overcome my fears. I'm sorry for spoiling your night, which was beyond my control," I said. If I had told him the truth, everyone in the hospital would know how terrible my situation was, and while the plight of gang-raped women would have earned a lot of symbolic sympathies, I would have been reviled and looked down on upon behind my back.

"Not to worry about anything; as long as you're okay, nothing matters. After our coffee, I'll drop you at your home on my motorbike," he said and went out, probably to check the coffee status. He was in a hurry to get rid of me, and I assumed he'd never want to meet me again.

When I reached home, I found Irina watching an American cowboy movie on the TV. She switched off the TV and said, "I wasn't expecting you so early; is everything alright, darling?"

"Everything is fine, I want to sleep now, and tomorrow I'll tell you the complete dinner saga," I said and went to my bedroom.

The following day, I told Irina the after-dinner details, with a supplement I'm sure Bob would never meet with me again. Unfortunately, my assumption was spot on, as he never met me again, and even when we crossed each other in the hospital corridors, he didn't bother to say hello or ask me about my health.

Irina constantly asked me to find another boyfriend, and one day I told her categorically, "I want to stay single as long as I'm alive, as I'm sure I wouldn't be able to enjoy the copulation. And I wouldn't approach a shrink to treat me as the torment of the brutal rape, and the near-death experience would never fade away."

Irina said, "Darling, give yourself some time and find another decent man. You're lucky that he showed you his true color before you could have settled with him. Look for another considerate, educated man who would stand with you when you need him."

I never attempted to enter into another relationship, nor did anyone chase me. Irina and I were happy with our routines, earning excellent money and buying all our desired luxuries. She looked after my needs in a way that even my biological mother wouldn't have done. As a result, I never missed anything in the wardrobe, on the dining table, ornaments, vehicles, or other luxuries.

Irina died when I was 44; even though she was fit as a fiddle in her late seventies, she couldn't fight a pneumonia attack. On the one hand, life became very lonely and boring; on the other hand, it became a massive pain. Irina cared for the house, cooking, laundry, and grocery shopping; I never had to worry about such responsibilities. After her death, I hired a full-time cook-cum-housemaid, paying a handsome salary. However, she was good only as a cleaner; her food preparation was awful. Still, I had to work like a mule to attend to various house chores that Irina was taking care of, resulting in pangs of depression and loneliness. All my worldly possessions could not give any pleasure or even assist me in overcoming the state of mind I found myself in. I had a beautiful mansion, numerous luxury automobiles, a large walk-in closet full of expensive outfits and accessories, an extensive diamond jewelry collection, a money-minting clinic, and a few million pounds in the bank.

But no worldly possession was of any use because my mental health made me feel like I was broken from the inside. I decided to bring a change, bought a luxury apartment in a newly built building, and got it furnished with the assistance of an interior decorator. The new environment was good only for a few weeks, but I found myself in the same boat again. For two years, I struggled, but my mental health further deteriorated. Finally, when I was 47, I decided to quit my practice and serve the needy in a developing country. While hunting for the right place to work, I saw an ad in a German daily newspaper from this hospital seeking doctors in various disciplines who believed in serving humanity and not aiming for a life of plenty. I sent my job application and got an offer within a few days, with a meager salary. I sold my house, practice, cars, and jewelry, and from that money, I donated a large sum to an Israel-based Jew NGO and relocated to this place. After joining the hospital, I noticed many areas that needed improvement, but they didn't have money for any development. So I decided to keep a little over a million pounds and donate the rest to the hospital. I put several conditions to offering my donation. I asked the management to construct a housing compound for the medical staff, buy the latest equipment, increase the number of beds, and change my employment agreement to a permanent lifelong job with a driver and a housekeeper-cum-cook. The hospital management gladly accepted and asked me to spend all my donation amount as I wanted, which I did and improved the facility to my liking and needs. Within a few years of employment, the hospital CEO retired, and I was asked to take his position; since then, I've been running this hospital; however, I stopped operating eight years ago.

The sad parts of my life are the four coward brothers who ran away to save their lives instead of standing before their aged parents. For this reason, I developed so much hatred for them that I never went to Berlin to claim my share of the inheritance, as I didn't want to take a chance of coming across the gutless scumbags. And the subsequent tragedy of my life was losing my daughter.

The bright side of my journey was meeting Irina, who made me what I'm today. She was everything to me and looked after me like her own daughter. Her death devastated me so much that I wouldn't have survived if I hadn't come here.

It's my journey thus far, and now I'm at a stage where, day by day, I feel like an old burned-up log that's turning into ashes; so every day, I'm begging *Adonai*, the Lord, to call me while I'm in my senses and on my feet."

"Please don't say that; you'll live for long and continue to serve humanity. And, thanks for sharing your journey, which has crushed my heart and soul into bits. But, unfortunately, everywhere, the story of humans is the same. The mighty rogues of any society hurt innocent people busy earning their living. Thus, I don't understand why God doesn't come to the rescue of the innocent or stop sending such brutes, murderous, barbaric humans to this world," I said.

"Madhu, I also don't understand God's business. I wasn't a Jew by choice, and to this date, I've no idea the merits or demerits of my faith and why some people have to kill us because we don't follow their religion. I've serious doubts about the existence of God, and I believe that it was created by humans to overcome the fear of diseases and death. Irina and I discussed religion for hours, read many books about atheists and theists, and studied almost all the faiths on the planet. She was a hardcore atheist, and I had also never been to a synagogue since I left Berlin. Irina was convinced that God is a human fabrication, probably by some good souls who believed that they could save the oppressed by bringing fear of punishment into the minds of ruthless scoundrels. I donated plenty of money to a Jew NGO, not because I'm a Jew but because Jews were killed, and their livelihood was taken away under fabricated beliefs spread by the people who benefited from such persecution. More than six million Jews were butchered, but no God came to their rescue, so I'm confused, and to this date, I've not made up my mind on the existence or absence of a supreme power controlling the world," Ilana said.

It was about four o'clock in the afternoon, and I thought Ilana might want to rest, and I should leave.

I said, "Thanks for lunch, and meeting you will go down as one of the best days of my life. Would you please call a cab so I can leave and allow you to take a rest, as I'm sure you have sacrificed your siesta time in talking to me?"

She didn't respond and instead said, "For how long you've planned to stay here?"

"I came intending to spend at least one or two months, but within 20 days, I've seen everything that Botswana had to offer, and I was thinking to either go back or find some activity to keep me busy for a few weeks. And for this purpose today, I came to your hospital," I said.

"I can offer you a temporary position to supervise the Hospice Department and assist the Irish nephrologist, loaded with patients and working ten or more hours daily. However, the job offer has a condition; you must work at least a month and stay with me," Ilana said with a chuckle.

"I don't want a job; just allow me to work, as I'm sure I would learn a lot from an experienced nephrologist and gain valuable experience in treating patients in the Hospice Ward. I'll spend as much time in your house as you want, but staying with you means causing you too much inconvenience," I said.

"Madhu, you would brighten my days and nights with your presence in the house. I want to talk to you, cook for you, and take you fishing or on cross-country rides. If you think staying with this old worn-out dame would be a pain for you, I'd still love to meet with you every day in the hospital," Ilana said.

"It would be a pleasure to spend with you as much time as you could spare, but I'm concerned my round-the-clock presence in the house could become a bother for you," I said.

"No darling, your stay would bring the zeal to live for some purpose; otherwise, just imagine the life of an old woman nearing her eighties, living alone. At times, the loneliness becomes so depressing that I start thinking about ending my life, as nothing makes any sense anymore. Everything has become meaningless, the money, the house, the car, the work, or even the food. So I'm just waiting for the day when I take my last breath; every moment you would give me will make me happy beyond words," Ilana said earnestly.

I hugged her and said, "I'd love to be with you as long as I'm in Botswana. Tomorrow morning, I'll check out from my hotel and come here."

"No, darling, I'll come with you to collect your luggage, but we've to wait for my housekeeper-cum cook, who'll come around 5:30," Ilana said.

"Fine with me," I said with a grin.

"Great, come with me, and I'll show you your room. You rest till the cook comes, and I'll also lie down for a while," Ilana said.

It's been almost three weeks since I stayed with Ilana, who was pampering me like her own baby. On the weekends, Eric took us fishing or on jungle rides leading to some tiny village of 50 or 100 houses and organized our lunch at the house of the head of the village. I tasted all the Botswana delicacies and loved the Braai lamb (barbeque), Seswaa goat meat, and the goat meat stew.

Every minute I spent with the knowledgeable nephrologist or with the patients of the Hospice Department was well worth my time in the hospital. The Irish nephrologist was a widower in his late 50s or early sixties. He joined the hospital after his wife's death due to cancer. He was a very accomplished and hardworking professional who worked for 10 to 12 hours nearly every day, six days a week. In every way, I learned a lot from him: his dedication, patience in listening to patients, detailed explanations of their health situation and treatment options, etc.

The Hospice Department was another learning experience. All patients were on deathbeds due to terminal diseases or old age. It was heart-wrenching to sit with them and give false hope of convalescence. But you must do what's needed; they knew that I was lying, and they were at the edge; still, they felt momentarily happy to hear my assuasive comments.

Daily, I came to the hospital with Ilana and spent the morning assisting the nephrologist and two or three hours in the Hospice Department after lunch. Ilana didn't change her timings of coming and going to the hospital; in the afternoon, Eric took me home.

I failed to remove Rama from my system; whenever I was unoccupied, I found him in front of me, smiling. Why this was happening, I had no idea. All my apprehensions had vanished; the visionary chamber of my body known as the brain had also taken a back seat, and it, too, seemed to be yearning to see him. Yet, every day, it was like another day had passed; he didn't show up; the eyes were paining with the constant stare at the door to see him walk in. I should have brought at least the chair on which he used to sit and pleads for forgiveness; sitting on it and remembering him would've lessened my pain. Someone should inform him how much he's missed; my eyes were locked on the door, waiting for him to step in and take me into his arms. I suppose I've lost him, but he'll forever remain in me as grief that I never wish to go away till my last breath.

He claimed that no matter where I was in the world, he would find out in no time. But, of course, it was all rhetoric, and in the most likelihood, he had forgotten about me. I presume he's right in ditching an uninteresting doctor like me who knows nothing about anything other than diseases; he must have chosen and married an attractive, polished, cultured, and gorgeous girl from a well-off family. But whenever I thought about him, an excruciating pain trickled through my body. Every day, increasingly, the eyes searched for him more and more, and the heart ached to see him and tell him to put the past behind and make a fresh beginning with love, care, and respect for each other. Being the obstinate jerk I am, I squandered my chance and will always regret not surrendering when his parents wanted me to be convinced for the plunge. I had no idea why my brain refused all my loved ones' pleas to forgive and why now every part of my body aches to see and embrace him, never to let him go. Every night reminded me that one more day had passed and he hadn't shown up, and before the brain shut for sleep, my uncontrollable falling of tears soaked the pillow.

When I arrived home from work one afternoon, a shiny black Mercedes was parked outside the gate. A chauffeur in a clean white suit and a security officer wearing a belt holding an automatic weapon were standing erect beside the vehicle. I asked the gatekeeper about the visitor, and he said, "A man has come to see Ilana Ma'am." I thanked him and wondered who could be the person but failed to figure it out.

I entered the house thinking the visitor must be a government official, or else he wouldn't come with a bodyguard. But, when I saw the man, my heart stopped beating, and my feet froze. Then, I heard Ilana's voice with a laugh, "Here is your girl, happy?"

With a herculean effort, I managed to bring a smile and said, "Hello Rama Sir, a real surprise to see you here; I hope all is well." He had lost weight; his several days' unshaven face looked rugged and drained out of the blood. Still, he looked very handsome in his jeans, half sleeves, white V-neck sweatshirt, and sports shoes.

He looked at me with wide eyes and said, "Now I'm fine, and everyone at home is also doing well. How about you? How have you been doing?"

Before I could respond, Ilana interrupted and said, "You have to excuse me for a few minutes to fetch tea and something to munch." She left the hall, even though I asked her to sit and I would get everything.

"Rama, Sir, I'm doing fine. Ilana must've informed you that I'm working at her charity hospital. I gained invaluable experience working with an Irish nephrologist. I also looked after patients in Hospice Department; it was a heart-wrenching and soul-crushing experience, giving the false hope of revival to the patients, even though they knew they would leave the hospital only to go to their graves. Ilana looked after me like my mother; every weekend, she took me fishing or to a remote village where we were entertained by the local tribe with their traditional dance and authentic delicacies," I ranted without thinking about what I was saying and why. Maybe it was the reflection of nervousness that had crept into my body and brain that caused me to verbalize inconsequentially; however, he didn't look at me; instead, all the time, he stared at his shoes as if they were hurting or something was about to come out from them.

"Glad to hear you got looked after well and gained excellent experience. How long are you planning to stay here?" Rama asked, still avoiding eye contact and focusing on his shoes.

"I've decided to stay here for good. This place is like heaven; no traffic, noise, or air pollution and no one to bother. You tell me why you're here." I said sheepishly.

"You're a genius person, and I'm sure you must've figured out the purpose of my visit," Ram said in a muted voice.

"Your assumption of my intelligence is way off the mark. I'm dumb and never understood anything other than diseases and prognoses. So please enlighten me on the purpose of your visit," I said boorishly. Instead of telling me how he missed me and how much pain he had to take to trace me, he's implying it is a casual visit and desirous of knowing my future plans.

Ilana entered the hall pushing a trolly, which had a teapot covered with a tea-cozy, two burgers, and assorted cookies and biscuits. "Hope you would find the tea is to your taste, and it's time for my siesta, so please excuse me. And, Madhu, don't let him go without having dinner with us," she said and left the hall.

"I'm waiting to hear your comments, Rama Sir," I said, emphasizing "Sir."

Still, he looked at his shoes, and I noticed a tear rolling down his cheek with a shock. Impetuously, I rose from the chair, grabbed tissue papers, sat beside him, and cleaned his face. Then, anxiously I said, "What happened to you? If I said something offensive, I apologize; tears falling from your eyes make you unmanly." Sitting beside him urged me to hold him tight and never let him go, but I suppressed the urge and returned to my seat.

"Sorry, I got emotional. It could be because I saw you after so long, which my eyes failed to believe, and they threw a few drops of water out of extreme pleasure. So the answer to your question is, I've come to take you with me, but you know I never forced you for anything. I want you to come back, and I promise I won't stop you from anything you want to do with your life; just continue your work in the hospital. Don't marry me or come with me anywhere, and I won't visit you even at your flat," Rama said. His voice reflected pain and genuineness.

Damn it, I missed him every day and cried every night for him to come and take me. His promise echoed in my ears every moment that wherever I was in the world, he would track and bring me back within a few days.

His tears crushed my heart, and I wanted to be in his arms and tell him to take me wherever he wanted.

"You said, within no time, regardless of where I'm in the world, you would find me, and I feared either you or some government officials would come to put me in a plane, which didn't happen. And when I decided to spend the rest of my life serving folks of this country, you showed," I said.

"Yes, I admit, I made exaggerated comments. Even with Dad's high-profile contacts, it took a few days to establish that you didn't depart from the railway station or the airport. And while exploring other search options, we learned that you'd contacted Vimi through a US service provider company. The service provider was conveying your messages with a masked caller ID.

"We contacted our US branch to find out the service provider. One of our senior American executives in our New York office had a close relative working in a high-ranking position in the New York Police Department, NYPD, and he asked for his assistance. Unfortunately, the officer refused to help, saying he couldn't oblige without a criminal complaint. However, he referred us to a private detective who could do the job, provided he wasn't heavily engaged. Our branch office reached the detective somewhere in Europe working on a case. He agreed to attend to the task upon his return which could take around four weeks or even a little more and refused to return for any consideration without fulfilling on-hand obligations. We decided to wait for his return as no other agency, or a reliable person was available to take up the job immediately. The NYPD police officer also suggested it is better to wait for his return, as he's an electronic wizard who could quickly track down the service provider firm. The detective took almost five weeks to return, and then he had to wait for a couple of days for your message to come. Within a few hours of your message, he tracked the service provider, an old retired lady in New Jersey working from home. The detective went to the service provider's house, accompanied by a couple of his police officer friends. The moment the lady saw the police officers, she got frightened and immediately blurted out that the calls were coming from Gaborone, Botswana. One of our head office executives called our Botswana distributor, who readily volunteered to take up the task, and in a matter of hours, he informed us of everything we needed to know. I learned this three days ago, and it took two days for the visa and other formalities to complete and one day to reach here. Your disappearance crushed my soul, and many a time, I thought of committing suicide to spare you from the agony of seeing me again," Rama said.

"Please spare me from your sufferings and intentions. Have you ever considered how you crushed my ego, disregarded my pleading eyes for your companionship, and proclaimed I'm a gold digger? Whenever I decide to bury the past, I get nightmares of my humiliations, worthlessness, and self-pity, all of which refuse to go away, preventing me from agreeing to marry you.

"You're a wonderful person; whichever way anyone wants to judge you, they probably won't find a single flaw that could be considered a weakness. God has bestowed you with looks, money, benevolence, and forbearing. So why didn't you show any of your traits and provide me a second chance to prove I wasn't what you'd witnessed on a morning that didn't start well for me? Allow me to confess; I appeared for the interview solely to look at you, and I wanted to see how well you're doing without me in your life. I also want to admit that I live with the regret that God didn't give me my love; hence I decided to punish myself and stay unmarried. My life's journey would've been incredible if you'd been beside me, raising our children, growing old together, and holding each other's hands till our last breath. But now it's too late, so allow me to die in peace, remembering you till I die and blaming none for the unfulfilled life.

"I've learned to live without you; please do the same or choose to live with a partner, but don't pressure me to marry you. I don't believe in revenge, but neither I believe in turning my second cheek. Thanks for coming all the way, but please forgive me and ask your parents and sisters for forgiveness. I'll seek my parents and brother's absolution for not obeying their wishes," I said, retorting with eyes dropping tears unceasingly.

Rama took a cloth napkin from the trolley, cleaned my face, and said, "Madhu, please tell me, is there anything I could do that would allow you to overcome your nightmares? And as I said, if you don't want to marry me, that's fine as long as you come with me and stay in Hyderabad and work for the hospital."

"I don't want to be in Hyderabad, as we wouldn't have peace, and it would become never-ending suffering for both of us. Please, I beg you to leave me alone, or else I won't have any option but to kill myself," I said and started crying loudly.

I had no idea why I was saying such stupid things while desperately waiting for him to come and take me every second. I probably lost control of my inner self, which caused me to blurt out the thoughts I had piled up over the years.

"Please don't cry; I'll leave, and my best wishes to you for everything you aspire to achieve. I'm not going to kill myself; I'll leave with the satisfaction that you're alive and happy. And, remember, I'm always a phone call away for anything you need," Rama said and took a couple of steps toward the door when Ilana entered the hall and said, "Rama, please sit down, have dinner with us."

Rama said, "Thank you for the dinner offer, but I'm tired and prefer to take a rest."

"Rama, no excuses; please sit down as dinner is not the only thing, but I want to talk to you," Ilana said.

Rama returned and sat without looking at anyone.

"Rama, first, my apologies; I overheard the conversation. I didn't snoop, but your discussion poured into my ears since I always keep my bedroom door open. Be that as it may, sadly, it appears my baby is grief-stricken and not likely to make amends with you. And, you know, Rama, I almost know every minute detail of what had transpired between you and Madhu, starting from the spat. She had commended you as a remarkable human being but an inflexible person who sees only black and white. Since you started chasing her, she's getting awful dreams that you left her again dead in the water for some senseless oversight. She heavily subscribes to the idiom 'If they've done it once, they'll do it again,' which frightens her to the bones.

"Rama, let me give you some insight into my life's journey before delving into resolving your issue. I was born in Berlin in an affluent Jew family; my father was a trader of fresh and dried fruits, and we had everything a wealthy family possesses. In 1944, I was transformed into a tall, gorgeous girl who had reached puberty even though I was a few months away from entering my teens. I had four brothers who left us fearing for their life as Gestapo was rounding up Jews and sending them to concentration camps. One day, Gestapo officers raided our hideout, the villa of Dad's retired police officer friend, and killed every occupant except me. Three officers raped me beside my mother's dead body and left me bleeding, probably thinking it was pointless to waste a bullet when I would eventually die a painful death. Luckily, the Russian Army saved me, treated me in their camp hospital, and the nurse attending to me became my foster mother; together, we escaped to England with some money I found in a suitcase Dad had kept in our bedroom. Irina Strokous, my foster mother, did everything a mother could do and motivated me to become a medical doctor.

"Unfortunately, after the rape, I developed a fear of men, which didn't allow me to marry or enter a relationship. Irina forced me to find a suitable man countless times, but the fear was so overwhelming that I refused to be in a relationship. Due to a few unpleasant relations, Irina didn't marry or try to have a boyfriend. Instead, she kept herself busy raising me like a mother, feeding me the right food, ensuring I dressed well, slept, woke up on time, didn't miss my grades, and so forth. When I got busy with my professional life and minting money, she ensured we were invigorated with a biannual vacation to an exotic place for at least two weeks. She took me to a movie, theater, or picnic every weekend. She was my mother, mentor, and friend, and she not only gave me a new life but made me who I'm today.

"She remained healthy and active even when she was in her advanced age and not only took care of me but handled everything, from house chores to clinic and banking matters. One morning she complained of a breathing issue and was rushed to a nearby hospital to treat the pneumonia attack, where she struggled to survive for four days and lost the battle. She left me without teaching me how to catch a fish. I only knew how to earn money, but the housekeeping and cooking tasks were beyond my grasp. I hired a professional cook-cum-housekeeping lady, but her services were nowhere near the service I was used to, and the food she was preparing was awful for my taste buds. And the worst part was upon my return from the clinic; there was no one in the house to talk to; the housekeeping lady kept the house clean and cold food on the dining table for me to warm and eat.

"The monotony and loneliness reflected in sleepless nights and started affecting my work to the extent that I consulted a psychiatrist. What I expected, the shrink suggested the same; find a partner, practice self-care, meet people socially, and get myself engaged passionately in hobbies or activities that could keep my mind and body occupied. Nothing had helped, and as a last option, I bought a high-end luxury apartment, thinking the change would be uplifting and help me not to remember Irina. I was happy with the new environment for a few weeks but soon began having bouts of anxiety, depression, and suicide ideation. I decided to leave England and go to an African country and help the underprivileged. I sold my practice, house, and all the worldly possessions that I could sell, and while I was doing that, I came across an ad in a German daily newspaper from this hospital. I immediately applied for it and got the job offer that I gladly accepted, and since the day I landed here, I've been at peace. The hospital became my family, and the loneliness bouts disappeared as serving the indigents and watching their gratified eyes became energizing and soul-satisfying.

"Rama, the purpose of me unfolding my journey wasn't to enlighten you about my sufferings or how successful I was. Instead, I want to tell both of you that nothing is more painful than loneliness. A loving and caring companion makes your life's journey pleasant and happy, not your work, money, or social status. As long as you're young and busy in your professional activities, you could possibly be okay. Still, loneliness will hit you so hard that life will become meaningless sooner or later. After the death of Irina, my journey became a miserable nightmare for me; had I not come here, I would have killed myself.

"Of course, exceptions are always there, and you would probably find a few strong-minded people who dedicated their lives to some cause and never married to avoid the distraction of family life. But, trust me, they would also find life depressing when age catches up to them.

"So, forget about remaining single; complete the lifecycle by enjoying the companionship and raising lovely kids like you, and be proud of living a fulfilling life.

"Madhu, don't follow my example; I didn't wed because of the psychological barrier implanted by three animals in the name of human beings, which was so cruel that I regretted my survival every day for several years. I would've committed suicide long ago if my foster mother hadn't come into my life to raise me. You can't imagine what it's like to be raped; the physical pain goes away, but the brain never forgets your powerlessness to defend yourself. Grief oozes out of you in waves, leaving you in constant despair.

"Your fears of suffering under the hands of Rama are ridiculous; his comments were a juvenile's condemnation, being in his fantasy world. Even if you decide to remain single, believing you would have smooth sailing till you pass away, you're absurdly mistaken. You may find yourself in hot water for unforeseeable reasons and unable to endure the pains inflicted by either fellow humans or so-called acts of God. So, forget the past, start your new journey with Rama, and be optimistic that it will prove to be the best decision of your life. If you love your non-biological Mom, then you must respect her desire to see you settle down. And, Rama, I know you've made many commitments to keep my baby happy and look after her with love and respect; still, you must commit to me that you would never mistreat her or fail to hold your promises to keep her fulfilled and content."

"I've committed to keeping her happy and content till my last breath and reiterate in front of you that I'll never disappoint you," Rama said.

"Madhu, I want you to forgive Rama and keep everyone happy, including yourself," Ilana said.

"Mom, you know I'm not ignorant to not understand life's ups and downs; however, knowingly, you can't take the plunge into a dry well," I said pleadingly.

"Madhu, I didn't lecture you to educate but brush up your knowledge. The dry well you're fearing is unsubstantiated, as you can't judge a person from his past behavior. Humans evolve, some for good and some for the worst. I've observed that successful persons generally better themselves, and please don't mix up power with success. Success enables you to improve, whereas power tends to corrupt you for the worst. I believe Rama has evolved for the better, left his ideal world of black and white behind, and become a successful doctor and humanitarian. If you allow yourself to suffer from one fear, then it will lead to another, and one day, you'll become a perfect case of panophobia. So come out of your anxiety, throw caution to the wind, and assure yourself that you've got the guts to fight. I was feeble, and at a tender age, I endured, which didn't permit me to emerge from my dread of men. Not only that, but I couldn't find someone who would hold my hand and walk with me, helping me overcome my fears. My one abnormality bout, a doctor friend, trying to get intimate with me, dumped me instead of treating me. You're pretty fortunate because most wealthy young men are undeserving of even a passing glance. The money degrades their soul to the extent that they fail to remember that even less fortunate humans have self-esteem and must be treated with deference and honor.

"An adolescent boy mistreated you because you behaved like a privileged brat, but he now seeks atonement and pledges to treat you nicely for the rest of his life. Be grateful to him, as such gems are hard to come by. Moreover, I would be hugely disappointed if you failed to catch hold of this opportunity and made all of your loved ones unhappy," Ilana stated emphatically.

From my first encounter with Rama boy, my love for him grew stronger each passing day, to the point that I was determined to die remembering him rather than marry a compromise for the sake of having a husband. What a tremendous down-to-earth man, blessed with a golden heart and no hauteur despite his bulging pockets. I adored him for every characteristic of his personality and always thought I would've found ways to marry him, come hell or high water if he were a pauper. I believe I should now surrender because he has demonstrated his genuine and sincere love for me by tracking me down and coming to get me.

"Mom, I don't want to disrespect you with my refusal; however, allow me to tell you he's an evil person, and I'll consider it my destiny to become his spouse. After marriage, even if he dumps me, I would be happier as everyone will know that my apprehensions were true," I said curtly.

"Madhu, I don't want you to begin your new life with an off-base front foot. Be thankful to your God for blessing you with such a wonderful partner. Remember, any girl across the globe would consider herself most fortunate to become his life partner," Ilana said reprovingly.

I didn't respond to her comments and did not look at her or Rama.

"Don't marry me under duress, Madhu; you won't be able to be happy in your married life if you do so. Take your time to decide, and whatever decision you make, I'll gladly accept," Rama said.

"Call duress or whatever you want, but now I've decided to marry you and stay happy and satisfied no matter what. And I won't allow you to back out or be ready for the eternal peace, as that's where I would send you," I said with a smile.

"That's music to my ears; I thank you for honoring my request, and I wish you to be always abundantly in love and contentment, and may God bless you with beautiful torchbearer babies. Now let me go and see what I can feed you for dinner," Ilana said and left the hall.

Rama stood up from his seat and came and kneeled before me, took my hand in his hand, and said, "Madhu, I don't want to make any tall claims, but I promise to treat you like a bubble blister on the center of my palm, which neither I nor anyone could dare touch. I'll always be beside you in your thick and thin, and please feel free to kill me whenever you notice I failed to keep you happy or if I philander. I know you're financially sound, but still, you'll legally own 50 percent of my shares in the group, and anything else you need now or in the future, you just need to tell me."

"Thanks, Rama; very comforting to hear from you. I don't want a penny from you, and I'll only marry you on that condition. However, I want one gift from you, Grace, my filly; I miss her terribly, and whenever I go to Hyderabad, I plan to go and first meet Grace," I said.

"You know Grace also misses you, as she's not allowing anyone to ride her. So I've instructed the stable hands to handle her with utmost care and not ride her. She's all yours; anything else, my love?" Rama said.

"Nothing else, whatsoever. Let's put behind the past and take a fresh start with loaded affection and regard for one another. However, tell me first, do you have a genuine and deep-seated love for me, or is it your ego that didn't allow you to accept that a run-of-the-mill girl could turn down the proposal of the crown prince of a multibillion-dollar empire?" I said teasingly.

"Whether you want to believe it or not, I missed you so badly that I was close to a nervous breakdown and was suicidal. Since you left, I hardly went to the hospital, and my entire family was mad at me for being so weak that a girl could destroy me to the extent that I became a nervous wreck. But the good to beat all my last few weeks sufferings is you've consented to wed the blockhead. And to say thank you for agreeing to become my wife is not enough, so I want to pay my debt by always remaining a loyal and loving husband," Rama said.

Rama sat beside me and took me in his arms; instead of getting uneasy with his tight hold, I felt elated, a river of happy hormones seeping through my body, giving me the utmost pleasure. Then, with a smile, he kissed my forehead and said, "Honey, if you ever disappear again, I'll put a bullet in my head, as I cannot retake the extreme pain and despair I encountered."

"You bet; it's not going to happen, and if you ever ditch me, I'll put a bullet in your head and then kill myself. And please ingrain in your brilliant upper chamber that once you've made my life miserable, I won't allow you to do it again, so be careful and handle me with extreme care and love," I said.

"Look, I'm human, and on a bad day, I may say something that I shouldn't have, which you shouldn't take seriously, and vice versa. However, if I turn my back like before or play around, you could empty the complete pistol magazine in my body," Rama said.

I felt indescribably happy with his words pouring honey into my ears.

To test the waters, for my reassurance, I said, "For how long you're planning to stay here?"

"As long as you want, my love, I'm not going anywhere without you beside me," Ram said.

"I've got a few obligations to fulfill, and that would take at least one to two weeks," I said to ensure what he said was what he meant, and he would take me with him.

"Okay, let me sort out this with Ilana," Rama said, smiling.

He's too intelligent to make him believe my silly excuse. "You don't believe me, right?" I asked.

"No, I very much believe you but to unshackle you from your obligations, I need to find a solution with Ilana," Rama said with a big grin.

"Your involvement is not needed; I'll handle it in my way to assign my obligations to the appropriate person," I said. Me, dumbo shouldn't have made a stupid excuse.

"It's your call, and you know better how to handle your obligations. Can I make a video call to Mom as she must be desperate to hear from me?" Rama asked.

"Sure, but first, give me a few minutes to freshen myself," I said and went to my room. When I returned, Rama was already conversing with his parents via his smartphone; they looked happy and smiling. I sat beside Rama and conveyed my greetings to them with an ear-to-ear smile.

Rama's Mom addressed me and said, "Madhu, you scared all of us terribly and never again frighten us this way; we've become old, and such shocks could result in disasters. We're not your biological parents but never think less of us either. If you've any issues with Rama or any of us, have a word with me, and I will sort it out."

"Please allow me to express my profound apologies for my irrational behavior, which has caused pain and distress to all my loved ones. However, I needed to hibernate in a tranquil environment before deciding whether or not to take the plunge, and not only that, but I wanted to figure out why I had become so timid and tense. During my time here, I've thoroughly examined my fears and discovered that my apprehension that everything would come to a grinding halt if my decision turned out to be a disaster was a false hypothesis. The pain I had experienced in the past had such a stronghold on my subconscious that I was unable to see that my future carries a glorious life among my loved ones and that the past had passed me completely. I'm glad I took this break that has allowed me to take a more logical approach toward life and not be overly concerned about a hypothetical disaster scenario," I said with a tinge of embarrassment.

"So, have you made up your mind on how you want to move forward?" Uncle asked.

"Yes, I've decided. It would be insane on my part to keep two loving families disappointed and dismayed. And, for sure, Rama would have become a headless chicken without this stupid girl standing beside him," I said with a grin.

"Madhu, you've given your parents and us a new lease of life. I thank you from the bottom of my heart, as your refusal would've curtailed not only our years of existence, but it would've been a miserable life without you beside us when we needed a hand to hold us in our phasing-out stage of life," Uncle said.

Aunty interjected and said, "So, what are your plans now?"

"I don't have any plans; Rama has to decide everything," I said.

"Mom, if you agree, can we meet in the US? I'll fly tomorrow and send you the plane to join us, and once you arrive, we can make all the needed decisions," Rama said.

"It's okay with me, provided your dad and Mohini agree to the trip," Aunty said.

"Mohini and her husband aren't an issue, but I could come only for three or four days max, as too much is going on because of the IPO, which is in its final stage," Uncle said.

"Come on, Dad, you could do everything online, and remember you haven't met with Nini and Vimi since they affianced, and I must remind you that Mom has promised to visit them at the earliest to give blessings," Rama said with a chuckle.

"Don't trap me with your emotional blackmail. Anyway, no issues, I'll come with everyone in the toe and put forth a laudable effort to spend as many days as possible," Uncle said, grinning.

"Okay, Rama, please call Madhu's family, as they're also stressed and worried about Madhu," Aunty said.

"Sure, Mom, bye for now and take good care of Dad and yourself," Rama said, and upon hearing the goodbyes of Aunty and Uncle, disconnected the call. He then called my dad, where it was mid-morning, and on the second ring, Dad answered the call. He looked frail and thin and must've lost at least four or five kilos, as reflected by his sagging skin. Life's uncertainty and disease must've transformed him from an energetic, healthy being into an infirm and apprehensive person. My eyes welled up with tears, and to put up a brave front, I immediately cleaned myself and, with a plastic smile, expressed my happiness in seeing him. After a while, Mom came on the screen and said how happy she was to see both of us and then voiced her disappointment about my reprehensible act. I apologized and promised never to behave irresponsibly and hurt them. When Rama gave them the good news, they were over the moon, and to top up their happiness, he informed them of our arrival in a couple of days.

Soon, both Vimi and Nini called and conveyed their happiness and eagerness to see us in the US.

The next evening, we left for the USA; I did my best to take Ilana with us to meet with our folks, but she refused to leave the hospital, stating the patients and staff were her family, and she couldn't be separated from them as long as she's alive. So, with tears flowing down my cheeks, I parted ways with her, promising to phone her regularly and visit her at least once a year.

Upon reaching our destination, Rama stayed with us for two days and then moved into a rented eight-bedroom magnificently furnished villa in an upscale neighborhood. In addition, he hired several armored cars with a chauffeur and an armed security man in each vehicle. Five days after our arrival, Uncle and Aunty, along with Mohini and his family, arrived. Rama pressured us to stay with them, but we declined since it would have been more inconvenient than the shuttling.

The following day, Rama took us to the villa for brunch, and after the meet and greet, we had yummy Italian lunch ordered from a famous restaurant. Vimi came for lunch and left immediately, informing us that he had an important meeting to attend. While sipping the black coffee, Uncle addressed me and said, "Madhu, please tell us when and where you want to marry and whether you want a grand ceremony or a small gathering of family and friends. We've discussed this issue with your mom and dad, and all of us have decided that it should be your decision, and we all would be happy with whatever you decide." I looked at Mom, and she said, "You decide, darling, and as Nageshwar Sir informed us, we will gladly go by anything you decide."

I told Rama, "Please decide on my behalf, and I'll go with your decision happily."

Rama said, "No, it's your call, and we all will be more than happy to go by your asking."

I felt a little uneasy, as I never thought I would be asked to decide what kind of marriage ceremony I wanted; I took a few moments to collect my thoughts. Then, finally, I said, "Among the immediate family and a few friends, I want to wed here in a temple; also, I want Vimi and Nini to get married the same day if they're okay with my suggestion. Rama was first to say he would be happy to go by my proposal, and then everyone followed in, giving their concurrence. Nini responded with an okay and an ear-to-ear smile when Uncle inquired if she was comfortable with the suggestion.

Aunty addressed me and said, "Madhu, it would be unfair on our part if we didn't share our happiness with our well-wishers. So, once when all of us, including Nini and Vimi, are in Hyderabad, I must organize a grand reception party. I'll push Vimi and Nini to come with us for a few days for the wedding reception. Following that, you'll be free to go wherever you wish for your honeymoon."

"Aunty, I'm okay with it," I said.

On the third day of our understanding, Nini and I got married in a local temple in the presence of a few colleagues of Vimi and some senior executives of Uncle's company.

After four days of our marriage, we flew back to Hyderabad. Vimi promised to come for at least a couple of weeks, along with Mom, Dad, and Nini, when he completed a few critical tasks that had a deadline.

From the airport, as per my request, Rama took me to the farmhouse to meet Grace. It was a sight to see; Grace greeted me with loud neighing sounds, and my caress and feeding her apples and carrots made her happy to rub her head with my body.

I played with her for over 20 minutes before riding; it was an absolute pleasure, as she took all my commands with ease and probably unequivocal happiness. Rama sat at the viewing gallery with his gaze fixed on me. The brain, void of apprehensions, was pumping ecstatic chemical messengers coursing through my veins, and my heart told me I couldn't have asked for anything better.

------------------END-----------------

www.ingramcontent.com/pod-product-compliance
Lightning Source LLC
LaVergne TN
LVHW041146150826
845673LV00001B/81

* 9 7 9 8 8 8 7 0 4 3 5 9 3 *